PRAISE FOR THE
STEEL BROTHERS SAGA

SPARK

SPARK

STEEL BROTHERS SAGA
BOOK NINETEEN

HELEN HARDT

WATERHOUSE PRESS

*In memory of everyone who lost their lives
during the COVID pandemic.*

PROLOGUE

Freed.

Finally.

Ashley is home, and we're going to make this work. Yes, it will take work. My past won't disappear. Not ever. Like Dad said, I have to live with it. That's not part of the choice. The choice is how I live with it—which road I choose to take.

I'm seeing Aunt Mel again to help sort everything out. The big question is whether I need to tell Donny what happened those last few days of our captivity. I waver on that. I want to tell him, to be honest with him, but he's happy. I don't want to destroy that.

Ashley made arrangements to finish her coursework online. By May, she'll be a true doctor of wine! Where she goes from there is up to her. She has my full support, whether she wants to use her knowledge at the Steel Winery or live her dream to become a sommelier at a fine restaurant in Grand Junction.

Willow is moving to Colorado. She'll be here by Thanksgiving for the big party for Uncle Ryan and Aunt Ruby. She'll stay with us until she finds a place of her own. Ashley has already found a place in town for her to open a salon. She's starting over in a new place, and Ashley couldn't be happier.

And Donny...

Donny's moving back home.

He accepted Mom's offer to become the assistant city attorney for Snow Creek. Yes, my little brother gave up a partnership track at a top Denver firm to come home. I can't help wondering if Callie Pike had anything to do with that decision. They were cozy the night of the reception.

The old-vine Syrah has finished fermenting. Now the aging begins. It's going to be an amazing vintage, and even though it should have been twice the amount, I'm living with it and my part in the tragedy. There's no way to know if my campfire truly started the fire. I've accepted that it most likely didn't, as I'm always very careful, and I remember being extra careful both mornings.

But I'll never know for sure, and I have to accept that.

Part of being free means I have to accept those things in my life that I can't change. It's not easy, but it's doable.

I'm doing it.

I'm at my office now, answering a few emails before I head to the winery to check on the Syrah and other wines, when my phone dings with a text.

Brendan Murphy?

Why is he texting me?

Dale, we need to talk. Important.
Tonight at my place. Bring Donny.

CHAPTER ONE

Donny

Moving back to the ranch isn't a huge issue. Sure, I was on a partnership track with a global firm in Denver, but my mother needs me.

I'll do anything for my mother. She raised me, took Dale and me in when she had no obligation to, gave us a life neither of us could have dreamed of—especially after what we'd been through at the hands of our captors. She was only twenty-five years old. Twenty-five and pregnant with Diana.

And she took on a troubled ten-year-old and seven-year-old. She's an amazing woman.

I love my dad, but I'm especially close to my mom. Dale is the opposite—really close to Dad, but he and Mom don't have the rapport that she and I do.

My place is packed up already. I don't have much here in the city, and I'm going to rent out my downtown loft. Tomorrow, I drive home. I'll be staying with Mom and Dad in the main house until Dale and Ashley's place is completed. Then I'll move into the guesthouse.

Home. To the ranch.

To Mom and Dad.

To my new position as assistant city attorney for the town of Snow Creek. An enormous pay cut and the only room for advancement is when Mom retires. She's only fifty, and I can't see her retiring anytime soon.

Mom has been the city attorney for decades, and her assistant, Mary, is retiring. Enter Donovan Steel, Esquire. Will it be the most challenging position? No. But like I said, my mother needs me.

And...

Callie Pike is on the slope. The Pikes own the vineyards to the north of our property. Callie's their third child. She's my cousin Henry's age, twenty-six. Yeah, a difference of seven years, but Dale and his new wife, Ashley, are ten years apart, so what the heck?

I love living in the city. Denver has so much culture and a great nightlife.

But Mom needs me.

Dale tried to talk me out of taking the job. He warned me the offer was coming. Unlike my big brother, though, I have a sense of family he doesn't share. He loves his family, just in a different way. I have more loyalty to the woman who raised me as her own son, who loves me as much as her biological children. She loves my brother too, but the two of them are like oil and water. Now that Dale's found happiness with Ashley, I hope he can heal his relationship with our mother.

That would make her ecstatic, and I think it would be good for him too.

I grab my laptop and connect to my phone's hotspot. Everything else is packed up, and I'm camping out in a sleeping bag for my last night here. Sure, I could have gone to the finest hotel, but for some silly sentimental reason I want to sleep here one last time. Time for some serious Netflix—

My phone buzzes. My brother.

"Hey," I say.

"Hey, yourself. You still driving home tomorrow?"

"That's the plan."

"Good. I just got a weird-ass text from Brendan Murphy."

"Gingers are always a little weird," I laugh. Brendan's a good guy, but Dale and I have been making fun of his Irish red hair for years. He takes it in good humor.

"He says he needs to see both of us right away."

"What for?"

"I don't have a clue. I didn't ask."

Classic Dale. Asking would require that he text back or call Brendan. As an introvert, he doesn't think in those terms. I'm really hoping marriage will bring him out of his shell. If it doesn't? I'll settle for him being happy. Ashley sure seems to do that for him.

"Well, find out what he wants, and let him know I'll be in tomorrow. We can meet him at the bar for a drink or something after dinner."

"Good enough. I'll text him."

"While you're at it, ask him what he wants."

"Yeah, yeah. Okay."

A pause. Such a long pause that I know Dale's considering his next words carefully. That's what he does.

Then, "You sure you want to do this?"

"Do what? Return to the ranch?"

"Yeah. I mean, you're leaving Diana in the city all by herself."

"Our sister is a grown woman, Dale."

"I know, but . . ."

"You don't get it. I know. Why would I leave a huge opportunity at my firm to return to Snow Creek in a dead-end job?"

"Yeah, pretty much."

"First, it's not a dead-end job. Mom will retire, and then I'll be the city attorney."

He scoffs. "You and I both know that Mom won't retire until she's six feet underground, and that won't be for decades yet."

I suppress a shudder. I don't like thinking about Mom's or Dad's eventual deaths. Another way Dale and I are different. He doesn't shy away from dark thoughts.

"Then I'll be assistant city attorney for a while. Not an issue."

"I guess not. I just thought you had bigger aspirations."

I sigh into the phone, exasperated. "You think it's unfair of Mom to ask me to do this."

"Well . . . yeah. I kind of do."

"Let me ask you something, then."

"Shoot."

"What about your wife? Ashley will be a doctor of oenology soon enough, but you've asked her to stay with you on the ranch. Working at the winery. What about her aspirations to be a sommelier at a Michelin restaurant?"

"She can still do that if she wants. Grand Junction has some—"

"Grand Junction is Grand Junction. It's not New York, LA, or Chicago. It's not even Denver."

"It's different. She's my wife, for God's sake. The person I'm spending my life with. She's not my mommy."

"You don't get it," I say, "and you never will. That's okay, Dale. I don't need you to understand. I just need you to support me."

"You know I always support you, Don."

Yeah, I know. Dale will always have my back. He's proved that tenfold. "Then we don't have an issue."

"I guess not."

"So I'll see you tomorrow. Find out what Murphy wants. We can catch him at the bar after supper."

"Sounds good. And Donny?"

"Yeah?"

"Drive safe, please."

"I always do."

CHAPTER TWO

Callie

Plans change.

My mom's sage words, only they're not sage to me.

I was supposed to begin law school in Chicago this winter. Now my law school money will go to help rebuild what was lost in the fire.

Our vines.

Three-quarters of our vines were destroyed through no fault of our own. We prepared. We used firebreaks.

They failed.

They all failed.

It's no one's fault. I know that. But I was so looking forward to getting off the ranch and out of Colorado.

I'm trying very hard to be understanding because I do understand. The money is needed for other things right now. In fact, I offered. If I'd insisted on going to school, Mom and Dad would have most likely relented. Deadlines for scholarships and grants have long passed, so no matter what happens at this point, I'll have to wait another year.

Another year to pursue my dream.

At the very least, another semester.

I love my parents, and I love our ranch.

But part of me is damned tired of putting my life on

hold because of it. I've waited five years since I completed undergrad, living at home and helping with the ranch because I was needed. In exchange, Mom and Dad put away money for my law school.

Money that's now needed elsewhere.

I'll do what I must, because I love my family and I always do what's best for the whole, not for myself.

That's how I was raised, and I have no problem with it.

Still, though... I'm pissed.

Pissed at the fire that ravaged our property even when we did everything right.

Pissed that it took from us instead of the Steels who can well afford it.

Where is the fairness in any of that?

I don't blame the Steels, of course. They're not at fault, and they're helping us rebuild through grants and loans from their foundation, which they certainly have no obligation to do. They offered more, but Mom and Dad turned them down. They don't want any more charity.

Ugh.

I'm not a spoiled brat. I'll do what I must for my family.

Doesn't mean I have to like it.

"Callie?" Mom knocks on my door.

"Yeah? Come in."

Mom peeks into my bedroom. "I just got off the phone with Jade Steel. Donny's coming home."

I perk up. Never mind that Donny Steel is living his big city lawyer dream that I want more than anything. Never mind that he's also gorgeous and rich. "For a visit?"

Mom shakes her head. "He's moving back to the ranch."

"What for?" Not that I'm upset by the news, but why

would he give up the big city life as a rising legal star? I certainly wouldn't.

"He's going to be the assistant city attorney, working with his mother."

I widen my eyes. "Instead of doing corporate law in Denver?"

"Apparently so. I'm as surprised as you are."

"I guess it'll be nice to have him back." I work hard to sound nonchalant. In reality, Donny Steel is a major babe who tried to get me in the sack the night of his brother's wedding reception. I probably would have succumbed, except for the tragedy that followed. A man collapsed and later died at the hospital. Dennis James, Dale's new stepfather-in-law.

The last month brought more tragedy than I ever care to repeat.

The fire. Then the death of a seemingly healthy thirty-three-year-old man.

What's next?

I don't want to consider the possibilities.

"He's coming in tonight," Mom continued. "The Steels are having a big welcome home party tomorrow night."

The Steels and a party. Those people celebrate every time one of them takes a good shit, I swear. Donny's mom, Jade, and her sister-in-law Marjorie are the sweethearts of the western slope. Between Marj's culinary skills and Jade's knack for event planning, their parties are legendary, and the Pikes never miss one. I certainly don't plan to miss this one.

"We're all invited," Mom says.

"Okay." Still trying for nonchalant. No need for Mom to know I'm feeling giddy at seeing Donny Steel.

Maybe Donny and I can continue where we left off.

Funny. I had a mega-crush on his older brother, Dale, growing up. Total puppy love, as I'm nine years younger than Dale, but he was such a conundrum. So quiet and withdrawn and magnificently good-looking with that long blond hair and those piercing green eyes.

I got over that years ago, and then I never gave Donny Steel a thought.

Until last week at their party.

His eyes are hazel, a warm brownish green, so much nicer than Dale's. He doesn't have that flowing mane of blond hair. His slightly darker tresses are cut in a lawyerly style, except for that thick lock that swoops over his forehead. Really sexy.

He's tall, about six-three, and like all the Steels, built to the nines.

Good genes plus the ranch work they all do when they're home make for amazing bodies, even for the ones who don't share their gene pool, like Dale and Donny.

Plus those good looks . . .

It should be illegal to look as good as every Steel does.

My brother, Jesse, calls them our western slope royalty. He's joking. Most of the time. He was in Donny's class at school, and they still have a good-natured rivalry today.

Good-natured, that is, except when it's not.

I'm not sure Jesse ever got over Donny being chosen as MVP in football their senior year. Jesse thought he was a shoo-in because he was the quarterback. He threw all the passes that resulted in Donny's touchdowns. Honestly, I always felt it could have gone either way.

My brother still has a chip on his shoulder about it.

I'm not sure how my big brother will feel if I start something with Donny Steel. Then again, I'm a big girl. What do I care what my brother thinks?

"So you're free?" Mom asks.

"For what?"

"The party at the Steels tomorrow night. Isn't that what we were talking about?"

"Right. Yeah. I'm free. What else would I be doing?"

Mom sighs. "I know you're disappointed about law school, Cal."

I return her sigh. "It's okay. I understand."

"I know you do, but I also know you're disappointed. This isn't how it was supposed to be. Dad and I had much higher hopes for you and your sisters and brother."

"Jesse and Rory are fine," I say. My older brother and sister had no desire for graduate studies. "And Maddie still gets to be in college."

"We talked about this..."

"I know, I know. College is one thing. Grad school's another. I get it. I'm trying, Mom."

"I know you are, honey. You've waited this long to pursue your dream, and it was within grasp. Trust me, Dad and I are just as frustrated for you."

"I don't mean to be selfish." I shake my head. "Truly, I don't. It's just..."

"It's just that you're twenty-six, and you've waited four and a half years already to go to law school. I know, sweetie."

"And you and Dad have waited so long to have a viable winery, and now it was yanked away from you. I'm happy to help you. I really am."

"You're a good daughter, Caroline."

Caroline. When Mom uses my given name, she's feeling extra guilty. I don't mean to make her feel that way.

"I try to be," I say. "I'm not sure I'm always successful."

Mom smiles. "You are. Shall I tell Jade you'll be at the party, then?"

"Sure."

Mom nods and closes the door, leaving me alone in my bedroom.

A party at least gives me something to look forward to. Right now, I'm stuck here. Nothing to look forward to. I can't even go help in the winery because the building was destroyed. Insurance claims have been filed, but the rebuilding probably won't begin for another month or so. Jesse and Rory are helping salvage what's left on the vines. Rory even temporarily moved back from Snow Creek so she could be more involved. And the Steels are letting us use their facilities to make what wine we can.

We're lucky, really. The fire didn't harm any of us, only our property. Our home is unscathed, as is Jesse's small house that he finished building last year on the eastern side of the ranch.

Yes, lucky.

Just not as lucky as the Steels.

CHAPTER THREE

Donny

I arrive at the main house right at dinnertime. My parents' cook and housekeeper, Darla, is in the kitchen stir-frying vegetables.

"Fajitas!"

Darla turns and smiles. "Your favorite. What else would I be making for your big homecoming?"

Darla's been with my parents since my senior year in high school, so she remembers what a huge appetite I have. She introduced me to her famous fajitas, and I swear, no Mexican restaurant in Colorado does them better. Ironically, Darla's Irish.

I inhale the fragrance of sizzling onions and peppers mingled with mouthwatering Steel beef.

"Dinner is almost ready. Your brother and Ashley are out on the deck with your parents."

"Thanks, Darla."

"Can I get you a drink?" she asks.

"Nope. I'll fend for myself."

"There's a pitcher of margaritas outside that your mother made."

"Sounds good." A margarita with Darla's fajitas is kind of a tradition.

Plus, I like sweet cocktails. There, I said it. Dale gives me three shades of shit about it because I'm not a wine snob like he is.

I open the French doors and walk onto the deck. Mom and Dad's two chocolate labs, Ginger and Fred, run toward me, nearly knocking me off my feet. Dale's rescue dog, Penny—an adorable heeler mix with black-and-white markings—adds her two cents.

"So the prodigal son returns!" Dad stands and gives me a hug.

"I was just home a week ago," I remind him.

"But now you're home to stay," he says. "It's great what you're doing for your mother."

"You'll never know how much I appreciate it." Mom stands and hugs me close, bussing my cheek.

"Anything for you, Mom."

Ashley, Dale's wife, hugs me then. "It's great that you're coming home. I'm finally used to all the hugging!"

"How's your mom doing?" I ask.

"She's okay. She's moving here as soon as our house is finished. We've got a room for her. A mother-in-law room. But I imagine she'll find a place in town once she gets situated with a salon."

Dale grabs me in his manly bear hug. "Good to have you back, bro."

I simply nod. Dale's not thrilled with my career decision, but he's definitely happy to have me here on the ranch. As much as I loved my life in Denver, I missed Dale terribly. After all we've been through, we like to be near each other.

"What time are we meeting Brendan?" I ask him quietly.

"Nine," he says. "I've already told Ashley, but you'll have

to figure out an excuse with Mom and Dad."

I nod, and we disengage.

"I swear," I say, "I could smell those fajitas a mile out."

As if on cue, Darla walks out the door carrying a sizzling platter. On the table are tortillas, pico de gallo, guacamole, cheese, and sour cream. All the fixings.

I pour myself a margarita. Dale and Ashley are drinking wine, of course, and Dad has his signature Peach Street bourbon. Only Mom and I are indulging in the cocktail.

I hold up my glass. "It's great to be home."

"It's great to have you here," Dad says, clinking his bourbon to my margarita glass.

Mom, Dale, and Ashley join in the toast, and then we dig in. I pile my plate high and take a seat between Mom and Dad, who are on the ends of the glass-topped patio table. Ashley and Dale sit across from me.

Conversation never lulls, as we talk about everything from the fire, Ashley's newly widowed mother, and Dale's fermenting old-vine Syrah, the progress of which he's extremely happy with.

My brother is more animated than I've seen him in... well, *ever*, to be honest. He just lost half his Syrah vines—his favorite and his place of solace—but his attitude shows strength and contentment. Marriage is clearly good for him. I'm excited to have a heart-to-heart with him soon, though apparently it won't happen tonight.

Tonight is for Brendan Murphy, a high school classmate of Dale's who lives in town and runs Murphy's Bar. He and Dale were never close—Dale was never close to anyone except Dad and me, and now Ashley—but apparently Brendan has information for us. I'm intrigued, though I'd rather head over to the Pikes' and say hi to Callie.

"Did you know that, Donny?"

I jerk toward Mom's voice. "I'm sorry. Did I know what?"

"Callie Pike won't be going to law school in January after all. Maureen told me they need the money to help rebuild."

"Callie was going to law school?" I raise my eyebrows.

"You didn't know? You seemed to spend a lot of time with her at the reception."

I'm not about to tell my mother that Callie Pike and I weren't talking about law school or the law or even the reception. We were speaking in innuendos, and I was hoping to get her between the sheets.

"I figured that was what you must have been talking about," Mom goes on. "You two have that in common."

"We were talking about other stuff," I say. "The fire. You know."

"Strange that law school didn't come up," Mom says.

I nod. Not so strange at all, but I'm so not going there. Not with my mother.

Dale smirks behind his wineglass, and Ashley gives him a good-natured punch on the upper arm.

My brother gives me all kinds of crap for my ways with women. So I like women. I like sex. What's the problem? If a woman gives me her consent, why shouldn't I take her to bed?

Dale and I have always had our own distinct ways of dealing with things. He goes inward, and I go outward. Just the way we're each wired.

"I didn't know Callie was interested in the law," I say. "She must be upset that her plans have gone awry."

Dale guffaws. "Who the hell uses the word awry?"

"High-powered corporate lawyers, apparently," Ashley says, smiling.

"She is," Mom says, ignoring Dale and Ashley. "Maureen feels terrible about it. I almost told her we'd gladly pay for Callie's law school, but I figured that was out of line."

"Yeah, Mom," Dale says. "That would be out of line. No one wants to feel like a charity case. Especially not the Pikes. They're proud people."

"They are," Mom agrees, "but we have so much to give."

"We have to let them be who they are, blue eyes," Dad says, looking at Mom with the love I've known since I came to this house twenty-five years ago.

"I know, Tal," Mom says. "I never forget my humble beginnings. Dad and I never took charity, and there were times when it would have helped."

"The Steel Foundation is helping them with loans and grants," Dad says. "They'll be all right. We can't force them to take our help, and I wouldn't want to anyway. They're entitled to their pride."

"Of course." Mom polishes off her second margarita. "I know. I just..."

"You want to help," Dad says. "You're just being you, blue eyes, and that's why we all love you."

Dale looks at his plate. He loves Mom, but he doesn't get her. To him, even thinking about offering the Pikes charity is an affront to his senses. I agree, but I also understand where Mom comes from.

It's a balance—a balance Dale and Mom don't have. They're both constantly walking a tightrope around each other. If one or the other of them could just ease up slightly, everything would be okay.

He has Ashley now, and he's opened up more than I ever thought possible.

I'm happy for my brother. He deserves the best. He was my protector all those years ago. I was so young and innocent. Without my big brother and his quiet strength, I have no doubt I'd have died in that horrific place.

Mom helps Darla clear the table, and then she brings out a chocolate cake, my favorite.

"This is a treat," I say.

"Nothing but the best for your homecoming." Mom smiles as she slices a huge hunk of cake and sets it in front of me.

Dale rolls his eyes. I don't even look at him, but I know he's doing it. I can feel it.

Mom serves cake to everyone else as I shove a succulent bite into my mouth. Moist and dense and perfect. Mom learned how to make cake from Aunt Marj, who's a chef. Somehow my mother, whose only culinary claim to fame is her grilled cheese and tomato sandwiches, perfected this amazing dessert. I told her once that it was my favorite, and that was all it took.

She gets me and I get her.

Call me a mama's boy. I can take it. It's the truth.

Dale gives me shit about it at every opportunity, but I'm used to it. I think deep down he wishes he and Mom were closer. He just doesn't know how to get close to her. He's three years older and has more memories of our natural mother than I do. That's probably a big part of the issue.

After cake and coffee, Dale rises. "We should go, Don."

"Go where?" Mom asks.

"We're meeting Brendan Murphy for a drink in town," I say.

"Maybe I'll join you," Dad says.

Dale gives me a side-eye.

"He wants to talk to us about something," I say.

Dad takes the hint. "I'll leave you to it, then. Let me know if you need anything."

Dale nods to him. "We will."

That's Dad. He knows when to back off, but he also makes sure we know he's always there for us. I don't have the first clue what Murphy wants with us, but it's got to be important. He wouldn't have asked for both of us otherwise.

"I have to grab my wallet," Dale says. "It's at the house."

"I'll walk over with you," I say. "We can go from there."

"Sounds like a plan."

Dale, Ashley, and I walk the half-mile path to the guesthouse, which will be my place of residence once they move out.

"I didn't want to say anything in front of your parents," Ashley says, "but Brendan told me some strange stuff that night he and I had dinner."

"That night he tried to move in on my woman," Dale says, only half joking.

Ashley giggles. "He didn't get very far."

"What did he say?" I ask.

"Not a lot, just that..."

"What, baby?" Dale asks, his eyes wide.

"That...people seem to disappear when the Steels are involved."

CHAPTER FOUR

Callie

Jesse and his band are rehearsing in the garage. Normally they rehearse in one of the winery sheds, but the fire took care of those.

They're great, but damn, they're loud.

My favorite pastime, reading, isn't possible when the bass guitar is thrumming in my head.

I put away my copy of *Little Women*. I know the story by heart, anyway, but it's my favorite go-to when things kind of suck. For some reason, diving into the world of Jo March and her sisters always makes me feel better.

"Cal, I've got to get out of here."

I look up. My sister Rory stands in front of me.

"What's up?"

"Jess and his band are giving me a headache."

"You? You sing with them half the time." My sister's a trained classical mezzo soprano, but she loves rock and roll too.

"I know, but I'm feeling more operatic today. Plus, they're doing some of Cage's music, and he's way too hard metallic for my tastes. Want to drive into town and see what's going on?"

"What could possibly be going on in town?"

She laughs. "Nothing. But it'll be quiet."

"You really hate Cage's stuff, don't you?" Cage Ramsey is our cousin, and he plays bass in Jesse's band, Dragonlock. The band is mostly old-school rock, except when they play Cage's compositions.

"Hate is a pretty strong word," Rory says.

My sister has a lovely voice but never made it in classical performing. Now she works in town, giving piano and voice lessons and sometimes performing with Jesse on nights when they stick to classic rock. She has her own place in town, but she's home for a while, helping out with the fire fallout. She and her girlfriend, Raine Cunningham, have been together for a year.

"Is Raine meeting us in town?" I ask.

"No. She's in Denver visiting her parents."

"Just us Pike girls, then."

"Minus Maddie."

I roll my eyes. I don't mean to. It just happens. I love Maddie. I love all my siblings.

"Your envy is showing, sis," Rory says. "You, Jess, and I all got to finish undergrad right out of high school. Maddie deserves nothing less."

"I'm trying, Ror."

"I know. If it's any consolation, Mom and Dad feel terrible about law school."

"Rory," I say, "that is absolutely no consolation at all."

★ ★ ★

We end up at Murphy's Bar. Pretty much because there's no place else to go in Snow Creek in the evening. Rory orders a draft, but I opt for Diet Coke. I'm not feeling the drinking thing tonight. I've never been big into alcohol. We find a table. Laney Dooley, one of Rory's friends from high school, is tending bar tonight. She joins us at our table when she takes a break.

"How's everything going?" she asks. "You know. With the . . ."

"Fire," Rory says. "You can say the word. We won't melt."

"I'm just so sorry about everything," Laney says.

I smile and nod. What am I supposed to say? *Yeah, I'm sorry too? Yeah, it sucks major dicks?*

"We're dealing," Rory says.

"Is there anything I can do?" Laney asks.

You can pay my law school tuition. The words hover on the tip of my tongue. I'm not a bitch. I don't say them. But seriously, why do people ask that question? *No, there's nothing you can do, unless you can regrow grapevines with a snap of your fingers.* Laney is a nice person, and yes, she'd help if she could. But she can't.

"No," Rory says, "but you're sweet to ask."

"Where's Raine?"

"In Denver with her parents."

"Right now? When you need her?"

I hold back a scoff. What is Raine supposed to do? All she can offer is support, and Rory doesn't need that. Besides, maybe her parents need her right now? My God, we Pikes aren't the only people with problems.

"It was a trip she had planned for a while," Rory replies. "I insisted she go."

"Oh." Laney smiles weakly.

"We can't put our lives on hold," I say.

Except I have. I've put my life on hold. Still, I feel I have to defend my sister's choice to let her partner leave town. I would have done the same thing.

Laney stands. "Break's over. Good to see you guys."

"You too," Rory says.

I simply smile and nod. My standard when I'm pissed and feeling bitchy for no reason. Well, I have a reason, but none of it is Laney's fault.

"Cal," Rory says once Laney's out of earshot, "you have that resting bitch face down to a T."

I sigh. "I really don't mean to."

"I know you don't. I get it. I do."

Rory tries. She does. But she gave up her opera aspirations long ago and loves teaching privately and singing with Jess on occasion. She's in a relationship with someone she loves. She no longer depends on Mom and Dad for help.

In short, she has everything, including thick dark hair and a body to die for. Why I'm the only Pike girl not to inherit Mom's great rack is beyond me. Rory and Maddie are both stacked to the hilt. The men of Snow Creek all gave a collective "damn it" when Rory came out as bisexual after high school. Now they had twice as much competition for the town brick house.

I drop my gaze to my breasts, which are B cups on a good day, and I can't help a sarcastic chuckle.

"What's wrong?" Rory asks.

I take a sip of Diet Coke. "Everything, sis. Just everything. I don't think I could be satisfied if the man of my dreams appeared in here and swept me off my feet. I'm just that damned mad at the world."

Rory lifts her eyebrows. "Really now?"

"Seriously. I'm feeling bitchy, and I don't see it ending."

"Too bad." Rory takes a sip of her beer and swallows. "Because I think that guy you're talking about just walked in."

CHAPTER FIVE

Donny

"Hey, Steel boys," Laney, a Murphy's staple, says from behind the wooden bar.

Laney Dooley is a hot little number and a professional bartender and waitress. She's tall and blond with legs that go on forever. Four years my junior, and ready and willing when we're both horny and available. She has that familiar glint in her dark-blue eyes. Unfortunately, I'm not buying tonight.

"What are you doing in town?" she asks.

Dale, of course, doesn't reply. I'm the spokesman when we're together. Always been that way, always will be, apparently. Marriage may have opened Dale up a bit, but some things will never change.

"We actually came to see Brendan," I say. "Is he here?"

"He must be upstairs. He's off tonight."

Brendan lives in the apartment above the bar. Must be nice to be able to roll out of bed and simply go downstairs to get to work.

"What can I get you?" Laney smiles at Dale. "Wait. Don't tell me. You're going to order your own wine."

I can't blame Laney for trying, even though she and I have been together. Women have been trying to come on to my brother since he hit puberty. I'm used to it. Must be that ridiculous long hair of his.

"Actually," Dale says, "just water for me."

"Donny?" Laney smiles knowingly.

Any port in a storm. Dale's off-limits for sure now, and I'm way more of a sure thing. He may be prettier, but I'm a hell of a lot more fun, and women are always more than happy to slip into my bed when they can't get Dale.

Yeah, I'm pretty okay with that. No time for it tonight, though.

"We had drinks with our dinner, so I'm going to stick with water for now as well."

She pulls out two bottles of Aquafina. "Here you go, then. You want me to call Brendan for you?"

I look at my phone. It's a quarter to nine. "Nah. We're a little early." I turn to Dale. "What do you think? Want to grab a—"

I stop abruptly as I peruse the tables. In the back sit Callie Pike and her older sister, Rory.

Damn. If possible, Callie looks even better than she did a week ago.

Her hair is the same color as my mom's—light brown—but there the similarities end. Callie is tall and slender, long and lean, and her eyes are the color of amber. Seriously. The lightest brown I've ever seen. Almost like an orangey-gold. Her hair is pulled into a low ponytail at the back of her neck. Classic and stylish, like Callie herself. While her mother and sisters are voluptuously built, Callie is perfect supermodel material.

Fucking gorgeous.

No time tonight, I remind myself.

"See something you like?" Dale says.

I clear my throat. "Maybe later. Right now, I want to see what Brendan wants."

"Right. You're aching to talk to Brendan Murphy when Callie Pike sits there, all gorgeous and ripe for the picking."

"You think she's gorgeous, huh?"

"Who doesn't? All the Pike girls are gorgeous, but Callie…"

"You're a married man now."

"I didn't say I want to take them to bed. I've still got eyes, you know."

"I can't believe I never noticed Callie before the other night."

Dale scoffs. "I can. You had your eyes on … easier prizes."

"What is it about her?" I say more to myself than to Dale. "Rory and Maddie are beautiful too—and built—but Callie…"

"It's the eyes," Dale says. "Rory's and Maddie's are brown, but Callie's are…"

"Golden," I say softly. "Big, round eyes of reddish gold."

Dale chuckles. "You're waxing all poetic, Don."

"She's thinner than her sisters," I say, though I'm not sure why. It's true, but in my book, Callie Pike has it all over her sisters. That gorgeous hair, and those eyes. I saw a flower that color once. I think it was a poppy.

Damn. What is wrong with me?

Dale nods. "And not as … well endowed."

"Are you a boob man?" I shake my head. "Ashley's beautiful, but she's hardly well endowed."

"First, you are *never* to look at my wife's tits. Got it?"

I hold my hands up in mock surrender. "Got it. Back off, bro."

"Besides, I have eyes," he says for the second time. "Rory

and Maddie Pike are fucking stacked."

I can't fault his observation. But Rory's involved with a woman at the moment, and Maddie's still in undergrad. Way too young for me.

Then there's Callie...

Man, I want her in my bed something fierce.

"She lives at home right now," Dale reminds me. "And so do you."

He's not wrong. Hardly the recipe for a romp in the hay. "I can work around that." I sip my water.

Dale eyes the staircase in back. "You'll have some time to think about your moves. There's Brendan."

I rise. "Hey, Murphy."

"Hey, Don, Dale. Good to see you guys." We all shake hands as if we're mere acquaintances, when in fact, we've known Brendan since we came to Snow Creek twenty-five years ago. Brendan and Dale were in the same class.

"So what's up?" Dale asks. "You've piqued our curiosity."

"Not here," he says. "We'll go up to my place."

I glance in Callie's direction. Damn. I have no idea how long we'll be, and she's liable to be gone by the time we come back down to the bar.

Though Dale's right. Where the heck would I take her? There's always the Snow Creek Inn, with its four guest rooms. Usually only one is ever filled at any given time except when someone in town has family visiting for a special occasion.

Dale and I follow Brendan up the stairs to his studio above the bar. He pushes the door open.

"Come on in. Excuse the mess."

The place is definitely a bachelor pad, but it's not messy at all. Even his bed is made, which is more than mine ever is.

Mom tried her best, but out of the four of us, only Diana got the neatness gene.

"You want some more water?" he asks.

I hold up my bottle. "Still good here."

"I'm good too," Dale says. "What's this about, Murphy?"

"Have a seat." Brendan gestures to a couch and a recliner.

"Do we *need* to be sitting down?" I ask.

"Your choice."

Dale and I plunk onto the couch, and Brendan takes the recliner.

Silence for a minute or so, until—

"I found something under a plank here. By accident."

"What's it got to do with us?" I ask.

"Not you two so much. But your grandfather. Bradford Steel."

CHAPTER SIX

Callie

"Dale's married," I say, "and I got over him long ago."

"I'm not talking about Dale."

I take a drink of Diet Coke.

"I saw you and Donny together at the wedding reception."

Had she? She and Raine had been hanging with Jesse's band most of the evening.

"Donny Steel's a known womanizer. Maybe I was just interested in talking law with him."

Rory smiles knowingly. "Did you talk about law at all that night?"

I can't help a chuckle. "Not once."

I find my gaze glued to Donny's tight ass as he and Dale follow Brendan Murphy up the stairs to his place. "I wonder what that's all about."

Rory sips her drink. "Beats me. I didn't know they were close to Brendan."

"They're not, as far as I know. He and Dale were in the same class, but that was"—I count on my fingers— "seventeen years ago."

"Dale comes in here to play pool sometimes," Rory says. "Raine and I see him every now and then. But Donny's hardly ever here."

"Because he doesn't live here," I tell her. "Until now."

"He does?"

"Yeah. Didn't Mom tell you? He's moving back and taking over Mary's position as assistant city attorney."

"Working with his mother?"

I laugh. "I know. Weird, huh?"

Though what's weird about it is beyond me. Rory and I are both living at home now, working with our own mother to help the family business. What's so different about what Donny's doing?

"They've always been close, from what I hear," Rory says.

"Just exactly what do you hear about Donny Steel?"

"Nothing. Just, it's pretty well known he's the closest to Jade of all his siblings."

"Closer than the girls?"

She nods. "Just what I hear. Town gossip. You know."

"What else do you hear in town?"

"You know me," Rory says. "I'm not a gossip hound. It goes in one ear and out the other."

I nod. Rory may not be a gossip hound, but her partner, Raine, is. She owns the hair salon in town, and she hears everything.

"Spill it," I say.

"Spill what?"

"Everything. Anything. Surely Raine brings home all the scoop on the Steels."

"There are about a million Steels, Cal."

"I'm interested in one in particular."

"Mostly she talks about Ashley's mother moving here. Apparently she's also a stylist and will probably open a competing salon, and that concerns Raine."

"Why? Raine's the one with the established clientele. She'll do fine."

"Sure, but she doesn't have Steel money behind her, and this Willow White will."

"Willow's Dale Steel's mother-in-law. That hardly means she has Steel money behind her."

"The Steels take care of their own."

"They're actually taking pretty good care of us at the moment." I can't help a snotty tone. I hate that we need taking care of right now. The Steel Foundation exists to help. Still . . .

"Yeah, it sticks in my craw too," Rory agrees. "But we're lucky to be getting the help from their foundation. Otherwise Mom and Dad would have to declare bankruptcy for sure."

"Would they? Really?"

"Yeah. Jesse and I were talking. They have contracts they can't fulfill and debt they can't pay if the winery isn't working."

"Why haven't they told me this?"

"Probably because they don't want you to feel worse than you already do about law school."

"Still, though . . ." My mind races. "Didn't their contracts have a force majeure clause?"

"Huh?"

"Act of God. The fire is a force majeure or act of God. It's basic contract law."

"You haven't been to law school yet, Cal."

"Doesn't mean I don't know a thing or two. It's been my passion since undergrad."

"I guess their contracts didn't have that clause, then. Or if they did, it didn't apply for some reason."

Mental note: Make sure I look over every contract my parents sign from now on.

"I suppose it's a good thing none of us are expecting to take over the business," Rory continues. "I have my students in town, and Jess has the band. You've got law school."

"If it ever happens." I sigh.

"It will. And then Mads is interested in history. I see her as a spectacled professor someday."

"Here's the problem," I say. "I'm the one who's been on the winery payroll for the last four years. I'm the one who's been saving up for school. I'm the one who won't be getting a freaking paycheck now and who has to live at home. I'm the one whose grad school money has to go toward the family."

"Find something in town," Rory says. "Surely there's something you can do. Don't they need an investigator at the city attorney's office? Something like that. You could stay with Raine and me until you find a place."

"I'm not sure Raine would appreciate that."

"Raine can get over it, then."

I eye my sister. "Don't tell me there's trouble in paradise."

She inhales. Takes the last sip of her beer. "We're okay. Let's just say it wasn't a hugely difficult decision to move back home for a while or to tell her to go ahead and visit family in Denver."

"Ror, what's going on?"

"She and I just seem to have different priorities lately. Plus, it's always bothered her that I'm bisexual. I told her that when I'm in a relationship I'm all in, but she can't seem to get over my attraction to men."

"I guess being bi comes with its own issues," I say.

"You don't know the half of it. Each side wants me to pick a team, but it doesn't work that way. I'm attracted to a person, not to their gender."

I nod. I can't claim to understand my sister's orientation, as I'm straight as an arrow, but I do sympathize. She's dated both men and women. Raine is the first person she's lived with, so I figured it was serious. I had no idea they were having problems.

"Suffice it to say," Rory continues, "you're welcome at our place. I'd do the same for Raine's brother if he needed it."

I nod. "Thank you. It's tempting, but I have to actually be employed first."

"Didn't I just mention the city attorney's office? Surely they need someone to do investigations."

"They have one."

"Maybe they need another."

"And how would they pay another?"

"I don't know. Snow Creek seems to have the resources to pay two city attorneys. Why not two investigators? Your criminal justice degree makes you more than qualified."

Rory's idea isn't a bad one. And if I worked at the city attorney's office ... I'd be working with Donny Steel.

Not a bad idea.

Not a bad idea at all.

CHAPTER SEVEN

Donny

"What the hell are you talking about, Murphy?" I demand.

Though I'm pretty sure I already know. Our conversation with Ashley while we walked to the guesthouse replays in my mind.

"I didn't want to say anything in front of your parents," Ashley said, "but Brendan told me some strange stuff that night he and I had dinner."

"That night he tried to move in on my woman," Dale said.

Ashley giggled. "He didn't get very far."

"What did he say?" I asked.

"Not a lot, just that . . ."

"What, baby?" Dale asked, his eyes wide.

"That . . . people seem to disappear when the Steels are involved."

Dale and I both stopped walking, our feet seemingly glued to the path.

"Excuse me?" I said.

"We were talking about his great-uncle, the original Sean Murphy, who his dad was named after."

"What about him?"

"Did you know that he died at your grandparents' wedding?"

Dale and I both dropped our mouths open.

"I'll take that as a no. Apparently the original Sean Murphy was your grandfather's best man, and he passed out while giving his toast. He died at the hospital."

Finally, Dale spoke. "That's sad. Really sad. But one death doesn't mean people disappear when we're around."

"I agree," Ashley said, "and I told him so. But apparently Sean the first's death was the reason Brendan's dad, Sean the second, originally came to Snow Creek. To try to get to the bottom of his uncle's untimely death."

"And did he?" I asked.

Ashley shook her head. "No. But he liked the town so much he stayed here. Bought the bar. Raised his family. A year later, his little sister moved here."

"Ciara Murphy," Dale said. "Did he offer any other example of someone who disappeared because of our family?"

Ashley shook her head. "No, but he did make the statement. I honestly didn't think anything of it . . . until he sent Dale that ominous text about meeting with you guys."

I jerk back to the present when my brother's voice breaks into my thoughts.

"I think I know," Dale says quietly.

"Ashley?" Brendan says.

"Yeah. She told me what you told her. I kind of filed it away at the time because I had a lot of other shit on my mind, with the fire and all. I guess I should ask Dad about it."

"Are you talking about the stuff Ashley told us earlier tonight?" I ask.

"Yeah." Dale's gaze meets mine, and an understanding passes between us. Dale knows something I don't, and he'll tell me later. I'll hold him to that.

"No one talks about it," Brendan says. "No one wants to get on the bad side of the Steels."

"The bad side of the Steels?" I shake my head. "What the fuck?"

"Look," Brendan says. "No one thinks you're bad people."

"We're fucking good people," I say adamantly. "This town wouldn't have survived without us."

"That's the point," Brendan says. "Everyone knows the Steels run this town."

"We don't run anything," I say. "You've got a lot of nerve, Murphy."

"Come on," Brendan says. "Your mother is the city attorney. You're soon to be her assistant. But that's not even why people say you run the town. Everyone knows when the coffers are low, the Steels add to them."

"That's not running a town," Dale says quietly. "That's taking care of our own."

"Potato, po-tah-to," Brendan says.

I stand then, anger boiling through me. "We're done here. Let's go, Dale."

Dale stays seated. Yeah, he knows some shit. Big brother will be spilling his guts later if I have to beat it out of him. Never in a million years would I think of physically harming my brother, but that's how mad I am at this second.

"I want to ask you both something," Brendan says.

"Ask it another time." I walk toward the door. "I'm so out of here."

"Donny," Dale says, "you need to sit down. We're far from done here."

I shake my head, pretty sure smoke is swirling out of my ears. "You know I'd do anything for you, Dale, but for God's sake—"

"Sit." My brother's tone takes on a sharp edge.

I swear. I know he has no genetic relationship to our father, but in that second, Dale sounded exactly like Talon Steel.

And what do I do? I do exactly what I'd do if Dad had said it.

I sit.

"Fine. What do you want to ask us, Brendan?"

"Just this." Brendan clears his throat. "We all know how much the Steels are worth. Billions. So here's my question. Why are you still living here? In Snow Creek?"

"We live on our ranch," I say. "There's a difference."

"Is there? You could be living the high life in LA or New York. London, Paris, Milan. Yet you don't. None of you. Why?"

I have to admit, Brendan raises an interesting query, and one I haven't thought about before. Dale and I weren't born into the Steel family, and once they took us in, our lives were so much better than they'd ever been, neither of us ever considered leaving. Why would we?

Why would anyone? We have everything we could ever want, right here on the ranch.

Still, I'm an attorney, so I play devil's advocate. "*I* left, Murphy. I went to Denver."

"And now you're back," he says.

"As a favor to my mother."

"Because your mother couldn't find anyone else to be assistant city attorney in this small town? Right."

"Because my mother wanted a good attorney."

"And you're the only good attorney in Colorado."

"For Christ's sake." I stand again. "This is getting nowhere."

"I swear to God I'm not trying to piss you guys off."

"Then you must just have a flair for it," Dale says quietly.

"Maybe," Brendan says, "but that's not why I asked you here. I like you guys. Both of you. I always have. I personally have no problem with any of the Steels. But the fact is that my great-uncle died in the middle of giving a toast at your grandfather's wedding. No one talks about it, but it happened. It's why my father came here to Snow Creek. He wanted to find out the truth. Why his uncle, who he was named after, died so suddenly at twenty-two years old."

"What did he find out?" I ask.

"Nothing. That's my point. No one knew a damned thing."

"But he stayed here."

"He did. He fell in love with the small-town life and opened the bar. He married a townie, my mom, and this is home now."

"So what's the issue, then?" I ask.

"The issue is this," Brendan says. "A young man dropped dead at a wedding, and no one ever talks about it."

"Because it's kind of a downer," I say.

"It is. I won't deny it." Brendan tucks a stray strand of red hair behind his ear. "But I've wondered for a long time if there's more to the story. More that maybe got covered up, and that's why what I found is so interesting."

"This is starting to get tedious," Dale says. "Tell us what you've got, or we're out of here."

"Yeah, definitely," I say. "Dale and I have a lot to talk about, and we're not going to do it here."

Dale gives me a side-eye. *Nice try, bro. You're not getting off the hook.*

"My dad didn't build this place. It was already here,

and the guy who owned it was a liquor distributor in Grand Junction. He ran a small bar here and staffed it with locals. As a distributor, he could get the liquor at less than wholesale, and he did even better by stocking the place with surplus stuff."

"And we care about this because . . . ?"

"Because the guy's name was Jeremy Madigan."

Dale cocks his head. "Madigan. Why does that name ring a bell?"

"It didn't ring a bell to me at first," Brendan continues, "but I found some documents that were hidden under the floorboards."

"You just happened to be looking under the floorboards?" Dale says.

"I'm redoing the floors, genius. Putting in new hardwood." Brendan gestures to an area rug. "See for yourself."

"Wait, wait, wait," I say. "Just who the hell is Jeremy Madigan?"

CHAPTER EIGHT

Callie

"They've been up there a long time." I gesture to the staircase leading to Brendan Murphy's apartment.

"Who?" Rory asks.

"Donny and Dale. They went up to Brendan's place."

"I'm pretty sure they're not having a threesome." She laughs.

"Ooo! Shut up. They're brothers. That's gross."

"Just trying to lighten your mood, sis. You're so down in the dumps."

The fact that Rory's relationship is on the rocks and she's not as down in the dumps as I am isn't lost on me. Time to do something. Get off my ass and stop the stupid pity party. It's no one's fault. It just *is*.

"I have to admit. I love the idea of working for the city attorney's office as an investigator. Or in any capacity, really. I'll answer the damned phones. I just want to get my foot in the door."

"And get closer to Donny Steel."

"That's a perk. I won't deny it."

"Head over tomorrow. Put on your best power suit and waltz right in there and ask Jade Steel for a job. She knows what our family has been through with the fire. She already feels terrible about it."

"What if there's no job available?"

"Show her how indispensable you are. Make her hire you."

"I'm not going to go in and convince her to hire me if it means firing someone else. That's not cool."

"She won't. Jade wouldn't fire anyone to hire someone. Convince her she needs two investigators. You're qualified."

"Being qualified won't help if there's no job available. Come on. How many crimes does a little town like Snow Creek have? There are only so many accidents to investigate. We have a police department of two."

"Three. We have a police department of three. And my God, Callie. The city covers part of the unincorporated county as well. Just go in and ask for a job. What's the worst that can happen?"

"She can tell me to fuck off."

"Which she won't."

"Okay. She can tell me she's sorry but there aren't any openings at this time."

"Exactly."

"That's rejection."

"For the love of God. We've all experienced rejection. Try auditioning for summer music programs and being forced to acknowledge that you're never going to sing Cherubino at the Met. You won't dissolve into nothingness. Besides, if there isn't a job, she's not rejecting *you*. She's telling you there's no job."

"Same thing."

Rory laughs. "You'll be a darn good attorney, Cal. I swear to God you argue every single point all the time. Even when you know the other person is right, like I am."

I join my sister in laughter. She's right, of course. I've been this way since I began forming syllables in toddler language. It still drives my family nuts.

"So you're going in tomorrow, right?" Rory gestures to Laney.

Laney approaches. "You need a refill?"

"Two beers," Rory says. "We're celebrating."

"Celebrating what?"

"My sister here is going after her dream."

Laney. "You're going to school in January! That's great!"

I bite my lip. "Not exactly."

"Good news sure travels fast in this town," Rory says. "No, that still has to wait."

"Oh, I'm sorry."

Great, now sympathy. I hate sympathy, especially when I'm the recipient.

"Don't be," I say. "I'm taking another road for now."

A road that will probably lead absolutely nowhere, but what the heck? I can go for a beer. We Pike kids are beer drinkers despite the fact that our parents produce wine. I gaze toward the staircase, where Donny disappeared into Brendan's place. I've known the Steels since we moved here when I was a kid, and not once have I seen any Steel drink a beer. They're all about wine and fine spirits.

God. And tomorrow I'm going to walk into the city attorney's office and ask Jade Steel to hire me.

That's going to take more audacity and courage than I have.

"I'll get your beers." Laney heads back to the bar, her cheeks red.

"What time should I come by your studio for lunch tomorrow?" I ask Rory.

"What? We don't have a lunch date."

"Yeah, we do." I smile. "After I get shot down by Jade Steel, you're going to buy me lunch. At Lorenzo's. I could go for some baked ziti."

CHAPTER NINE

Donny

"I asked the same question," Brendan says. "I mean, sure, someone had to sell this place to my dad, but why would this Madigan dude leave papers hidden under the floorboard?"

"Who gives a fuck?" Dale says. "What does any of this have to do with your great-uncle's death?"

"Give me a minute. I went to my dad and asked him about his purchase of this place all those years ago. He said yeah, he purchased it from Jeremy Madigan, and right after that, Madigan left town with his brother and sister-in-law. Their names were Warren and Marie Madigan."

"Again," Dale says, "so what?"

"Dad didn't think a lot about it at the time, but when I showed him what I found..."

"Yeah, this is getting tedious," I say. "What exactly did you find?"

"A deed. A quitclaim deed, actually, transferring your entire ranch, including all buildings, improvements, and livestock, to a trust for the benefit of Ryan Steel."

"Wait, wait, wait." I try to wrap my head around Brendan's words and find that I can't. "What?"

"It's signed by Bradford Steel, but here's the thing... It's not dated."

"Give it to me. I can tell you if it's real or not."

"It's in a safe place."

"I'm a damned attorney, Murphy. You let me see the thing or my brother and I are out of here."

"I made a copy." He rises.

"A copy doesn't do any of us any good. I want to see the real thing."

"It's at the bank. In a safe-deposit box."

For God's sake. "Fine. Give me the copy."

Brendan walks to an end table and pulls open a drawer. He withdraws a large manila envelope and hands it to me.

I open it. Inside is indeed a copy of a quitclaim deed.

"What do you think, Don?" Dale asks.

"Fuck it all. It does look legit. We'd have to verify Brad Steel's signature. Why would he leave everything just to Uncle Ry? That doesn't make any sense."

"He *didn't* leave everything to Uncle Ry," Dale says. "When he died, all four of his kids inherited in equal shares."

"Have you seen his will?" I ask.

"Well . . . of course not. None of us saw it. We weren't even born when he died. Well, you, Henry, Brad, and I were, but we were kids."

I glance over the document once more. "If there's a trust, that means there's a trustee. There's no trustee mentioned on this document."

"Maybe there was never a trust," Dale says.

"The deed isn't dated, and it obviously was never recorded," I say. "Or if it was, Uncle Ry may have quitclaimed everything to his siblings in equal shares."

"Why did you call us here for this?" Dale asks Brendan.

"Because that's not the only part of the story."

"Okay . . . spill it," I say.

"Dad and I did some digging into the Madigans. Seems your grandfather had an affair with Jeremy Madigan's niece, Wendy. That affair resulted in . . ."

"In what?" I demand.

"Shit . . ." Dale says.

"What? I know there's something you're not telling me, Dale."

"Later," my brother says quietly.

"Their affair resulted in a child," Brendan continues.

"So we have another uncle or aunt out there somewhere," I say. "Someone who might want a piece of the Steel pie. Is that it?"

"It's not that simple," Brendan says. "There's another document in play."

"Oh?"

"Yeah. Apparently Brad Steel, your grandfather, had another sibling."

"I thought he was an only child," Dale says.

"Another sibling came out of the woodwork when your father and uncles were younger. He made contact with your uncle Jonah, but then he disappeared again."

"Where's this other document?" I ask.

"It's also in the safe-deposit box."

"I suppose you have a copy, though?"

"I do."

He reaches back into the drawer and removes another envelope, this one smaller. He hands it to me.

I pull out the copy—a birth certificate.

William Elijah Steel, father George Steel. Mother is blank. I hand it to Dale.

"It's been tampered with," I say. "I've heard of the father's name being left blank, but never the mother's. The kid had to come out of a woman."

"Unless she didn't want to be named," Brendan says.

I wrinkle my forehead. "So we've got a quitclaim deed transferring everything to Ryan, which is neither dated nor recorded. And we have a birth certificate for William Elijah Steel, supposedly fathered by George Steel, our great-grandfather, and who apparently came out of thin air."

"Birth certificates are easily forged," Dale says.

"And you know that how?" Brendan asks.

Dale says nothing.

Yeah, my brother has knowledge I don't, and it's pissing me off majorly.

"Why call us down here for this?" I ask. "Why not give it to our dad? To Ryan?"

"Dad and I talked about that. We figured you two were the best to approach first, because . . . Well, you know."

"Because we're not really Steels," I say flatly.

"Well . . . yeah."

"You know, Murphy, that shit pisses me off to no end. Dale and I *are* Steels. In every way that fucking matters. Our parents don't differentiate between us and their natural kids. Why are you?"

"I don't mean any disrespect," Brendan says. "I've got nothing against any of you. But these documents could pose problems for your family."

"Not if you board them back up underneath your floor," Dale says in a low voice.

Classic Dale. He's spent his life burying his emotions. He's opened up since Ashley came along, but he still doesn't want to deal with this can of worms.

Truth be told, part of me doesn't either—the part who's a devoted son and nephew who'd do anything for his family.

The problem is the other part. The lawyer part. I have to know the facts, *especially* where my family is concerned. Investigate facts, come to a conclusion, and if it's harmful, make it go away by any means possible, including a payoff. In corporate law, we call that a settlement.

"I can't do that," Brendan says. "My dad already knows about it."

"So the two of you can keep quiet," Dale says. "No sweat off either of your backs."

"It's not that simple," Brendan says. "We know, and . . ."

"Oh, for fuck's sake," Dale says. "You're looking for a payoff, aren't you? The fucking nerve."

Anger rises in me. Seriously? That's what this is about? A fucking payoff? Sure, I've settled many a case in my day, but not until the facts are known. "Boy, are you barking up the wrong tree, Murphy." I clench both hands into fists.

"That's not what this is about," Brendan says. "We did some research. Not much came up, of course. Your grandfather was a genius at making documents disappear."

"Just wait a minute," I begin.

"Again, no disrespect. Ask your parents if you don't believe me."

"I intend to," I say. "For now, though, I'm asking you. If you don't want a payoff, what do you want?"

"All I want is the cloud off the title of this place."

"There's a cloud on the title?" I ask.

"Yeah. Has been since Dad purchased it all those years ago. It's a lien. Held by the Steel family."

I look around the tiny room. It's been updated with contemporary appliances and decor. The bar downstairs is equally modern. Sean Murphy clearly did a lot of remodeling when he bought it, and Brendan's taken great care of it. Why would the Steels hold any kind of lien on a building in town?

"I didn't even know about it until Dad told me," Brendan says. "He said he'd all but forgotten about it until these documents showed up."

"I see," I say. "You want us to give up the lien in exchange for these documents. Why should we?"

"You know why. The Steels don't need whatever value this property has. Why is the lien there, anyway?"

I draw in a breath. "Liens are usually a way of securing debt. Did your father ever owe the Steels anything?"

"He says he didn't."

"Did the Steels hold a mortgage when your dad bought the place?"

"No. Like I said, he bought it from Jeremy Madigan," Brendan says. "I don't want any trouble with the Steels. I like all you guys. But Dad and I want this place to be free of the lien. Once the lien is gone, Dad and I will hand over the originals."

I nod. "Fair enough."

CHAPTER TEN

Callie

I drink my beer slowly. I'm not a big drinker. Truth be told, I prefer Diet Coke to just about anything. I shake my head when Laney comes by asking if we want another.

"Yeah, I'm done too," Rory says.

"I should get home. Apparently I have a big day tomorrow."

Rory smiles. "Not every day you go after your dream job."

I scoff. "It's hardly my dream job, but without a law school education or a license to practice, it's the best I can do—at least the best in Snow Creek, Colorado."

"You'll get it."

I scoff again. "We don't even know if there's a job to get."

"Make there be a job," Rory says. "You can convince anyone of anything."

"I think Jade Steel probably has the upper hand. I may be able to win an argument with Mom and Dad, but Jade's been an attorney for twenty-five years. Besides, I'm not going over there to argue."

"Nope. You're going over there to—" Rory shifts her gaze to the staircase and waggles her eyebrows. "Here come the Steel boys, back from whatever they were doing up there with Brendan."

"God, sis, you make everything sound dirty."

Indeed, it's Rory's gift. She can make any sentence sound dirty just with her tone of voice. Another reason the men of Snow Creek all held a vigil when she came out. Although, really, it was because of her boobs.

I look over my shoulder . . . and then instantly regret it.

Donny Steel meets my gaze. Man, those hazel eyes! He's dressed in Levi's and a white button-down, which accents his tanned skin nicely. He's slightly darker in skin and hair from his brother, and the effect is . . . Well, my flesh is heating.

He walks toward our table, his gaze never leaving mine.

"Good evening, Pike women," he says nonchalantly.

"Hey, Donny." Rory nods. "Dale."

"My brother and I would love to buy you two lovelies a drink."

Rory stands. "I'm just leaving, but I'm sure Callie can be convinced."

"Actually, I—"

"Sit, please," Donny says. "In fact, I'm pretty sure my big brother has a wife to get home to."

"I do." Dale nods. "But I'm your ride, remember?"

"I could probably talk Callie into driving me home to the ranch. It's not that far out of your way, right?"

I don't speak. I'm stunned. Sure, we hung out at the wedding reception, flirted big-time, but we didn't even kiss. I sure wasn't expecting to see him tonight. I figured I'd go to his mom's office tomorrow, beg for a job, and possibly run into him. Maybe he'd offer to take me to lunch, and I'd have to break my date with Rory.

"Where's Raine?" Dale asks Rory.

"In Denver with her parents."

"Stay, then," Dale says. "Let my brother buy you a drink."

Rory laughs. "I'm done for the evening, but thanks. I'll hitch home with you, if you don't mind, Dale."

"No problem," Dale says.

"Great. See you, sis." Rory heads toward the exit.

O-kay. Now what? Three's a crowd, but I'm suddenly squirming at the thought of being alone with Mr. Steel the younger.

"Tell you what," Donny says. "If you let me buy you a drink, I'll let you drive me home."

"Tempting," I finally say, "but it's getting late."

"It's ten forty-five," he says.

"Don, Rory and I are out of here," Dale says.

"See? I need a ride home, Callie."

"Fine. Let's have a drink." It's not like we can go anywhere. He's staying with his parents, and I'm staying with mine. This isn't going to lead anywhere except with both of us horny.

Dale follows Rory toward the exit, and Donny takes her seat. "What are you drinking? Beer?"

"I had a beer. Now I'm drinking Diet Coke."

"Caffeine'll keep you up."

"Are you kidding? I'm so addicted to caffeine that I sleep like a baby."

He laughs. "Me too, actually." He signals Laney. "Two Diet Cokes over here, please."

"You're not drinking?"

"Don't tell my brother or my father, but I'm not really into wine or bourbon."

"What's your pleasure, then?"

He lifts his eyebrows.

Did I really just say those words? I was talking about his drink of choice, and he thinks I'm flirting.

Not a huge deal, but I'm usually not quite so overt.

"For now?" he says. "Diet Coke. Later? We'll see."

Not that I'm averse to having a quickie with Donny Steel, but again, where does he think we'll go?

"Good enough," I say simply.

"So I'm back for good. Have you heard?"

I nod. "Mom told me. Your mom invited us all to your big welcome home bash tomorrow night."

He laughs. "My mom will take any excuse to have one of her bashes."

"They're always fun. Jesse says she booked his band again."

Donny lifts his eyebrows. "I thought they were going to LA for a tour."

"They were. The fire changed some stuff, and Jess decided to stay here."

"Oh. I'm sorry to hear that."

I sigh. "It is what it is."

"Dale's bummed about his vines." Then he bites his lip. "Sorry. I know you guys have it a lot worse."

Please, don't pity us. I can't take it. "We'll deal. We always do."

"If there's anything we can—"

I raise my hand. "Please. Just don't."

"I just mean—"

"I know you're trying to help. I do. But think about how you'd feel if our situations were reversed."

He pauses a moment. Then, "I understand. I'm sorry."

I smile. "No need to be sorry. We appreciate the fact that your family wants to help, but the Pikes have always made their own way, you know?" Tried, anyway.

"I do know. Believe me."

I cock my head slightly. Truth lies in his words somewhere. Donny wasn't always a Steel. No one really knows where he and Dale came from originally, but they were both old enough to have memories of their former life.

Maybe one day I'll know him well enough that he'll want to share those memories with me.

I'm busy thinking about how to reply, when he continues.

"Tell me, Callie. Where have you been?"

I wrinkle my forehead. "Uh . . . right here?"

"I mean, why haven't I noticed you until now?"

My cheeks warm as I ponder what to say.

Laney returns with our drinks and sets them down. "Anything else?"

Donny doesn't reply. He's too busy gazing into my eyes, making my insides melt.

"I'm good. Thanks, Laney." I pick up my glass and take a sip.

"So," Donny continues after Laney leaves, "you were saying?"

I swallow my drink. "I wasn't saying anything."

"I asked where you've been."

"And I told you. Here. You're the one who *wasn't* here. You've been in Denver for the past"—I calculate in my head—"fifteen years." Geez. I was only thirteen when Donny left for college fifteen years ago.

"I've been back to visit."

"Now and then, but when you went to Denver for school, you were gone. You never came back permanently."

"Until now."

"I suppose not."

"So why haven't I noticed you?"

Because you were busy chasing anyone else in a skirt. Nope, not the right thing to say to strike the mood I'm going for.

"That's on you," I finally say. "I've been here, except when I was in the city attending undergrad. Plus, I was ..."

"You were what?"

"Too young, Donny. When you left for school, I was thirteen."

He smiles. "You're not too young now."

I bite my lip as sparks skitter across my cheeks.

"And I'll be honest," he continues. "You Pike women have always been beautiful."

My God, I'm going to be scarred from the fire consuming my cheeks.

I clear my throat. "Good genes, I guess. My mom was Miss Grand Junction when she was young."

And yeah, I want to jump in a hole. Why did I bring that up?

"Oh?" he says. "I didn't know there was such a thing."

"There isn't any longer. It was a county fair thing, but they stopped it a while ago. A bunch of people signed a petition saying it was degrading to women. Pageants are kind of outdated, but my mom got some great benefits. A full year of college tuition paid for, and a trip all around Colorado doing promo gigs."

And why again am I talking about this? Like Donovan Steel, Esquire, gives a crap that my mother was the winner of a local beauty pageant. *Geez, shut up, Callie.*

"If it still existed, you'd win for sure."

Not likely. Not against either of his sisters, nor any of his cousins, for that matter. We Pikes may be pretty, but the

Steels are gorgeous.

Am I supposed to respond to his observation? If I say no, I'll seem self-deprecating. If I say yes, I'll seem conceited.

There's just no easy response.

So I take another sip of Diet Coke.

"I'm noticing now, Callie."

His words are slow and raspy, and they tug on me, landing in all the places that make me hot. *This* is the Donny Steel I know. Seducer of women.

Yeah, I was headed to bed with him a week ago at the wedding reception. But I was drinking that night. It was a party. Jesse's band was playing. We were dancing, laughing, in the moment, until the unthinkable happened.

Clearer heads are prevailing now.

I want him. I mean, I *really* want him. I haven't had sex in a while. It's kind of tough when you live at your parents' place. My last serious relationship was five years ago, when I was still in college.

"I know you spent your adolescence mooning over my brother," Donny says.

My God, surely my cheeks are burned to a crisp by now, yet the sparks keep erupting.

"You weren't the only one. Dale has that brooding thing going on that seems to be irresistible to women." Donny takes a drink of soda. "Frankly, I don't get the appeal."

"It's the hair," I say.

He chuckles. "That long hair? Really? Man, I couldn't do it. But then, a lot of you ladies do it. Isn't it a pain in the ass?"

I laugh then. "Yeah, it can be. That's why mine is out of my face most of the time. Part of ranching too."

"My sisters both wear their hair long. Not an issue for

Diana, since she doesn't do much ranch work, but Bree's out in the orchards with Dad all the time when she's home."

"She wears it up. It's not an issue."

"It'd be easier to cut it off."

"I've thought about it," I say truthfully. "What do you think? Should I cut it off? Wear one of those short styles?"

His eyes widen then, and he looks almost frightened. "God, no. You should *never* cut your hair."

"Then why'd you bring it up?"

"Because of your comment about Dale. I don't get the appeal of long hair on men. But he refuses to cut it. It's not like any of the rest of the guys in our family wear it like that. Henry and Brad wear theirs a little longer than most, but not down past the shoulders like Dale does."

"It's sexy," I say. "I'm not sure why, but it is."

"Your brother wears his long."

"Oooh! That's not what I mean. My brother is *not* sexy. He's my brother. Besides, he's a rocker. That's how rockers wear their hair."

"Not all rockers."

"But a lot."

He takes another drink.

Yeah, sexy convo we're having. Talking about his brother's hair. *God, Callie. Get a grip.*

Silence reigns for a few awkward moments, until—

"You want to go to dinner tomorrow?" he asks.

"Isn't tomorrow evening the big welcome home bash?"

He blushes. Donovan Steel, Esquire, actually blushes! And man, it makes him even handsomer.

"Right," he says.

"How quickly you forget."

He meets my gaze then, and I feel like those gorgeous hazel eyes are penetrating my soul.

"Easy to forget when I'm sitting across from the most beautiful woman in Colorado."

CHAPTER ELEVEN

Donny

Callie's cheeks are an amazing shade of pink. Like the petals of a dusty rose. God, who talks like that? Since when do I wax poetic?

Again I remember the red-gold poppy I saw once at a benefit in Denver. So close to the color of her eyes.

She says nothing.

"The night after, then?" I prod.

That gorgeous blush? It's extending down her neck to the tops of her breasts, which are visible due to the V-neck T-shirt she's wearing. It's black, with an imprint of a dragon and Jesse's band's name, Dragonlock, embroidered in bright red.

She takes a sip of Diet Coke, trying to pull off coy, but her blush gives her away. "Sure. That'd be fun."

"Awesome. It's a date, then." I polish off the rest of my soda. "You want another?"

"No. I'm good. Thanks."

I pull my wallet out of my pocket and leave a few tens on the table for Laney. "Ready?"

"Sure."

She stands, and I get a great look at her body. The T-shirt is formfitting, and her skinny jeans adhere to that marvelous ass. She may not have the breast size of her sisters, but that ass... She's got them both beat on the posterior. I'd like to slide my tongue between those cheeks and give her the rimming of a lifetime.

I drop my gaze lower. She's tall and lean-legged, and I imagine those shapely gams wrapped around my neck as I pound into her.

Fuck. My groin tightens.

She walks toward the exit, and I follow. I feel like a high school kid about to make out with my girlfriend in the car. Crazy shit.

I'm definitely getting the vibe from her. She may talk a good game, but I've seen her body react. That blush... Those swollen breasts... She's turned on.

And so am I.

I follow her out the door of the bar, and my other head takes over.

In an instant, I push her back against the brick of the building, and I crush my lips to hers.

She gasps softly and then parts her lips, letting me in.

She tastes sweet—a mixture of hops and diet soda—and I sweep into her mouth, finding her tongue and tangling it with my own.

Callie Pike knows how to kiss, and it's refreshing. So many women are passive kissers, but not this one. She invades my mouth as I invade hers. I go deeper, and she goes deeper, until our tongues are engaged in a duel for control.

Fuck, she's hot.

My cock is already hard, and I push it against her belly. A groan vibrates from her throat and through my clothes, taking over my body. Just one little groan from her, and I'm on fire.

I'm ready. I could fuck her right now up against the outside wall of Murphy's Bar.

Wouldn't be the first time I've had sex in a public place.

But Callie Pike deserves better.

I brace myself to break the kiss, when she grabs my ass and pulls me closer into her.

That being a gentleman thing? The idea that she deserves better? Just flew straight out the window.

The Snow Creek Inn is a block around the corner.

If I can just disengage my mouth long enough to get there.

But this kiss… This amazing, soul-crushing kiss…

I love kissing. I do. But it's never been more than a prelude to better things. This kiss, though?

I'm so hard I'm ready to burst. From a kiss.

Now that would make sense if I were sixteen. At thirty-two, it's a different story.

Except right now it's not.

The high school isn't far from here. Man, I feel like a horny kid ready to take his girlfriend under the bleachers.

Can't do it. Can't…

But my thoughts are jumbled. I tell my mouth to stop kissing her, but it doesn't want to listen.

Hell, *I* don't want to listen. I could kiss Callie Pike all night and still want more of her full, sweet lips, her silky tongue, her perfect flavor.

I deepen the kiss, exploring every millimeter of her sweet mouth, and—

She pushes at my chest, breaking the kiss with a loud pop of suction.

"My God." She gasps, her breath coming in rapid puffs.

"You said it," I say, rearranging things inside my jeans.

Callie's mouth hangs open, her breathing still rapid. Her

nipples—oh, God, her nipples. They're poking through that black T-shirt like hard little knobs. I itch to reach toward her, cup one of those perfect tits, give that nipple a pinch.

"I can't..." She shakes her head, squirming.

I inhale. Yeah. The scent. The scent of a woman's sex.

Fucking intoxicating.

She's wet, and I want to slip my tongue between her legs and have a feast.

"You want to go somewhere?" I ask.

No response. She's still panting. "That kiss..."

"Was pretty fucking spectacular," I finish for her.

"I'll say..."

"So...you didn't answer my question."

"What question?"

Good sign. She's in a buzz of hormones, not thinking clearly.

"Do you want to go somewhere?"

She blinks a few times, clearly trying to regain her rational thought. That's okay. It's rational for her to want to go to bed with me. Right?

Her breathing slows, and she exhales a long breath. "Wow."

"Yeah, wow. You're beautiful, Callie."

"So are you."

I smile. She's not the first woman to use that word to describe me, but she's the first who made it sound desirable.

So are you. Those three words, in her sultry voice, mean everything to me in this moment.

I won't press her on the going somewhere issue. I've asked twice, and I won't ask again.

I buss her quickly on the cheek. "Where's your car?"

"About a block over." She pauses a moment. "By the hotel."

Oh my God . . .

I grab her hand—it's small and warm in mine—and we walk toward the hotel.

The hotel.

The Snow Creek Inn.

The neon sign looms in the distance, seeming to pulse with each rapid beat of my heart.

Va-cancy. Va-cancy. Va-cancy.

Dare I ask one more time?

But she heads straight to her Chevy sedan and clicks her fob, unlocking the doors. "Your chariot awaits, my lord."

I chuckle. "Are we being British now?"

"It's always a good time to be British," she replies in a perfect royal accent.

I slide into the passenger seat, all smiles. So much I don't know about Caroline Pike, but what I do know, I like.

I like it a lot.

Maybe getting her into bed right away isn't the way to tackle the lovely Caroline.

Maybe I should take it slow with her.

And maybe I'm sounding nothing like myself by having these thoughts.

She starts the engine and pulls out of her spot.

I rearrange the bulge in my pants discreetly.

Fuck, this is going to be a long night.

CHAPTER TWELVE

Callie

It isn't lost on me that I was parked right by the hotel.

It also isn't lost on me that Donny wanted to get a room.

So did I.

But then I figured maybe it wasn't the best idea, when I'm heading back into town first thing tomorrow to ask his mother for a job.

Donny Steel will still be here after I meet with Jade. She'll give me a position, or she'll let me down easily. Either way, I have to get that over with before I start anything with her son. I have to be professional, and Donny's about to be sworn in as her assistant city attorney.

Not cool to be sleeping with a potential boss.

At least not yet.

And yeah, I'm horny as hell. I've never had a kiss like that. Right now, my whole body is awash in flashing sparks.

I'm not sure what to say. I never did answer Donny's question—the one where he asked if I wanted to go somewhere.

Yeah, I heard him both times. I just played the hormonal fool the first time to get out of answering. Said the amorphous "wow" the second time.

Because if I actually answered the question, it would have been a resounding yes.

But clearer minds prevailed, thank goodness.

First, talk to Jade Steel.

Second, sleep with her son.

In that order.

If he's still interested tomorrow.

With Donny Steel, you never know. He could meet someone else between now and then. He could easily drive back into town, hook up with a local, and be at the party tomorrow night chasing another skirt.

"So . . ." Donny says.

"Yeah?"

"Where do you want to go?"

I wrinkle my forehead. "You mean now?"

"No. I mean on our date. The night after tomorrow."

"Oh, right. Whatever you want is fine. I eat anything."

"There are some great places in the city, or we could eat here in town. Up to you."

"I'll love whatever you choose."

"Good enough." He pauses a moment. Then, "Did I come on too strong?"

Really? We have to talk about this? Can I drive off a cliff now, please?

"No. I was into it, if you couldn't tell."

He chuckles. "I could tell."

Damn. Those sparks are dancing over my cheeks again. I swear I won't have skin left by the end of this night.

"So where'd I go wrong?"

"You didn't."

"That's not true, or we'd be hitting the sheets about now."

This time I giggle. I can't help myself. "Pretty sure of yourself, aren't you?"

"After that kiss, baby, yeah. I am."

"Maybe I don't go to bed with a guy on the first... whatever this was."

"Oh." He nods. "That's cool."

I don't sleep around, but in truth, if I weren't waltzing into his mother's office tomorrow, I probably would have gone with him to the hotel.

Sure, I'd be one of a whole lot of notches on his bedpost, but that's okay. I enjoy sex for the sake of sex. I just don't do it nearly as often as he does.

I'm not looking to fall in love anyway. Law school first, if I ever get there. That's what I want, and that's what I'm going to do. I can't focus on that if I'm in a serious relationship with an older man who's probably thinking about settling down and starting a family. The Steels are all about family.

Funny. I've never thought about denying myself sex before. I've never been afraid of falling in love before, because frankly, I don't think about love after a date. Or after a kiss.

This is different, though. Different in a way that makes me pretty darned uncomfortable.

I tell myself I'm thinking about sex for the sake of sex with Donny, but if that were truly the case, I'd be in bed with him right now.

The potential job with his mother is just an excuse. There probably isn't even a job, and if I were doing the horizontal tango with Donny right now, I just wouldn't go see Jade tomorrow. It's not like I have a scheduled interview with her. It's a cold call. Simple as that.

No, the reason I'm not in bed with this gorgeous man right now is simple.

So simple.

I don't want to fall in love.

I don't have time to fall in love.

And I could *so* easily fall in love with Donny Steel.

CHAPTER THIRTEEN

Donny

After another scorching hot kiss, I hop out of Callie's car, wave goodbye, and head into Mom and Dad's house. I'm horny as hell, but taking care of things myself doesn't appeal to me at the moment.

Mom goes to bed by ten, but Dad's usually up until midnight, so I head to his office. To my surprise, he's not there. He must be in bed already.

I walk behind his desk and sit down in his comfy leather chair. This house and office once belonged to my grandfather, Bradford Steel.

Who apparently signed a quitclaim deed transferring all his property to his youngest son, Ryan.

Dale knows something. I don't dare bother him at this hour. He's still a newlywed, and he's in bed with his wife, either sleeping or doing the thing that I wish I were doing with Callie Pike.

I've been in Dad's office many times, but things look decidedly different from this angle. Sure, I sat in his chair sometimes when I was a kid, but this is the first time I've sat here as an adult. Seems strange, but I've never been in here without Dad. I love the ranch, but I chose a different path. Mom, of course, was thrilled—that I chose the law, not so much that I left the ranch.

And here I am, back again.

I never thought I'd come back permanently. I thought the powerful law partnership in the big city was what I wanted.

But Mom asked.

And I said yes.

I don't ever have to worry about money. My love affair with big city life had nothing to do with the money I was making—and I was making some decent cash.

It was all icing on my already abundant cake.

Being a Steel means never worrying about money, which is pretty darned nice, frankly. Even if the fire destroyed everything we own, we'd still be okay. Grandpa Steel made sure of that. During his reign, he apparently diversified into all kinds of investments, including some amazing tech start-ups, and we're all set for at least four lifetimes. Still, the heartbeat of the Steels is still Steel Acres Ranch.

My father taught Dale and me the value of work. Even though we don't have to, we have a work ethic that doesn't quit.

Even before work ethic, though?

Comes family.

So when Mom asked me to come to work with her at the city attorney's office, it was a no-brainer.

Dale doesn't get it, and he probably never will. His work ethic is as strong as mine. Perhaps even stronger. But while he loves his family, he's isolated. He won't do something just because his family wants him to. He'll weigh the pros and cons and then make an informed decision. Usually family wins, but sometimes, it doesn't.

Perhaps being married will change that. Doesn't really matter, since his chosen path kept him here on the ranch anyway, so he's around whenever the family needs him.

I'm happy for Dale. He has someone who will help him be less isolated. But Dale will always be Dale. I wouldn't have him any other way.

I don't think about our past much, but sometimes it creeps in anyway.

I owe my big brother a huge debt I'll never be able to repay.

Maybe that's why I value family so much.

It began with my big brother.

But it's also from the Steels.

Dad, Uncle Joe, Uncle Ry, and Aunt Marj, along with their significant others, have instilled in all us kids that sense of family.

I always assumed it came from their father, Bradford Steel.

Now I'm not so sure.

Why would Grandpa Steel quitclaim everything he owned to Uncle Ryan? Leaving his other three children with nothing?

Clearly, it wasn't dated, and it had never been recorded.

But it *was* signed.

I suppose it could be forged. I'll have to look at other documents Brad Steel signed to know for sure, but . . .

This is a mystery.

I sigh. Okay. I'm going to find out why we have a lien on the Murphy property, get rid of it, and then Brendan and his dad will give Dale and me those documents. We'll destroy them, and our family never needs to know they exist.

They'd just cause problems we don't need.

First, though, I'll find the truth.

So . . . if I were a document pertaining to a lien on a bar in town, where would I be?

Nosing around Dad's office feels all wrong. I could just ask him in the morning.

Of course, in the morning, I have to go into the office with Mom.

Why not have a look around now?

Dad has two file cabinets in his office, both of which are locked. No help there. His desktop computer is password protected, of course.

I stand.

Ethics take over. I can't go nosing around Dad's documents without his permission. I just can't. I'm ready to walk out from behind the desk, when—

"Donny? What are you doing in here?"

Shit. Dad's still awake, apparently. He stands in the doorway, clad in lounge pants and a white T-shirt.

"Nothing," I say.

He chuckles. "Nothing? You sound just like you did when you were a kid and had done something wrong. What's going on?"

"I didn't look at anything."

"No one's accusing you, but you came in here in the middle of the night for a reason."

"I just got back from the bar."

"And instead of going to bed, you came into my office."

I have no response.

"What do you want, Don?"

Fuck it all. "Murphy says the Steels hold a lien on the bar."

He widens his eyes slightly and then nods. "We do."

"What for?"

"Honestly? I don't know. It's been there forever. No one really thinks about it."

"Dad, you expect me to buy that?"

"No, Don. I don't." He gestures. "Have a seat."

I sit back down, but not in his chair this time. I walk out from behind his desk and sit in one of the leather chairs on the other side.

The office looks completely different from this vantage point—the one I'm used to.

"How'd you find out about the lien?"

"Brendan mentioned it tonight."

Dad rubs the graying stubble on his chin. "Seems a strange thing to bring up over a drink."

"Not so strange," I say quickly. As a lawyer I know well how to bullshit. Whether it will work on my dad, though, is another story. "We were talking about our respective families."

Dad clears his throat. "Oh? What about your respective families?"

What the heck? The death of Sean Murphy is no secret, is it? "Apparently Brendan's great-uncle and your father were friends."

Dad nods. "They were."

I raise my eyebrows, expecting him to go on.

He doesn't.

Why am I not surprised?

"Dad, what's the story? With your father and Sean's uncle?"

"I think you know," Dad says. "I think that's why you brought it up."

Yeah. Should have known he'd see right through me. I can pull anything over on Mom. She's a soft touch. Dad? Not so much.

"Did he really drop dead at your father's wedding?"

"He did. It's not something we talk about because, as you can imagine, it's a horrible thing."

"It is. But we just had another man drop dead here in our own backyard a week ago, Dad."

Dad rubs his chin some more. "We did. But Dennis had a stroke and subsequent heart attack due to undiagnosed hypertension. That's different."

"How is it different?"

"Because Sean Murphy was drugged and poisoned."

My jaw nearly drops on my lap. "By whom?"

"We don't know. The police never found a suspect."

"That's crazy."

"It happens. Crimes go unsolved all the time."

I shake my head. "Doesn't that bother you? Didn't you look into it?"

"Would that change anything?"

"Well . . . no, but—"

"Don," Dad says in his *I'm your father and don't contradict me* voice, "the young man died. Nothing will ever bring him back. He'd most likely be dead by now anyway. This all happened over half a century ago. Why are you dredging it up?"

"Because it sucks, Dad. The guy dropped dead at a wedding. Right here in our backyard."

Dad sighs. "I didn't find out about it myself until I was well into adulthood. By that time, nothing could be done. Any trail was long cold. The cops did what they could at the time, and I'm sure my father had the best PIs on the job."

"For God's sake, Dad."

"I understand. This is new to *you*. But it's not new. It happened a long time ago."

"Brendan says his dad came here to Snow Creek for

answers, but all he found were dead ends."

"That doesn't surprise me."

"He seems to think ..."

"He seems to think what?"

"He seems to think something nefarious went on. He thinks—"

I stop abruptly. I almost said, *he thinks people seem to disappear when the Steels are involved.*

But Dad's right. This was decades ago, and nothing we do now will bring Brendan's great-uncle back.

More to the point, though, I realize something about myself.

I trust my mother and father. I trust them with my life. I always have.

But there's one person I trust even more, who I'd take a bullet for in a minute without hesitation.

Dale.

My brother.

And he asked me to keep mum about this until the two of us talked about how to deal with it. As much as keeping something from my father feels foreign to me, I make the decision to do it this time.

I'll speak only to Dale—and Brendan, when necessary— about these developments.

Tomorrow is Friday. Mom said I didn't have to go into the office until Monday, but I told her I'd go tomorrow.

I'll renege in the morning.

Instead, I'll take the day to do some research. Dale will be busy with his old-vine Syrah and the other wines, so this is on me for now.

Where will I start? I have no idea.

But I *will* find what I'm looking for.
I always do.

CHAPTER FOURTEEN

Callie

I park a block away from the tiny city courthouse and administration building. The tiny police department and fire department sit across the street. I leave my car, nearly stumbling in my black pumps.

I want to be an attorney more than anything in the world, but I hate dressing the part. I'm a jeans, tank, and cowboy boots girl. Western all the way.

But today? Full power. Navy-blue linen skirt and jacket, white blouse, pantyhose—ugh!—and black leather pumps. I walk slowly, my pulse racing, toward the administrative building. It's ten a.m. on the dot. I draw in a deep breath and pull open the door.

"May I help you?" a receptionist asks.

"I'm here to see Jade Steel."

"I'm pretty sure she's in court right now. Did you have an appointment?"

Court. Crap. Of course she's in court. It's not like she sits around twiddling her thumbs, waiting for Callie Pike to waltz in and demand a job.

"No, I . . . I'll just come back later."

"Oh . . . wait. Here she comes now."

Heels clack on the tiled floor.

"Jade," the receptionist calls. "This young lady is here to see you."

Kill me. Just kill me now.

"Oh?" Jade's voice. "Good morning... Callie! Hi there."

Jade looks like a fashion plate in her straight black skirt and silk blouse. Suddenly I feel like an idiot in my suit.

"Hi," I say, trying not to sound too timid.

"What can I do for you?"

"Well...I was wondering... You know, about law school... And I'm not going yet because of the... So..."

I'm a bumbling idiot. My humiliation is complete.

"You want to talk about something?" Jade asks.

I breathe in. I've already made a complete fool of myself. May as well go for broke. "I was wondering if you have any jobs available in your office. I'm home for now, and my parents can't pay me for obvious reasons, so I need to find a job, and, you know, my interest is in the law, so I figured it wouldn't hurt to come in and talk to you."

There. I got the words out without stammering. Huge run-on sentence, but still... Nice job.

I brace myself to get shot down.

"Sure, let's chat about that. Come on up to my office." Jade leads me to a staircase to the left of reception. "All our offices are upstairs. The courtrooms are down here. Have you been here before?"

"Only once, when I had to pay a speeding ticket."

"You've probably never been upstairs, then."

We reach the top of the stairs, and she leads me down a hallway. We walk past Alyssa Dean, the secretary. Alyssa and I went to school together. My cheeks redden.

Jade gestures to an empty office. "Mary's already moved

out. This will be Donny's office. He was going to start today, but then he decided to wait until Monday."

I'm both disappointed and relieved. A weird combination that makes me want to smile and vomit at the same time.

Jade opens the door to another office. "Come on in and have a seat." She walks behind her desk and sits.

I take one of the three chairs opposite hers.

She smiles. "So . . . you need a job."

I nod. "Yeah. And I can get something else easily, but my interests are here."

"I understand. With Donny starting next week, my funds are limited, but we do need someone to do basic stuff, like filing, running errands, and such."

"Oh." I try not to sound too disappointed. After all, she could have easily said she has nothing.

"I'm sure you're way overqualified, though," Jade says.

"My undergrad degree is in criminal justice. I'd love to do some investigating, if possible."

"We have a full-time investigator," she says.

"Oh! I wasn't suggesting—"

Jade smiles. "I know you weren't. Frankly, you're probably more qualified than Troy, but he's been with me for ten years now, and he does a good job."

"I understand. About the other position . . ."

"Forget I suggested it," Jade says. "You won't be happy being anyone's errand girl."

I clear my throat. "Actually, I'd love it. I'd at least be in a law office, and I hope you'll feel free to give me any assignments you think I could handle given my education and background."

"I'm sure sorry about law school, Callie."

Please, please, please don't pity me.

"It is what it is. My family needs me now, and I'll be there for them. I'll be a lot more help if I can support myself, so if you're offering... I'd love to accept the position."

"Don't you want to know what I'll pay?"

I force out a chuckle. "Whatever it is, it's more than I'm making now."

"Good enough." Jade rises. "Alyssa can get the paperwork for you. When can you start?"

"Today?"

Jade laughs. "Monday will be fine. Besides, I'm leaving after lunch today anyway. I have a lot to do before the party tonight."

Right. The party. Donny's welcome home party.

I stand. "I can't thank you enough, Jade. Or should I call you Ms. Steel here?"

"Don't be silly. Everyone calls me Jade. We're pretty casual."

"So the suit's a bit much?" I let out a nervous laugh.

"Are you kidding? You look amazing. But feel free to dress more casually. I only wear a skirt when I have court."

I nod, not sure what to say.

She glances down at her desk. "You know what? I think I'll just take off now. My calendar's clear for the rest of the day. What do you say to an early lunch?"

"I'd love it, but I'm meeting Rory at Lorenzo's at noon." I bite my lip. "Would you like to join us?"

"No, that's okay, but it's sweet of you to offer. I'll head over to Ava's for a sandwich and then get home. Marjorie will be thrilled I'm home earlier to help. We'll see you and Rory tonight, I hope. Along with the rest of the family."

"As far as I know, yeah. Except Raine's out of town. She's

visiting her parents in Denver."

"We'll miss her," Jade says. "Glad the rest of you can make it. Your brother's band is playing."

"Yeah, he told me. So . . . what time should I be here on Monday?"

"We start around eight. I'm usually here a little earlier. Talon has me on ranch time."

I smile. "Sounds good. Thanks so much."

"You're very welcome. I'm thrilled you're coming on board. See you tonight?"

I nod, smiling, and leave Jade's office.

★ ★ ★

"Earth to Cal," Rory says over Diet Coke while we wait for our lunch at Lorenzo's. "When your new boss offers you lunch, you go."

"But you and I had plans."

"We've only had lunch together . . . what? About a thousand times? And we'll do it a thousand more times in the near future."

I twist my lips. "Did I really just make a huge faux pas?"

"Yeah, a little."

"Crap."

"Of course, the main thing is that you got a job. You did what you set out to do. Nice going!"

"The job is grunt work."

"It's still a job, and it's in your chosen field. There are no small jobs, Cal. Just small people."

"Nice, Ror. Throwing my own words back at me."

"Well, they're good words. They worked when you said

them to me, and I came to find out that, yeah, I'm a good opera singer, but I'm a *great* voice and piano teacher and pretty darned awesome rock singer too. That's my true calling. If you hadn't goaded me into hanging out my shingle, I'd never know."

The server arrives with our baked ziti. I inhale the spicy tomato and cheese fragrance.

"Do you need anything else?" The server raises her eyebrows.

"I'm good. Ror?"

"Nope. Good here."

"Will you guys be at the Steels' party tonight?" the server asks.

"Yeah," Rory replies. "We'll be there."

"I'm so excited," she says. "It's my first Steel party. I can't believe they invited me."

I smile. "They're very generous."

"I'm Nora, by the way. I met Ava over at the bakery. That's probably why I got an invite. She was talking about all her hot cousins. Except one recently got married, but his brother . . ."

I lift my eyebrows. "You mean Donny Steel?"

"Yeah. The hot lawyer who's moving back here. I can't wait to meet him."

Rory clears her throat. "All the Steel men are hot, Nora. And all are unmarried, except for Dale."

"I'm kind of a sucker for blond hair, though. Ava says most of them are dark."

My stomach is clenching. Yeah, it's jealousy, which pisses me off. I'm really not the jealous type. At all.

Nora is blond herself. Platinum blond. And young. And clearly she stuffs her bra. Nineteen at most, I'll bet.

"Are you new in town, Nora?" Rory asks.

"I've been here a few weeks. I'm surprised I haven't met either of you. It's such a small town."

"I'm Rory Pike, and this is my sister Callie." Rory holds out her hand.

Nora takes it. "Ava mentioned you guys. You're the music teacher and singer."

Rory nods.

"And what do you do, Callie?"

"I work with Jade Steel at the city attorney's office." I'm shocked at my own words. They just tumbled out without any thought at all.

"Oh! So you *know* the Steels."

"Yes. Plus our ranch is adjacent to theirs," I say.

Nora's blue eyes widen, the pupils nearly encompassing her blue irises. "I'm about ready for my break. Can I join you for a minute? Tell me everything."

"I'm sure you got the scoop from Ava," Rory says.

"Sort of. But she's their cousin. It's not like she's going to tell me how hot they all are."

Oh, God. This so isn't happening.

"How old are you, Nora?" I ask.

She smiles. "Just turned twenty-one last week."

I hide my surprise. The chick looks like she's barely out of high school. At least the Steels don't have to worry about serving her alcohol. And the Steels serve a *lot* of alcohol.

"All the Steels are great," Rory says. "But all the men are older than you."

"Not a problem for me."

"It may be for them," I say. "And Donny's the oldest, except for his brother, who's married."

"How old is he?"

"Thirty-two."

She beams. "I think older men are crazy sexy."

"Henry Simpson," Rory says.

I raise my brows at my sister.

"He's Marjorie Steel's son," Rory continues, "and he's blond, blue-eyed, and gorgeous."

Rory, I totally love you. If you ever need a kidney, I'm your girl.

"Henry, yeah. Ava did mention him when I told her I prefer blond men." Nora frowns. "But she said he has a girlfriend."

"I heard they broke up," I say.

Yeah, it's a lie. I don't feel bad about it.

Well, maybe a little bit, but I'd rather have Nora chasing Henry than Donny.

Nora looks down at her watch. "Break's over. It was totally awesome meeting you guys. I'll see you tonight!" She flounces off.

"Somewhere there's a guy with a huge butterfly net and a rock-hard dick looking for that woman." Rory laughs.

"Nice try with Henry," I tell her.

"I'm pretty sure he's still with Darlene," Rory says.

"I know. This will be a monumental test of their love."

"You just don't want her chasing after Donny."

"Really? Am I that transparent?" I say sarcastically.

"Callie, you have it all over that fluttering blonde." Rory smiles. "And tonight's your chance to prove it."

CHAPTER FIFTEEN

Donny

"Spill it," I say to my brother.

I've managed to steal him away from the winery for a quick lunch in town. We sit in a booth in the back of the Bluebird Diner, a Snow Creek staple.

"Couldn't this have happened at home?" Dale says.

"Ashley might be there."

"So?"

"I know she's your wife and you have no secrets, but I want this between us. At least for now. I love your wife, but I hardly know her."

He nods. "Okay, got it. But if she asks, I'm telling her. She and I have this thing between us called trust."

"Dude, I'm happy for you. I really am."

"It's crazy. I never thought this would happen for me. I thought I was too fucked up."

"I hear you. I worry about that too."

"You?"

"Sure I do. Why do you think I've never had a serious relationship? I just deal with it differently than you do. I have a lot of sex. You did a lot of yanking hank."

My brother chuckles. Actually chuckles.

"Man, marriage has been great for you. A couple months

ago, that comment would have pissed you off."

Dale smiles. "You're right. And I'll tell you, it's been nice to give the hand a rest."

"I doubt your hands have had any rest lately."

"Not a lot, but what they've been doing is a lot more fun."

"Seriously, bro. Ashley's great. I love her."

Dale reddens slightly. My big brother is happy, and deservedly so.

"So . . ." I begin. "I'll repeat myself. Spill it."

He draws in a breath. "Okay. But this goes no further than you. Got it?"

"Got it." I take a bite of burger and chew.

And Dale starts talking.

And with each word, my jaw drops farther.

"What do you mean Uncle Ry has a different mother? How does that even happen?"

"Dad didn't elaborate, and I didn't push because I had other things on my mind at the time."

"Yeah, I know. The fire. Ashley."

"To name two."

"I think we need to talk to Dad. Get some real answers."

"I agree," Dale says. "But Dad and his siblings kept all this shit secret for a reason. What would it do to Ava and Gina to know they're not our full cousins?"

"I don't know. We got over it. We're not their cousins at all. Biologically, that is."

"But we've *always* known that. What if we didn't? What if we just found out now? As adults?"

"I don't know. Would it matter?"

"Yeah, it would matter. It'd be like finding out you're not who you think you are. I don't want to do that to them."

"Do you think Aunt Ruby knows?"

"Honestly, I have no idea. Dad and I didn't get very far with the talk. Dennis had his stroke in the middle of our conversation."

"So that's where you disappeared to that night."

"You actually noticed? You sure seemed busy with Callie Pike."

"We were hanging out, that's all. Nothing happened."

"I didn't ask."

"Good, because before I tell you about Callie—and there's precious little to tell—I want the rest of what you know."

He takes a bite of his cheeseburger, chews achingly slowly, and finally swallows. "The next part is tough, but when you find out, it'll make a lot of sense."

"Okay . . . Freaking out a little here."

He clears his throat, eyeing the burger on his plate.

"No, no, no. Not another bite until you fess up."

He sighs. "All right. It's not like you and I ever talk about . . . *it.*"

It. No, we never talk about *it.* I've done my best for the last two decades to forget *it* ever happened.

"No, we don't. But why does that have—" I drop my mouth open. "Oh, God . . ."

"Yeah. Dad had a similar experience when he was young. My age, actually. He was ten."

"And Uncle Ry was my age. Seven."

Dale nods. "Except Uncle Ry got away. Apparently he and Dad were attacked, but Uncle Ryan somehow escaped. Dad thought it was because he kicked the guy holding Uncle Ry and then he told him to run."

"You would have done the same thing for me."

"I would have, if I'd had the chance. But it turns out Dad didn't do anything. Uncle Ry was never meant to be taken because of who he was."

I go numb. Seriously. I want to say something—I'm not even sure what—but my throat closes. My tongue goes limp.

"Whoever his real mother is was behind it all."

"Is she still alive?"

"I don't know. I didn't ask."

"Why the hell not?"

He shakes his head. "I can't really explain. I was going through some shit right after Ash and I got married."

I nod. When Dale says he's going through *some shit*, we both know what that means. He had it a lot worse than I did during that time. He protected me as much as he could. He wasn't always successful, but he was more than not. I owe him everything. I'm not sure I could have taken what he took. I'd be dead now. He was older, stronger, tougher.

He still is.

"I understand," I say. "But we do need to figure this out. Grandpa had an affair with the Madigan chick. That's got to be Ryan's mother, right? She's probably behind that quitclaim deed. She wanted everything to go to her kid instead of all of them."

"They—Dad and the others—don't talk about their father. Ever."

"Then we ask, Dale. He's our grandfather. We have the right to know."

"Sometimes, ignorance is bliss," Dale says, staring down at his half-eaten burger.

"Bull. Facts are important. Every single fact."

"In your line of work, yes, they are."

"I'm not talking about my line of work," I say. "I'm talking about life. Knowledge is power, Dale. Ignorance is lack of power, not bliss."

"I get that you believe that," Dale says.

"So do you, in your heart. What's eating you? I know you're still upset about the fire, about the vines, but—"

"This has nothing to do with that."

"Right. Those vines meant everything to you."

"They did. They do. But Ashley means more. *You* mean more. The family means more. I've always known that, in the back of my mind. I understand why you think it's about the vines, but it's not."

"What is it, then?"

"All I can say is that I was going through some shit."

"That didn't have anything to do with the fire or the vines."

"Correct." He picks up his burger and takes another bite.

He *is* dealing with something, and he isn't ready to tell me about it. Okay, I can deal with that. I know him. This is Isolated Dale—the term I use when he gets like this.

"I'll accept that," I tell him, "until the time comes that I need to know. Got it?"

He finishes chewing and meets my gaze. "Understood."

CHAPTER SIXTEEN

Callie

My little sister, Maddie, hitched a ride home from the city with Gina Steel, Ava's sister. They both go to Mesa State College in Grand Junction. The Steels always come home for the big parties if they can. Brianna Steel, Donny's sister, and Angie and Sage Simpson, Marjorie's twin daughters, also go to undergrad at Mesa. They drove home separately.

So all the Steels, save Diana, Donny's other sister, who works at an architecture firm in Denver, will be in attendance at the welcome-back-Donny shindig. She must have plans she couldn't break, or she couldn't get off work in time to drive or catch a flight. It's a five-hour drive from Denver.

"Let's go!" Maddie urges.

"Don't you know about being fashionably late?" I say.

"I'm starving, and they'll have tons of food. Plus . . ."

"What?"

"Steel guys, Cal. Come on."

One Steel guy in particular has my attention. "Oh? Aren't they all too old for you?"

"A gal can dream."

"Spill it, Mads. Which one do you have your eye on?"

"Not Donny, sis. Don't worry."

"Yeah, well, he's *definitely* too old for you. Which one?"

"Does it matter? As long as it's not the one you want?"

"I don't—"

"Spare me, please. I saw how you made googly eyes at him at the last Steel party. Plus, Rory already filled me in."

"This isn't you answering my question. Which one?"

"Honestly? I'm not sure. Henry and Brad are both gorgeous, but they're taken."

"For now," I say.

"Oh? Do you have intel I don't?"

"Not really. There's a certain blond waitress who I think will be following Henry's every move tonight."

"Who?"

"Nora something or other. She's new in town."

"Brock, then."

"Brock Steel? Eminent seducer of women? I don't think so. Not with *my* sister, he doesn't."

"*Your* sister is twenty-one. Way past legal. And Brock is sex on a stick. So is Dave."

She isn't wrong. All the Steels are gorgeous. Even Talon and his siblings still look amazing at their ages. Marjorie is Jade's age, and she doesn't look much older than Rory.

Mom sticks her head in my bedroom. "We're heading over. Want to come along?"

Maddie jumps off my bed. "Absolutely."

"Thanks," I say, "but I'll go over later with Rory."

"Rory's gone," Mom says. "She went over early to help Jesse set up."

Thanks for telling me, Ror.

I sigh. "Okay. Give me two seconds."

I head into my bathroom to check things out. I don't wear makeup as a rule. My skin is clear—now, anyway—and I was blessed with naturally long eyelashes. Tonight, though, I swipe on some blush and apply a dark-pink lip gloss. My hair is pulled back in my signature low ponytail, but I wonder…

I tug the scrunchie off and let my hair fall over my shoulders. It's light brown and sleek, and it falls nearly to my butt.

Dare I?

"Let's go!" Maddie prods.

That settles it, then. Hair down it is.

"Coming." I head out of my bedroom and outside to my parents' car.

★ ★ ★

I've been here for an hour, and I haven't even seen Donny yet. I'm hanging with Maddie, who's gossiping with Angie, Sage, and Gina. Brianna, the last of their fivesome, is busy flirting with my brother and the rest of his band members. Never took her for a groupie.

They're gossiping about classes and professors and guys, oh my. I'm surprised Maddie hasn't latched on to a Steel guy yet, but she seems happy hanging with her friends for now.

I answer when they speak to me, but I'm otherwise engaged with scoping out the place. Where's Donny? For that matter, I haven't seen Dale and Ashley yet, either.

But Donny should be here. This party is for him.

Jade approaches us then, looking gorgeous as usual, in a crimson maxi dress. "Did you girls get drinks yet?"

"We're good, Aunt Jade," Sage says.

"How about you, Callie? I don't see a drink in your hand."

"I'll get something. I'm more of a soda than alcohol person."

"Nothing wrong with that. There's a huge selection over in the cooler on the deck. Can I get you something?"

"I'll get it myself." I nod to the others. "Back in a minute."

Jade walks with me to the deck.

"Where's Donny?" It's okay to ask, I tell myself. After all, this party *is* for him.

"He and his brother are inside with their father," she says. "You should go in and rout them out."

I open the giant cooler and choose a Diet Coke. "That's not my place."

"Nonsense," Jade says. "You have my blessing. The three of them will stay in there all night talking business if someone doesn't force them out."

"Donny's not the shy type," I say.

"Not at all. Talon and Dale, on the other hand, would just as soon stay inside and avoid the crowd."

"Is Dale's wife here yet?"

"She should be here soon. She had to pick up her mother at the airport in Grand Junction. They're on the road now."

"Ah. Got it. How is Willow doing?"

"Okay, I think. It's been a struggle. She was going to wait a while longer before moving, but Ashley talked her into coming out earlier to get settled. Her car and RV and the rest of her things will arrive in a week or so."

"If there's anything we can do . . ." I say.

"I'm sure Ashley will ask if there is. Time is really what Willow needs, and she'll have plenty of that."

"I hear she's opening a salon in town."

"That's her plan."

"Raine's a little worried about it."

"Raine has an established clientele. I doubt there's any reason to worry."

"That's what I told Rory."

Marjorie Simpson races toward us. "Jade, there you are. I need your help with some stuff. Hi there, Callie."

"Hi."

"Duty calls," Jade says. "Go on in and tell my husband and sons they need to get their butts out here, will you?"

"Sure. If you say so."

Diet Coke in hand, I walk through the French doors and through the gigantic kitchen. I've been here before, so I know Talon Steel's office is down the right hallway, second door on the left. If they're talking, that's probably where they are.

I inhale deeply, trying to slow the race of my heartbeat.

Just being this close to Donny Steel has me on high alert already.

I walk toward the closed door.

CHAPTER SEVENTEEN

Donny

"You really thought you could keep this from me?" I yell at my brother.

"I wasn't keeping anything from you, Don," Dale says. "I just found out myself."

"A *week* ago."

"Yeah, a fucking week ago. It was a lot to process."

"Fuck you!" I yell.

"Donny," Dad says, "you're not angry with Dale. You're angry with the situation."

"No, I'm angry with Dale."

But Dad's right. Dale is just taking the brunt of my rage because he's the messenger. Plus, his wife's stepfather died right after, and—

I can't help it. I'm still pissed as all hell.

"This is ancient history," Dad says.

"Okay," I say. "Sure, it's ancient history. But I just fucking found out that my birth father sold us off to psychopaths for five grand. Just how am I supposed to feel? Happy?"

"You're the one who pushed, Don," Dad says. "Neither Dale nor I wanted to tarnish this party."

He's right, of course. I'm the one who forced the two of them into this office for a *talk*. I'm the one who knew Dale didn't level with me at lunch.

This is all on me.

I'm still pissed.

Pissed at the fucking world. Pissed at Floyd Jolly, now dead. Damned good thing for him, or I'd be on my way to Grand Junction to kill him with my bare hands.

So much for never thinking about *it*.

"Yeah, yeah. My big welcome back party. Fuck it all. Send everyone home. I'm not in the mood."

"That would kill your mother," Dad says.

I have to hand it to Dad. He knows my weak spots. I'll do anything for my mother.

"For God's sake, Dad," Dale says. "It would hardly *kill* her."

"I'm not being literal, and you know it."

"It's okay," I relent. "I won't ruin Mom's party. But damn." I rub my temples with both hands.

"None of this changes anything," Dad says. "Dale didn't want you to ever have to know."

Classic Dale again. Willing to bear this burden alone. Always thinking he has to protect me.

Why did I push? I could be out there right now flirting with Callie, having one of Mom's froufrou drinks. Talking to Jesse and the band about our old football days.

"Dale," I say, my tone serious, "you've got to stop protecting me."

Dale shook his head. "I can't do that, Don."

"I'm thirty-two years old. We're not being held captive in a concrete room anymore."

Dale winces. Very visibly.

"See? You still can't shake our past. Part of you still lives in that room, Dale."

Dale clears his throat. "You're wrong. I can see why you might think that, but you're wrong."

"Am I? You've been carrying the world on your shoulders for the last twenty-five years. Let it go, man. For Ashley. For your future. For yourself."

"I've let it go," he says.

"You haven't."

"Actually, I have."

Dad speaks then. "The two of you handle things differently. That's not to say one of you is right and the other wrong. It's just how it is. There's a reason you're so close to your mother, Don. It's because you're so much like her. You always see the glass as half full. Dale is more like me."

"You're not that way at all," I say to Dad.

"No. Not now. But I was. Long ago, before I met your mother. I was a lot like your brother, for reasons—"

I nod. "I know, Dad. I know, and I want to know more, but I just as much *don't* want to know more."

Dad sighs. "I'm afraid some of these new developments are going to open up old wounds. Wounds I thought I'd buried forever."

"I'm sorry," Dale says.

"Not your fault. Neither of you. Please trust that your uncles and I thought we were doing what was best for the family. We had our spouses' support. We wanted to wipe the slate clean, start fresh. The two of you would always have a past to contend with, but you didn't need *my* past as well. The others? We thought we could spare them all of it."

"You can't run away from the past, Dad," Dale says.

"I never thought I could. That part of my life is always

with me, as it will always be with you. Your mother helped me a lot. Gave me something wonderful to live for. But even she couldn't erase my past."

"I understand that so much better now," Dale says. "Because of Ashley and my feelings for her."

"I may not have a Jade or an Ashley," I say, "but I've chosen not to dwell on that horror. Is that so bad? And now, it's all coming crashing back."

"It doesn't have to," Dad says.

"How the hell can you say that? Our own father..." I exhale slowly, but my attempt at relaxation doesn't slow the angry racing of my heart.

"See?" Dale says. "This is why I didn't want to tell you. How do you want it, Don? You say you no longer want my protection, but now you're pissed that the horror is coming crashing back. If I hadn't told you—"

"Shut up." I thread my fingers through my hair. "Just shut the fuck up!"

Truth be told, I don't know what I want. Do I want to go back ten minutes and have no clue about my birth father?

Yes.

No.

I don't know.

"Don..." Dale begins.

"What? What now?"

"There's something else."

Dad shakes his head slightly at Dale. Does he really think I won't notice?

"Keeping something else from me?"

"No," Dale says. "It's just... I had all of Floyd's stuff hauled away to the dump. Without asking you. And I'm sorry."

"Is that all? I don't want any of his shit."

Dale nods. "Good. It wasn't really my place to do it all without you. If I'd known you'd be back to stay so soon, I'd have waited."

"No big deal."

Seriously. Like I care. Now that I know what the man did to us, I don't want any remnant of him. If I could erase his DNA from my body, I would.

Dad sighs. "I shouldn't have allowed this conversation to take place until after the party. This is all on me."

Maybe he should have waited. Maybe I shouldn't have been so adamant.

Maybe a lot of things.

"Come on, Don," Dale says, not quite meeting my gaze. "Let's put on a good show for Mom."

I know my brother. I know that look in his eye.

There's more. He hasn't told me everything.

Well, he's going to. Maybe not at this particular moment, but he will, damn it.

My blood is boiling. I want to strike out, but striking out at my brother and father won't help. They're the wrong targets.

I want to strangle the life out of my birth father.

But he has no life to give me. He's gone.

I want to . . .

I want to . . .

I want to . . .

I jerk at a knock on the door. Probably Mom, wanting to know where I am. "For Christ's sake, I'm coming!" I yell as I throw open the door.

But it's not Mom.

Callie Pike stands on the other side, her mouth dropped open.

CHAPTER EIGHTEEN

Callie

Donny's hair is mussed, and his lips and cheeks are dark pink.

His hazel gaze sears into mine.

Still, though... I've never seen him look sexier.

"Your mom..." I draw in a deep breath. "She asked me to come get you guys."

"Fine," he says, grabbing my arm. "Let's go."

He drags me down the hallway and into a room. It's a library. I inhale the leathery scent of bindings, the crisp scent of pages.

"What's going—"

But then his lips are on mine.

Hard, fast, and needy.

I open, and his tongue slides into my mouth.

A kiss. This one just as scorching as the night before, but with an extra dose of aching rage.

He's angry.

Angry about something. I don't know what.

I don't care what.

I care only about this kiss.

He walks forward, inching me backward until I hit a bookshelf. It grinds into the small of my back, but I ignore it.

We kiss and we kiss and we kiss, and just when I think he

can't kiss me any more deeply, he somehow does.

His groan rips through me, sets sparks skittering across my flesh.

Desire overwhelms me.

My nipples harden into tight nubs. My knees weaken.

My inner core lights on fire.

I feel him everywhere. In my mouth, my breasts, between my legs.

He's everywhere. All at once, he's in me.

And all we've done is kiss.

Can't breathe. I inhale frantically through my nose, getting enough air to keep the kiss going.

Until—

He breaks away, leaving my lips burning.

"Fuck," he grits out.

My fingers make their way to my bottom lip. It stings. In a good way. A really good way.

"I want you," Donny says, his low voice more like a growl.

I want you too.

The words don't come.

He pulls a condom out of his back pocket. "You deserve better than a quick fuck, but I'm going to give you one. Right here. Right now."

I open my mouth to speak, but again nothing comes.

"You'll have to tell me no, Callie. Otherwise, I'm going to—"

"Yes," I say without hesitation. "Please. Now."

"Fuck," he says again.

Does he want to undress me? Does he want—

His mouth is on mine again, and he lifts my shirt up, exposing my breasts. He pulls one out of my bra and pinches my hard nipple.

I groan into his mouth, nearly losing my footing again. I want to be naked. Naked under him, over him, beside him, on top of him.

Everywhere and nowhere all at once, as long as it's with him.

He rips his mouth from mine and inhales sharply. "Damn. This is wrong."

No. He can't change his mind. If he does, I'll die an untimely death right here in the Steel family library, against the agriculture books.

He gazes down at my exposed breast. "God, you're beautiful." He fumbles with my jeans.

Why did I wear cowboy boots tonight? Sandals would have been a much better choice. I could have them off by now, my jeans halfway down my thighs . . .

Donny drops to his knees.

Actually drops to his knees.

He removes my boots and socks quickly, and within another two seconds, my jeans are in a crumpled heap of denim on the Mediterranean area rug.

One tit hanging out, my shirt around my chest. I begin to remove the shirt and bra, but in a flash his own jeans are midway down his thighs, and his cock—his giant cock—is sheathed in the condom.

He lifts me into his arms, my back still aching from the shelf, and thrusts into me.

"Oh!" Then I bite down hard on my lower lip, stopping the noise.

My whole family is here. The whole community is here. All to welcome Donny Steel home.

He should be out there, mingling.

Instead, he's fucking me in his library.

He's huge, and he tunnels through me as if he's drilling into steel. I'm far from a virgin, but his sheer size spikes into me with a sharp pain.

Good pain, though. *Really* good pain.

"You okay?" he whispers against my ear.

"Yes," I say through clenched teeth. "Fine. Please. More."

He pulls out and thrusts back in.

Yes, pain. Glorious pain that soothes my emptiness—emptiness I didn't know existed.

He thrusts again.

Again.

Again.

The pain dissolves into pure pleasure. I cry out despite myself. My body takes over, and I let it happen.

Let the desire and overwhelming passion take me.

Thrust.

Thrust.

Thrust.

"Baby, I can't hold out," Donny grits against my neck. "I've got to come. Got to—"

He thrusts hard into me, holding himself there.

I feel every spurt in time with my heartbeat.

Time passes in a warp. He stays inside me, holding me against him. My legs are wrapped around his waist as if they belong there.

My breath comes in spasms. I wriggle against him, looking for the friction I need. If I can just—

Then a knock on the door.

"Shit!" Donny pulls out of me and sets me on the floor.

"Donny, are you in there?"

Jade's voice.

Please don't open the door. Please don't open the door.

Did Donny think to lock it? I doubt it. He was in a hurry.

He snaps up his pants and buckles his belt. Then he gathers my jeans and boots and pushes them into my grasp. "Get in the closet."

I drop my mouth open as he takes my hand, walks quickly across the room, shoves me into the large closet, and closes the door.

And I stand here.

In the dark, one boob still out, holding my jeans and boots.

My socks. Where are my socks?

I strain my ears, trying to hear what's going on in the library. Is Jade coming in? Will she see my socks?

Donny will tell me when the coast is clear.

This is the right thing. I mean, I'm going to work for the woman beginning on Monday. I don't want her to find me half-naked in her library with her son, the brand spanking new assistant city attorney.

I don't dare try to get my jeans on. I don't want to make any noise.

So I wait.

I wait for Donny.

He'll come when it's safe.

CHAPTER NINETEEN

Donny

I open the door to face my mother.

"What are you doing in here?" she demands. "The party is underway. The food's all set out. People are starting to wonder where you are. Dad and Dale said you were right behind them."

"Yeah, I was. I just had to go to the bathroom."

"In the library?"

"I just stopped in here to ..." Right. What the hell am I going to say to my mother? *I stopped in here for a quick fuck with Callie Pike because my adrenaline is on speed. You and Dad have been lying to me for years.*

"I don't care, Donny. Let's just go. For God's sake."

"Right, Mom. I'll be there in a few."

"No. Now. Come on. This party is for you." She grabs my arm and pulls me into the hallway.

Damn. Callie. Callie in the closet.

I'll come back for her.

I follow Mom out to the deck. Dad has taken over for Darla at the grill, and Dale is talking to Bree and Jesse Pike by the stage where Jesse's band will perform later.

"Here he is!" Mom calls. "The man of the hour!"

And then they're on me.

Everyone. Hugging. Kissing. Shaking my hand.

"Good to have you home, Don!"

"An exciting career move!"

"Will you be taking over for your mother soon?"

"The Snow Creek ladies will be thrilled you're back!"

I talk to everyone who greets me, answering their questions as best I can as seconds turn into minutes. Ten. Twenty.

Darla brings me a plate containing a double burger and a heap of Aunt Marj's special potato salad, which everyone knows I love.

Mom brings me a margarita, and Uncle Ryan taps on a champagne flute.

"Does everyone have a drink?" Ryan asks. "It's time for our toast."

Dale leaves Jesse and Bree and helps Uncle Ryan fill flutes of Steel sparkling wine.

Callie. I've got to go get Callie.

But I can't get away. Someone is hugging me or shaking my hand, and then Uncle Ryan and Dad somehow get to the microphone on the makeshift stage for the band.

"Hey, everyone," Dad says, his voice amplified. "Thanks so much for coming. I hope you've all filled your plates. There's plenty more for seconds. We'll have Jesse and Dragonlock performing up here in a bit, but first, Jade and I would like to welcome back our second born into the Steel family fold. Donny, come on up here!"

Crap. I'm sorry, Callie.

I make my way to the stage, where Mom has also joined Dad and Uncle Ry. She grabs me in a hug and whispers, "I'm so glad you've come home."

I kiss her cheek quickly and stand beside Dad.

"I'll have Ryan do the toast," Dad says, "since he's much more eloquent than I am. Plus he made this awesome sparkling wine."

"If that's the case," Ryan says, "I should have Dale come up here. He's our new winemaker after this season. And he's Donny's brother. Come on up, Dale."

"Sorry," Dale says from the peanut gallery. "Just got a text from Ashley. She and Willow just got to the guesthouse. I have to help with the luggage."

I force a laugh. "Good one, bro," I say into the microphone. "Anything to avoid making a spectacle of yourself."

Dale smiles, holds up his phone, and begins to walk toward the guesthouse while everyone laughs.

Yeah, I'm still pissed at my brother, but I won't ruin my mom's party for anything. All I want right now is to get this toast over with so I can get back to Callie. Will she leave the closet and come back out without my okay? I hope so, but what if she doesn't?

"So Donny," Ryan begins, "when you went off to college thirteen years ago, determined to become a high-powered lawyer, none of us thought you'd return to Snow Creek for good. But here you are, and we couldn't be happier. I know your mom is especially thrilled that you'll be working together. So here's to you. Welcome home!"

Glasses clink.

"Speech, speech!" someone—I think it's Brock, damn him—yells.

Ryan moves out of the way to give me access to the mic.

And all I can think about is Callie holed up in that closet. How long has it been now? A half hour at least, probably longer.

"I just want to thank all of you for coming over tonight.

Part of me feels like I never really left the western slope, and it's great to be back. Thanks to my mom and Aunt Marj for planning this affair. Thanks to Jesse, my old football pal, for the music to come. It's honestly great to see all of you and to know I'll be here for a while. Cheers!" I take a sip of my margarita.

"Cheers!" come the shouts.

"We've got plenty more food," Dad says after the applause dies down. "So please help yourselves. Marjorie's cake will be out soon as well, and you all know she does it up right. So eat, drink, and be merry, and we'll have some music in a little while. Thanks to all of you for coming!"

I make my way through more congratulatory hugs. Why are people congratulating me, anyway? I left a partnership track in a global firm to come here and work for pennies.

On the other hand, they all do seem glad to have me back, and in truth, I'm thrilled to be back. My anger at Dale and Dad dissipates. Sure, I'm giving up a lot, but family first. Talon Steel drummed that lesson into our heads from day one, and he's right.

Step by step, I make my way back to the deck, and I'm four feet from the door when—

"Donny." Mom grabs me. "Can you help Marj and me with the cake?"

But Callie's in the library . . .

I can hardly say that. I'm an adult, but still . . . I don't particularly want to tell my mother that I left a half-naked woman hiding in a closet.

I can't say no. The cake is for me, after all.

"Sure," I sigh.

I follow Mom into the kitchen where the cake is set out and Aunt Marj is putting on the last touches.

"Wow," I say. "It's beautiful."

"Nothing but the best for my favorite nephew." Aunt Marj giggles.

It's been a running joke since we were all kids. Aunt Marj refers to each and every one of us as her favorite niece or nephew.

"I thought I was your favorite," Brock jokes.

I turn to face him. "Can you help Mom and Aunt Marj? I've got to—"

"Sorry," he says. "I've got to piss like a racehorse. I'll be back in five if you can wait."

"Never mind," I say.

"We're done!" Aunt Marj wipes her hands on a dish towel.

I take a second to appreciate her handiwork. It's a two-tier creation with golden frosting and the scales of justice sculpted out of white and black fondant.

"I don't know how you do it, Marj," Mom says. "Each cake you make is more beautiful than the last. Why you took so long to get into baking is beyond me."

"I was too busy creating real food," Marj replies. "I like dessert as much as the next person, but I'm much more into savory than sweet. I have to admit, though. Cakes do let me stretch my creativity. It's fun!"

"You should sell these at Ava's bakery," I tell her.

She laughs off my comment. "That would take all the fun out of it."

The three of us carefully set the cake onto a catering trolley and wheel it through the French doors and out onto the deck.

"Talon," Mom says. "Tell everyone the cake is ready and, if they want to see it before we cut it, to get over here."

I love my mom. I do. But my God, does everything have to be a major event? Though the cake *is* a work of art. No lie.

Dad makes a quick announcement, and sure enough, people gather to ooh and ahh over the dessert.

A good time for me to sneak away and get Callie.

Except—

"You do the honors, Donny." Aunt Marj hands me a serving knife.

"I'll screw it up."

"Just the first slice, so your mom can get a photo. Then I'll take over."

Photo op. Of course. Can't ever miss a good Steel photo op. I paste on a smile and try not to think about how angry Callie's getting in the closet.

I slice into the cake as camera phones click.

I'll be up on twenty Instagram accounts within seconds.

And all I want is for this party to be over so Callie and I can pick up where we left off.

CHAPTER TWENTY

Callie

"Finally!" I say, as the closet door opens.

Then my jaw drops.

It's not Donny but his cousin Brock who stands on the other side of the closet door.

Thank God I went ahead and got dressed after so much time passed. Boots without socks aren't particularly comfortable.

Brock gives me a dazzling smile. "Well, well, well. What have we here?"

"I was just . . ." Just what? *Oh, just fucking your cousin, and he left me here for . . .* Damn. How long has it been?

"I thought it was your sister who came out of the closet," he jokes.

"Yeah. Funny."

"Seriously," he says. "What are you doing in here? The party's in full force."

"There's really no good answer to that question."

He laughs. "Now come on. There's got to be some reason why you're hiding in a closet. Seriously."

"That's the second time you've used the word seriously."

"Seriously?" He waggles his eyebrows.

I like Brock. He's a few years younger than I am, and even

though my family didn't move here until I was in elementary school, Brock was one of the first Steels I got to know.

He was the boy who chased all the girls on the playground.

While all the other little boys were in their *I hate girls* phase, Brock Steel was a skirt chaser even then.

He's still a skirt chaser now. He, Donny, and Dave Simpson, Marjorie and Bryce's second son, are the Steels known as the womanizers. In town they're called the Three Rake-a-teers. I remember when Rory coined the term after high school. Donny's quite a bit older than his cousins, but once Brock and Dave were legal, the three of them could be found at Murphy's whenever Donny was in town, picking up women and heading to the Snow Creek Inn.

I was almost one of those women once.

And it was the man in front of me who almost made me a notch on the Rake-a-teer bedpost.

Brock Steel is a hunk, no doubt.

All dark, gorgeous, muscular, and he can turn any woman's knees to mush.

As I gaze at him now, though—his incredible height, his thick dark hair, his searing black eyes, and his beefy broad shoulders—I think only of one man.

And it's not him.

"You coming out or what?" Brock smiles deviously. "Or I could join you in there. It's a big closet."

I step out. My phone died earlier, or I'd have texted Rory or Maddie to see if it was safe to emerge. "What time is it, anyway?"

"It's nearing eight."

My jaw drops. Seriously? I've been waiting in this closet for almost an hour? I'll kill Donny Steel.

"Seriously"—he chuckles at his own word—"what are you doing in there?"

"Nothing, clearly." I head toward the door, glancing around quickly for my socks. They seem to have disappeared. Just as well. I don't want to field the questions they'll produce from Brock. "Any food left?"

"Aunt Jade and Aunt Marj always make sure there's enough for at least a thousand people. You won't go hungry."

"I'm not hungry," I say, more to myself than to Brock.

Nope. Not hungry. Just angry.

I just got fucked in more ways than one.

Though I'm tempted to march out with smoke unfurling out of my ears, I decide on an alternate strategy. I link my arm through Brock's.

"Let's go. I'm ready to party."

"Now those are fighting words, Callie. I'm your man. Let's get you a drink."

We stroll together through the house and out onto the deck. The party is in full swing, and Jesse and his band are tuning up on stage.

Brock steps up to the redwood bar. "What's your pleasure?"

"Diet C—" I stop. "Screwdriver. Heavy on the screw."

Brock smiles at my double entendre and mixes me a drink while I scan the crowd, looking for one blond head in particular. I find him with his brother and Ashley. A beautiful older woman stands with them. Willow. Ashley's mother, who was widowed such a short time ago.

My cheeks warm when he turns my way and meets my gaze.

So when Brock hands me the drink, I can't help but look

up at him admiringly and grab his arm with my free hand.

Donny's full lips purse into a thin line.

Really, though, what does he expect? He freaking left me in a closet. Half-clothed. Not knowing whether it was safe to come out. For all I knew, Jade and Talon could have been right outside the door of the library. Or any number of others who would wonder why the heck I was in the Steel library by myself while a party's going on.

"Let's get you some dinner," Brock says.

"I wasn't kidding when I said I'm not hungry. Unless you want to eat."

"I've had two plates full," he laughs.

"Good. Then let's mingle a little."

"Your wish is my command, gorgeous." He leads me off the deck and into the swarm of people.

We head toward the stage, where Rory is working on the sound system.

"Hey, sis," I say.

"Cal, Brock." She looks around. "Where've you been, anyway?"

"Long story." I roll my eyes.

"Which she's keeping mum about," Brock adds.

Dark-haired and blue-eyed David Simpson joins us then. The silky dark hair is from his mother, Marjorie, and the blue eyes from his father, Bryce Simpson. And of course, he's gorgeous as all get-out, just like everyone with Steel blood.

"Callie Pike," he says jovially, "what are you doing with this moron?"

"I saw her first, dude," Brock returns.

"I think the lady is the one who gets to choose," Dave retorts.

I take a sip of my screwdriver and smile in what I hope is a flirtatious way. "The lady isn't up for grabs, guys."

Though having two of the Rake-a-teers attending to me isn't such a bad thing. I've never been one to play games, but Donny Steel is on my list at the moment.

And the sad thing is?

If he came up to me right now and dragged me back into that library to fuck, I'd go.

It was *that* amazing.

"We'll see about that before the night is over," Dave says. "I get first dance."

"Uh . . . the lady's with me." Brock smiles.

"Tell you what." I try the flirtatious grin again. "Jess never starts with a slow song, so you can both have the first dance."

"Baby, we don't share," Dave says.

"Except that one time," Brock replies.

I stop my mouth from dropping open. They shared a woman? A threesome? I can't decide if I'm grossed out or turned on.

Rory, who witnessed the exchange, is laughing her ass off. I give her a stink eye.

Jesse takes the mic then. "Hey, everyone! Who's ready for some rock and roll!"

Cheers galore.

"We're going to start with a few covers and then move into our original stuff. Most of you know the band, but I'll introduce them to you anyway. My cousin Cage on bass, Dragon Locke on drums—and yeah, his name's so cool we named the band after him—and Jake Michaels on lead guitar. I'm Jesse Pike, vocals and second guitar, and tonight we have a treat for you. I've managed to talk my amazingly talented sister Rory into joining us with her pipes. You may know her as an operatic mezzo, but the girl can also rock!"

I widen my eyes and meet Rory's gaze. Her eyes dance. I had no idea she would sing tonight.

"Rory's singing?" Dave says. "Awesome."

More cheers for Rory and the band.

They start with some oldies that are great to dance to.

"Ready, guys?" I ask.

"Absolutely," Brock says, taking my arm.

Dave takes the other, and we join several others on the portable dance floor. It's a fast song, but both Dave and Brock dance close to me. I'll give Dave the edge on dancing, but they're both good dancers. Better than I am, to be honest.

I paste a smile on my face and pretend I'm having the time of my life.

And hope Donny's watching.

CHAPTER TWENTY-ONE

Donny

Damn her.

Okay, I did leave her in a closet, but I didn't want to. People kept grabbing me, and it's my party . . .

Yeah, I'm a dick.

A big one.

I should have made some excuse.

And now she's the delicacy in a Brock and Dave sandwich— and I'm sure they're thinking the same thing.

I love my cousins. Hey, I've partied many times with the two of them, picked up women with them. They're many years my junior, but I taught them everything they know.

Now they're using my moves on my woman.

Okay, not *my* woman. But strangely weird that I just thought of her in those terms.

That fuck in the library . . .

I needed it. Needed it badly, to work off the tension and anger from the talk with Dad and Dale.

But I also wanted it. Wanted Callie. I've been thinking about her since the last Steel party. Funny how I never noticed her before. She was so much younger. She was jailbait for a long time, so I just got used to thinking of her in those terms.

No longer.

"What do you think, Don?"

I jerk my gaze to my brother. "Sorry. What?"

"You were a million miles away." Dale shakes his head. "I asked if you think Raine might help Willow get set up with a salon in town."

"Oh. I don't really know Raine that well." True enough. I sure didn't want to say Callie already told me Raine was worried about the competition.

"I don't want to put her out," Willow says.

"Mom," Ashley adds, "there's no hurry. You need to get settled. Deal with your loss. It's still so new."

"The best thing for me is work," Willow says. "Always. I love having work to do."

"Snow Creek's a small town," Ashley says. "You're not going to be nearly as busy."

"I understand," she says. "But there's only one stylist in Snow Creek. There are thousands in LA."

"For thousands more people, Mom."

Willow sighs. "Ash, I'm just not happy unless I'm working. You know that. All those years . . ."

She didn't finish, but I know where she was going. Dale confided in me about Ashley's and Willow's years in the tent city in San Francisco. Of course she wants to work. She knows all too well how horrible it is to be out of work.

Willow hasn't realized, yet, that her daughter is a Steel and she no longer has to worry about money.

Of course, that doesn't mean she won't want to work. None of us have to worry about money, and we all work. It's kind of our thing.

"I can ask Raine," I say.

Ashley's eyes widen. "Do you know her?"

"She's Rory's partner. I know Rory. And Callie."

And it'll give me a chance to wrench Callie away from my lothario cousins.

"I haven't seen Raine tonight," Dale says.

"She's in Denver visiting her parents."

"Oh. Okay." Ashley smiles. "See, Mom? Relax. Raine isn't even in town. There's plenty of time for you to set up shop."

"Excuse me," I say to them.

Time for me to take action.

I head toward the dancing—

When another of my cousins grabs me. This time it's Henry.

"Don," he says, "I need your help."

"Sure. What's up?"

"There's this hot waitress named Nora who's coming on strong."

"Really? Where's Darlene?"

"She's in Vegas with friends, a girls' trip. She already had the plans in place before Aunt Jade scheduled this party. Not that she'd have stayed in town for a party, even a Steel party."

"So flirt with the hottie. No one has to know."

"Dude, she wants to do more than flirt."

"Do you want to do more than flirt?"

Henry laughs. "Spoken like a guy who's never been in a real relationship."

He isn't wrong.

"I was hoping you might be able to take her off my hands," Henry continues. "She's just your type."

"I have a type?"

"Yeah. Double X chromosome, ready, and willing. Right?"

Again, he isn't wrong.

Except for tonight. I have one type tonight. Her name is Callie Pike, and at the moment, she's sandwiched between my two horny cousins who aren't above sharing.

At least they did once.

It sounded hot when they relayed it to me, but I couldn't get past being naked and hard in front of a family member. Brock and Dave were in college then and acted like it was no big deal. To them, it probably wasn't. They were total frat brats.

To be young again . . .

"I can't help you, Henry. Sorry."

"There you are!" A bubbly blonde with amazing tits— Nora, I presume—latches on to Henry. "Let's dance. This band rocks." She drags him out into the moving people before he has a chance to turn her down.

Yeah, he's on his own.

Normally, I'd be happy to take pretty Nora off his hands. She's hot, she's horny, and she's female.

But she pales in comparison to Callie Pike.

I resume my path toward Callie and my cousins.

And—

"Donny!" Uncle Joe claps me on my back. "Melanie and I haven't had a chance to talk to you the last couple times you were in town."

I'm here for good now, so we have all the time in the world.

The words don't leave my mouth, of course. Uncle Joe is Brock's father. I'm this close to telling him to haul his son off my woman, when I realize she's not my woman.

She's pissed as all get-out at me.

And she has good reason to be.

"Assistant city attorney," Uncle Joe says. "That's great. Your mom is tickled, but you already know that."

"I'm happy to be able to do this for her."

"You know, I—"

Mom arrives then. "Excuse me, Joe. Can I borrow my son for a minute?"

"Sure, sure. Don, you and I need to get out on the golf course soon. Before snowfall."

"It's a date, Uncle Joe," I say, as Mom drags me to yet another group of people.

Frank and Maureen Pike, Callie's parents, and Frank's sister, Lena Ramsey. Another woman stands with them.

"Donny," Mom says, "I want you to meet Lena's niece, Kaia. She just flew in from Montana to help out while the winery is rebuilt."

I smile and hold out my hand. "Nice to meet you."

"You too. Thanks for inviting me tonight. Oh, and welcome home, I guess."

"Are you a niece on Scott's side?" I ask.

She nods. "Yeah. My dad is Uncle Scott's brother."

Kaia Ramsey has shoulder-length dark-blond hair, and she's tall and beautiful. In fact, looking around, I see that everyone here is tall and beautiful.

"Kaia's a paralegal," Mom continues.

"Oh? Taking some time off from legal work?"

"The firm I was working for just had a breakup. Both sides courted me, and I realized I wouldn't be happy working with either one, so I decided to come to Colorado and help with the winery and ranch. There's a lot to do right now."

"That's nice of you," I say, searching for Callie in my peripheral vision.

"I was telling Kaia if she chooses to stay on, we might have room for her at the office," Mom says. "Though I just hired someone this morning."

"You did?" I ask.

"Yeah. Callie Pike, actually."

I suppress a shiver at her name. "Oh?" I say as nonchalantly as I can. Weird that Callie didn't mention a new job. Of course, we didn't really talk earlier . . .

"Yeah. Poor thing. She can't start law school this winter like she was planning, and she wanted a job in the industry while still staying in town."

I nod. Again trying to be nonchalant while my dick is reacting just to the word *Callie*.

"Don't feel you need to make room for me," Kaia says. "I'm here to help Uncle Scott and the others. It'll be a nice break in routine."

"Oh, I know that," Mom says. "Just, if you want to get back into your chosen field, be sure to holler at me. Or at Donny here. He's the assistant city attorney beginning on Monday."

Kaia smiles at me, and . . . Yeah, I see something behind her smile. I'm an expert at reading women. She's interested.

I'm not.

"Will you all excuse me?" I say. "Nature calls."

Not the best excuse, but it works every time. I say goodbye and head toward the house. I have to go in to keep up my cover. I whisk past Darla and Aunt Marj in the kitchen and head to the nearest bathroom.

After two minutes, I stage a flush, wash my hands, and return to the deck.

Just in time, too. Jesse's gearing up for a slow song. No way is one of my cousins getting Callie into a clench.

I hurry toward them, where Brock has somehow managed to edge Dave out and has his arms around Callie.

I tap his shoulder. "I'm cutting in."

He turns around. "Hey, Don."

He makes no move to let me have Callie, though.

"I said I'm cutting in."

"Up to the lady, I think," Brock says.

I meet Callie's gaze. Man, she's angry. Her eyes shoot darts at me. But she says, "It's okay."

Brock doesn't look happy, but he has no choice but to back off after she says it.

I take Callie in my arms.

And wonder what to say to her.

CHAPTER TWENTY-TWO

Callie

I hate this. I hate that I feel so at home in Donny's arms. I hate that I want to forgive him so easily.

I hate that this is what I wanted all along.

I had the attention of the two best-looking men here—okay, second-best-looking, because no one is better looking than Donny Steel at this moment—and I gave it up for a guy who left me stranded in a closet for nearly an hour.

Not my finest move.

I want to say so much. Words jumble in my head in an angry black cloud.

But I refuse to speak first.

He needs to say something to me. Even if it's not an apology, it has to be *something*. No way will I talk first.

Damn it! We move slowly to the music, and he still says nothing.

I should let go and move away in a huff, but I can't.

Physically, I can't separate myself from him. It feels so . . . good. So . . . right.

Finally, he moves his lips toward my ear. I wait for his sweet words begging my forgiveness.

Instead, he nips the outer shell of my ear.

That's it. I yank myself out of his arms and walk away

from the dance area.

Brock and Dave have moved on to someone else—the woman Donny was talking to before he cut in on my dance. I have no idea who she is, but she's tall and beautiful, so she's just their type.

So now I've got no one. I head toward the house before tears arrive. I'm so not a crier. Rory and Mads have been known to break down, but not I. Never. I steel myself against tears.

Still, my eyelids are stinging. I hate that feeling. Hate it with a burning passion.

I will not cry. I will not cry.

Is it sadness? Anger? Hopelessness? Rage?

Yeah. All of it wrapped into one.

I'm not sure where I'm going. I've been to the Steel house many times, but it's so huge. Whether it's my subconscious or something else, I end up back in the damned library, wishing I stopped for a drink at the bar first.

Even though I'm not a big drinker, that screwdriver went down pretty smoothly, and I'm wishing for another. A double, even.

I zero in on the bookshelf that dug into my back earlier—and then my socks crumpled on the floor next to it. I walk forward and stuff them in my pocket.

The door opens, and I jerk toward it.

Donny.

"Callie," he says.

I inhale deeply, willing back those stinging tears. Never will I cry in front of this man.

Never.

I don't respond.

"Hey." He walks toward me. "What's wrong?"

I can't help it. I scoff softly. "What do you *think* is wrong? You left me in here for an hour!"

"I know. I didn't realize how much time had gone by. Why didn't you come out?"

"I didn't know who was waiting for me in the hall, and my phone died, so I couldn't text anyone to come get me."

He's only two feet away from me now, and my body is on high alert. Goose bumps erupt on my flesh. My nipples harden.

God, the memory of him inside me, burning through me.

"I'm so sorry, Callie." His voice is deep—deep and laced with sincerity. "I tried. People kept grabbing me, wanting me to say something, wanting to welcome me back."

"I get it. You couldn't spare a minute and a half to come in here and get me. After I—" I shake my head. Damn, my eyelids are stinging again.

"What will it take?" he asks. "What can I do to make this up to you?"

"You can't. I'm humiliated. Brock found me in here. Brock!"

"And he took advantage of the situation in true Brock Steel style."

"You mean true Rake-a-teer style. Same as you would have."

"I'm not Brock."

"No, but you're one of the three. I'll bet Brock and Dave learned every move they have from you."

He doesn't argue the point.

Which makes me feel even worse.

"Callie, please. I'll ask again. What can I do to make this up to you?"

"And I just said that you can't."

"Does that mean you're breaking our date for tomorrow night?"

Wow. I forgot. He's right. I accepted a dinner date with him for tomorrow. I should break it. I should tell him I never want to see him again.

Except I don't *want* to break it. I want to go out with him. Even after his despicable behavior tonight.

"Yes," I say, "I'm breaking it."

He moves toward me, closing the gap between us. "No. You're not breaking it."

"I am—"

Then his lips. On mine. Prying mine open. His tongue. Finding mine and tangling with it. His groan. A sweet vibration I feel to my toes.

Push him away, Callie.

Do it.

Don't let him get away with this.

Instead, I respond to the kiss. I kiss him back. My arms go around his neck of their own accord. He presses into me. He's hard. Hard as a rock. And those sparks ignite again beneath my flesh.

If he wants to fuck me again, I'm going to let him. Already I know this.

The word *no* doesn't seem to be in my vocabulary when it comes to Donny Steel.

I melt against him, deepening the kiss, until—

He pulls back. Him.

"Tell me you'll go to dinner with me tomorrow evening," he whispers against my ear, his breath igniting me.

I say nothing.

He nips my earlobe. "Please, Callie. Tell me."

Be strong, Callie. Please, be strong.

He presses a kiss to that sensitive spot right beneath my ear. I suppress a shudder that boomerangs through me and lands between my legs.

"I'll make this up to you," he says softly, brushing his lips over the sensitive spot once more and then trailing downward to my neck. "Please."

Despite myself, I moan softly.

He trails his lips over my neck and to the top of my chest. "I'll make it up to you. We'll go anywhere. We'll go to Aspen if you want. I'll take you to the best restaurant there. Or we'll drive into the city. Drive into Denver, even. I know all the best places. We can spend the night at a hotel and drive back on Sunday. Whatever you want."

"Donny..." I'm quivering.

He presses a kiss along the edge of my shirt, where my breasts are only an inch below. "Anything, Callie. Please. I'll do anything to make this up to you."

"For God's sake, Donny."

He lowers his head and closes his teeth around my nipple—right through my shirt and bra.

I'm going to erupt in a moment if he doesn't stop this.

"What?" he asks.

"Just fuck me, will you? Please."

He chuckles against my still-clad boobs that are aching to be freed. "Only if you forgive me."

Oh. My. God.

The man is...

The man is fucking irresistible.

"Fine. Fine. I forgive you. I'll go out with you tomorrow night. Now please. Please."

To my utter shock, he pulls away. "Not here."

"Why not here? It was good enough earlier."

"Because there's a party outside. I won't take the chance of you having to hide in the closet again. I'm so sorry about that, baby. Please believe me."

"But..."

"Please. My only thought was getting back here to you."

I sigh against him. Every cell—the ones controlled by my pussy, anyway—in my body aches to accept him at his word.

Every cell in my brain urges caution.

I could fall so easily for this man.

And to him, I'm a notch on the bedpost.

I thought I was okay with that.

Turns out, I'm not.

I want more.

"Okay," I say finally. "I forgive you."

He smiles then—a dazzling smile that lights up his whole face and ignites a spark in my already hot loins.

How did I ever think Dale was the handsomer of the two?

Donny is beautiful. He could be modeling between the pages of *Esquire* and *GQ*.

"I won't let you down again," he says. "Just tell me what you want for our date tomorrow, and it's yours."

"You choose," I say.

He shakes his head. "Nope. We're not playing that game. I want to know what *you* want."

"Dinner. Just dinner. Where doesn't matter, as long as it's with you."

Part of me wants to puke a little at my words. Even more so when I realize how much I truly mean them.

I'm so not the romantic and mushy type.

But I mean those damned words with my whole heart.

"Aspen, then?" he says.

"Don't be silly."

"What's silly about it? We have a place there. A couple, actually. They're unoccupied at the moment. It's a two-hour drive. We can drive back or stay the night. Your choice."

"Dinner in Grand Junction is fine. It doesn't matter where, Donny."

"Aspen it is, then. I'll make a reservation at my favorite place. They serve our beef and our wines."

I can't help a laugh. "You Steels. Always paying good money to eat and drink your own stuff."

"Because it's *that* good." He smiles slyly.

"You said you're not much of a wine drinker," I say.

"I'm not. Doesn't mean I don't know good wine when I taste it." He smiles. "Want to know a secret?"

"Sure."

"My cocktail of choice is a margarita."

I can't help it. I laugh out loud. "A sweet drink?"

"It's a manly drink," he says.

"Manly with an umbrella."

"Manly because it's made with tequila."

"And a buttload of sugar."

"And it's also delicious."

I nod. "I can't argue with you there. I prefer a sweeter cocktail myself, when I drink at all. That or a beer." I don't mention how good the screwdriver Brock mixed for me earlier tasted.

Donny gives me another searing kiss and then backs away. "Tomorrow. And I owe you."

I cock my head. "What? Other than an apology, which you

already gave me, you don't owe me anything."

"You're wrong." He presses his lips to mine once more. "I owe you an orgasm."

CHAPTER TWENTY-THREE

Donny

I don't leave Callie's side the rest of the evening. We share a few more dances, and then I take her home, give her a scorching kiss, and drive myself back to the house with a hard-on.

So strange how badly I want to make this up to her. Any other woman, and I'd be screwing her right now. I sure didn't come home to Snow Creek to get serious with someone.

My crush on Callie Pike will probably be short-lived, but while it's here, I'm going to treat her right.

I get back to the ranch house, and Dale is still there, which doesn't overly surprise me. He and I still have a lot to discuss. I'm still angry about what our birth father did to us, but it's not Dale's fault. His only crime is that he didn't tell me—was never going to tell me.

Which isn't a crime.

He's so overprotective. Always has been. I'm not his baby brother anymore. I'm a grown man. Try telling him that, though.

"What's up?" I say to him.

"Just figured we had more to talk about."

Mom and Dad are out on the deck, hanging with Aunt Marj and Uncle Bryce. Everyone else has gone home, it seems.

"I'm fine, Dale," I say. "Sorry I went off on you. None of this is your fault. It's our fucking birth father. But damn, it's all so long ago, and I hate having to think about that time."

"I know," he says. "You've done a great job of getting past it all. Much better than I have."

I shake my head. "We just have different ways of dealing. It's still with me. Always. I just push it to the back of my mind."

"You compartmentalize," he says.

"Yeah, if you want to put a label on it."

"Do you ever worry that it will come barreling out?"

"Not really. It's not like I've blocked it out. I know it's there, and sometimes I do think about it, but I just choose not to."

He smiles. "You have a brilliant mind, Don. The way you can choose what to think about. That's why you were so good in school. Why you could deal with college and law school."

"Don't put yourself down," I say. "College isn't for everyone. No one can blame you for not wanting to be stuck in a room."

"No one can blame you, either, but you were able to do it."

True. We're two different people. That became clear soon after we arrived at Steel Acres.

"Don't get me wrong," Dale says. "I don't feel like I missed anything. It's just that I never considered so many things until Ashley came along. She really helped me see clearly. She and..."

"She and what?"

"She and Floyd, to be honest."

"Say what?"

"Not Floyd, really. Just a Robert Frost poem I found at his place."

I shake my head. "Dale, you surprise me sometimes."

"I surprise myself more. This is getting awkward, so let's change the subject. What's the story with you and Callie Pike?"

"There isn't one. Though we're heading to Aspen tomorrow for dinner."

"Aspen?"

"Yeah. I owe her one."

"Say what?" This time from Dale.

"I'll tell you sometime when we're drinking. I've only had one margarita tonight."

Dale chuckles. "You and Mom and your margaritas. So this is a drinking story?"

"I'm going to change the subject again," I say.

Truth is, I'm not ready to talk about Callie and me. I originally thought it'd be a hookup, but I don't usually take my hookups to Aspen. I'm certainly not planning to get serious with anyone, but something about Callie Pike makes me want more than a simple hookup. I've already had her, and now I think I want her even more.

"Okay." Dale grabs his phone out of his pocket. "Let's talk about what's on both our minds—other than women."

"How to get the lien off the Murphy property. Should only require a simple release. I can file the paperwork first thing Monday morning."

"Why didn't someone take care of this long ago?" Dale asks.

"Beats me. Someone in the family would have had to sign off on the transfer of the property when Murphy's dad bought it from that Madigan dude. That happened back when... I don't know. It would have been our grandfather, most likely, but we'd have to check the timeline."

"This doesn't sit well with me," Dale says. "The whole thing. Why would Grandpa Steel have allowed the transfer without Madigan paying off the lien?"

"Maybe he didn't care. It's not like he needed any money from the sale."

"Yeah." Dale rubs the blond stubble on his chin. "Good point. Still, there's something we're not seeing. I feel it in my bones."

I nod. I can't fault my brother's observation. Something here doesn't quite meet the eye.

"I'll do some research Monday when I get to the office. I'll have access to all the databases for the city and state. Maybe I'll find something. Of course, if anything was there, Mom would probably have already found it."

Dale stays quiet, but his eyes lower slightly.

"Say it," I say.

"What?"

"You want to say something. I know you better than anyone else does, bro. That look on your face says you're holding something back."

"I know how close you are to Mom," he says.

"What's that got to do with anything?"

"Because that's what I want to say. You said Mom would have found it if there was anything to find. And the first thing that jumped into my mind when you said that was *she might have hidden it.*"

CHAPTER TWENTY-FOUR

Callie

Rory, Maddie, and I sit on the deck at our place, drinking Diet Coke. Mom and Dad went to bed, and Jesse and his buddies headed into town for a drink at Murphy's. They invited us along, and Maddie almost went, but when Rory and I turned them down, she stayed behind.

"Thanks a lot," she says.

"For what?" Rory asks.

"For making me stay here with my sisters when I could be having a drink with Dragon Locke."

"I don't recall either of us forcing you to stay," I say.

"How would it look? You two staying but me going alone?"

"I'm in a relationship," Rory says, "and Callie is . . ."

Maddie's eyes widen. "Callie is what?"

"Callie's not interested in hanging out with her brother and his bandmates, one of whom is her cousin," I say. "Besides, Jesse won't let Dragon near you. I thought you were after a Steel man, anyway."

"They all seemed otherwise occupied," Maddie says. "Not fair that you, dear sister, had *three* of them salivating over you."

I ignore that last comment. "It's late. I'm exhausted."

"I am too." Rory polishes off her Diet Coke. "It's too late to give Raine a call. I'm going to head to bed and wake up early to call her. Night, girls."

Maddie pounces on me then. "Please? Come with me to Murphy's?"

"It's midnight, Mads."

"So? I'm not even slightly tired."

"I am. Call Bree. Or Angie and Sage. Or Gina. I'm sure one of them will be up for it."

"I'm kind of a third wheel with them." She scoffs. "Make that a fifth wheel. They're all Steels."

"You five have been inseparable since fifth grade," I tell her.

"True. But they don't have to worry about the things I have to worry about. It's a drag after a while. They're all the same age."

"You're the same age as they are," I remind her.

"You just don't get it."

"Actually, I do. So does Jesse. The Steels... Well, something shined on them long ago. But they do work hard too."

"I know. I have nothing against them. I love all the Steels. It's just..."

I give her a smile. "It's just you're feeling a little sorry for yourself."

"So what if I am?"

I open my mouth to tell my sister to stop having a pity party, but I can't bring myself to. I should be looking for an apartment in Denver right about now. Getting ready to move there for law school.

I should have started the fall semester, but no. I decided to stay and help with the grape harvest.

If I'd gone, no way would Mom and Dad pull me out now.

Of course, I'd have come home anyway to help.

Because that's what Callie Pike does.

She takes care of her family first.

Not a bad thing, but damn, can't I catch a break? Even my big date with Donny tomorrow evening doesn't put me in a better mood when my little sis is pouting. I'm looking forward to it, but it doesn't mean I get to go to law school.

Maddie sighs. "I'm sorry."

"For what?"

"For being a brat. I'm so thankful we're all here. No lives were lost in that fire. Things can be replaced. People can't."

I nod. She's right, of course. Except the things that were lost are the things that the people need to make a living.

"You know what?" I rise. "I changed my mind. Let's go into town."

"Really?" Maddie squeals.

"Yeah, why not? We can drown our sorrows together."

★ ★ ★

Murphy's is hopping. It's Friday night, after all, and it's the only bar in town if you don't count the quieter bars that are attached to restaurants.

Jesse and his bandmates are playing pool, and—

Uh-oh.

Hanging around them are the awesome foursome themselves. Brianna and Gina Steel and Angie and Sage Simpson.

"Let's sit at the bar, Mads," I say.

"No, I want to—"

Well, there's no protecting her. Her four best friends are

already here, and they didn't invite her.

Maddie is twenty-one—way too old for high school drama. Still, I feel for her. She wanted to be included.

"Maddie!" Angie waves. "Hey! Come on over."

My sister meets my gaze with a hopeful look.

I get it. She dragged me down here, and now she really wants to hang with her friends and the band.

"Go ahead." I plunk onto one of the only two available bar stools.

Brendan Murphy is tending bar. "Hey, Callie. What'll it be?"

"Screwdriver. A double." What the heck? Maddie can drive home. Or I'll hitch a ride with Jesse or Cage.

"Coming up."

"I didn't realize you were working tonight."

"I got back here an hour ago after the Steel party started dying down. I'm wired, so I told Laney and Maryanne to go on home. I'd tend bar and close up."

I nod as he slides my screwdriver to me. I take a sip.

"Wow! That one's stronger than the one I had at the party."

"You said double."

"I did. You're right. I guess I just didn't realize a double was so . . . *double.*"

Brendan laughs. I've never been overly attracted to redheads, but Brendan Murphy is in a class by himself. Slap a kilt on him, and I swear he'd be Jamie Fraser with a ponytail.

Yeah, a hottie.

"What are you two doing out so late?" he asks.

"Blame Maddie. She twisted my arm."

"I'm glad she did. You and I haven't talked in a while."

"Brendan," I say, "we've never talked."

He laughs. A big boisterous Irish laugh. "You may be right about that."

"Last I heard, you're kind of mooning over Ava Steel."

He reddens. And on his fair and freckled face, it's really obvious.

"Where'd you hear that?"

"A little bird told me."

"You mean Rory."

"Yeah." Rory knows all the gossip from Raine, of course.

"There *is* something about her," Brendan says, "but she's way too young for me."

"She's twenty-four."

"And I'm thirty-five."

"So?"

He laughs. "You make a good point. Where is she tonight?"

I look toward the back. Sure enough, Ava's nowhere to be found. "Don't know. I imagine she's home in bed. I hear she gets up early to make all her bread for the day herself."

He nods. "Doesn't surprise me. She's got one hell of a work ethic."

"All the Steels seem to, despite the fact not one of them needs to work."

"That's not a bad thing, Callie."

"Did I say it was?" I take another sip, willing myself not to be so defensive. I'm getting used to the strength of the drink.

"Hey," he says. "I'm sure sorry about law school."

"Don't be. It was my decision."

True enough. Mom and Dad would have backed me if I'd pressed about going. But the money... They need the money, and I'm young. Law school can wait.

"I'm young," I continue, echoing my thoughts. "Law

school can wait."

"It may not have to," he says.

My eyes widen. "What's that supposed to mean?"

"You seemed pretty friendly with several Steels earlier tonight. Brock, Dave, Donny."

"That better not mean what I think it means."

"It only means that your financial struggles will be over if you snag a Steel." Brendan smiles broadly, and his blue eyes twinkle.

He's so cute I can't be angry, even though his comment is way out of line.

"I have no plans to snag a Steel. Those seem to be *your* plans." I give him a smug smile of my own.

"Ha!" He throws his head back. "I should be so lucky."

"You've got as good a chance as anyone else."

"Not when the one I want doesn't know I'm alive."

"Brendan, everyone knows you're alive."

"Not so."

"Do I really have to spell it out for you?" I take another sip of my drink, the alcohol lessening my inhibitions. "H. O. T. You're hot, Brendan. Have you ever thought about wearing a kilt?"

Another uproarious laugh spills out of him. "That's a Scottish thing, lassie. I'm Irish through and through."

His fake brogue makes me smile. I pull out my phone and search for Murphy Tartan. Sure enough, a gorgeous dark-green plaid pops up. I shove my phone in his face. "Check this out. Murphy Irish plaid. Get a kilt, Murphy."

"You seem pretty invested in this idea, Callie."

"Kilts are hot."

"They're skirts, Pike. I don't wear skirts."

"You want Ava Steel to take notice of you?" I sip the screwdriver again. "Get a skirt."

"She's not the type to get turned on by a guy in a dress."

"Who said anything about a dress? It's a kilt." I tap some words into my phone. "Look. Get one of these Jacobite shirts. Totally sexy."

He takes my phone from me and stares at the photo of the guy in a kilt and the long-sleeved shirt with a lace-up neck. Yeah, he's thinking about it.

"Ava likes to look different," I say. "She colors her hair pink and has a lip ring."

"She also has the body of a goddess," Brendan says, "and the face of an angel."

"Oh my God, do you have it bad! Listen, as a woman, let me tell you a secret."

He leans in, his eyes mockingly wide. "Okay," he whispers. "What's the secret?"

"She probably thinks you're too old for her. That you'd never notice her. Trust me. She *does* know you're alive, Murphy. Every woman in this town knows you're alive. You're *that* good-looking."

He winks at me. "Want to go to my place?"

"Ha! Nice try."

"Right. You've got your heart set on a Steel."

We're smiling and joking, but Brendan doesn't know how right he is.

Which pisses me off.

I'm *not* ready to fall in love.

And the realization that I'm halfway there already sticks in my craw like a blade.

CHAPTER TWENTY-FIVE

Donny

"Mom wouldn't do anything like that," I say automatically.

Already, anger is rising in me. I hate it when Dale says anything negative about Mom. He loves her. I don't doubt it. But their relationship is different.

Still . . . something in what he says rings true.

Which makes me even angrier.

"I don't want to believe anything negative about Mom," Dale says. "And I'm not even sure this is negative. If Mom *did* hide something, she did it with the best of intentions. But let's take a look at the facts. They've hidden a lot of shit from us. Maybe not us so much as from the rest of the kids. No one knows why we were adopted. What we went through before."

"They wanted to spare our sisters and cousins that horror," I say.

"Of course they did. I get it. My point is that Mom—and the rest of them—aren't above hiding stuff when they think it's for the greater good. The good being the lives of their children."

"Not such a bad thing," I say.

"Did I say it was a bad thing? Did I?" Dale rakes his fingers through his mass of hair, making it so unruly he looks like a wild man. His green eyes light on fire.

"Easy, Dale. I wasn't criticizing. Just observing."

"Right. I can tell by your tone that you're pissed off."

I breathe in. Out. He's not wrong. "Okay, I'm pissed off. But not at you."

He gives me the patented Dale Steel side-eye.

"Okay, a *little* at you. But more so I'm pissed at this situation. At our grandfather for putting us in this situation. That quitclaim deed has me bothered. It's got to be about Grandpa's affair with Wendy Madigan, like we talked about at the Bluebird. The kid that came out of it has to be Uncle Ryan."

He sighs. "Yeah."

"We can find out for sure. Or we can at least access the files necessary to get more information."

He lifts his eyebrows. "What are you suggesting?"

I pull out a key card Mom gave me earlier. "We go into town."

"What's that?"

"The key to get into the courthouse," I say. "And into the databases."

★ ★ ★

I slide the card through the reader at the courthouse. I'm not breaking in. I'm the assistant city attorney. So what if it's the wee hours of a Saturday morning? I worked through the night many times at my firm in Denver.

"Wait," Dale says. "Let's not go in yet."

"Why?"

"What if it's not safe? What if there's surveillance or something?"

"There probably is. It's a courthouse. But I'm the assistant city attorney. I have the right to be here, to access the files."

"What if the files are hidden? Deleted?"

"Since when are you a conspiracy theorist?"

"I'm not. Except here's the thing. If Mom and Dad are hiding this much, what else might they be hiding? A secret quitclaim deed—that they may not even know about. A secret lien. A secret uncle. It's all too much."

He's not wrong. "Tell me," I say. "How did you find out about Dad's childhood? About..." I don't even want to say the words.

"He was sharing some stuff with me. I was going through a rough time, with the fire, and Floyd, and Ashley... I think he thought it would help me to know some family secrets or something. To explain that I wasn't the only person in the family with struggles."

I sigh. "Sounds like Dad. Always trying to make things easier on us. He never seemed to understand that we just have to get through it on our own."

"That's what I thought too, but now, I think he understands better than we ever knew."

I nod. "You may very well be right."

"Anyway, back to the original point. The quitclaim deed was probably something that Uncle Ry's birth mother demanded. Got Grandpa to sign or something. I don't know."

"Maybe. At least now we have a theory as to why such a deed even exists. The birth mother wanted everything to go to Ryan, her offspring."

"Right," Dale says. "But it was never dated or recorded. So we have no idea when Grandpa signed it."

"First thing we need to do is find all the deeds pertaining to the Steel property. If Dad and the others inherited via joint tenancy on a deed, then they all legally own the property. If the property went through probate, we may have a problem."

"There's no problem if we get the quitclaim deed from Murphy and destroy it."

"True. But until we get the lien released, we don't have the deed. And even if we can get the deed, there are still so many questions it raises. We're going to have to approach Dad at some point."

Dale nods. "I know," he says, his voice soft and resigned.

I get it. Dale is close to Dad like I'm close to Mom. He doesn't even want to think that Dad may have done anything even slightly unethical.

"Maybe it's time," I say, "that you stop thinking Dad is perfect and I stop thinking Mom is perfect."

"I never thought—" He stops.

"Yeah, you did."

"Yeah, I did."

"And so did I. About Mom."

"You still want to go in?" Dale asks.

I look up at the two-story building. The window to my corner office on the second floor is visible.

What secrets does this building hold?

More than I ever imagined, it seems.

"Yeah," I say. "I still want to go in." I slide the card back through the reader.

I pull the door open and follow Dale through. This is a small town, so we don't have twenty-four-seven security. I look around. No cameras watching me, at least not that I can see, though I'm sure they exist.

"Here goes nothing," I say.

Dale eyes the stairwell to the second floor. "Mom's office is up here."

"Yeah, I know." I walk toward the stairway, rethinking what I'm about to do.

"Having second thoughts?" Dale asks.

"How did you know?"

"How can I not know? I've known you longer than anyone else in your life, Don. I can read you like a book."

True enough. I can read Dale as well.

"We can turn around," Dale says. "No one even has to know we were here. You can begin your search on Monday."

I nod. "You know what? You're right. I'd like two more days of innocence. I have a big date with Callie tomorrow. I don't want to taint it with anything I might find out if we go up there."

"I understand." My brother nods. "Let's go."

We walk back to the entryway and leave the building. My car is parked a block over, near Murphy's Bar. Dale and I begin to walk—

I widen my eyes.

Callie. Callie is walking on the other side of the street, her arm linked through Brendan Murphy's.

What the fuck?

"Please tell me you didn't see that," Dale says.

"I'd sure like to."

"He's probably just walking her to her car. Feel like a nightcap?"

"You know? I do."

Dale and I head to the bar and walk in. It's still pretty packed for nearing two a.m.

"My brothers!" Brianna squeals and comes barreling toward us.

"What are you doing out so late, sis?" I ask.

Dale just glares at her.

"Playing pool. Hanging with my cousins and Maddie. You know."

"Because you don't get enough of that at college, huh?" I say.

"We have certain things here that we don't have in college."

Right. Jesse Pike, Cage Ramsey, and Dragon Locke. "Don't even think about it," I tell her.

Dale continues to seethe.

"I'm actually glad you guys are here," Bree says. "Don't ruin it."

Dale and I walk toward the back, where the band is playing pool with our youngster cousins.

"Steel," Jesse says, meeting my gaze.

"Pike."

Our standard greeting. Jesse's a good guy. I like him, actually, but some wounds never heal.

The bell on the door jingles when Brendan returns. Good. He's not off somewhere heating up the sheets with Callie. Dale's probably right. He was walking her to her car. I should thank him for that.

Except what was Callie doing here in the first place?

I leave Dale to deal with Bree and the gang and head toward the bar, where Brendan has grabbed a rag and is wiping it down.

"Hey, Don." He meets my gaze.

I nod. "Isn't it closing time?"

"Nah. As long as the place is hopping, I may as well make a buck, right?"

Brendan's a good guy. At least I always thought he was. But he's basically blackmailing Dale and me with that quitclaim deed and other shit. Heck, I might do the same thing if the situation were reversed. Why do we even have a lien on this place? A tiny building in town. The Steels own some of the most expensive property on the western slope. What's so special about this building?

"I talked to my dad," I say. "About the lien."

Brendan looks around. "Not here."

"Dude, we're the only two at the bar right now."

"I said not here," he enunciates in a whisper.

"Fine. I'll have a margarita."

Brendan smiles. "You and your mother are the only people who ever order margaritas in here, and even Jade usually orders wine."

"You got a problem with my order?"

He laughs. "Not at all."

"Good. I'd hate to have to kick your ginger ass."

"I'd like to see you try."

Truth be told, Brendan and I are pretty evenly matched. Still, I could take him. "If I see you with Callie Pike again, you might get your wish."

Fuck. Did those words just come out of my mouth?

Brendan juices a lime into a stainless-steel shaker. "You got designs on Ms. Pike?"

"She's a friend."

"She's my friend too."

"Since when? I've never seen you in the same room with her."

"It's a small town, Steel."

He's not wrong. "She and I have a date tomorrow night."

"You mean tonight, I think."

"Yeah. I guess I do." Good thing it's Saturday. I'm going to need the extra sleep.

Brendan adds simple syrup, tequila, and a dash of triple sec to the shaker. "If you're concerned, don't be. My interests lie elsewhere."

"Good."

Brendan shakes the margarita and then pours it into a salt-rimmed glass. "Enjoy."

"Put it on my tab."

"No problem."

Brendan wipes down the surface quickly and then heads out into the sitting area, taking drink orders.

I sit alone and eye the staircase leading up to Brendan's apartment. What else is hidden up there?

When Brendan returns, I ask, "Found anything else underneath the floor?"

He scowls at me. "I said, not here."

"Sunday, then. Your place. We're removing your entire floor."

"Uh . . . no, we're not."

"Yeah, we are. Don't worry. I'll pay for everything."

"Yeah, you will. But what's the point?"

"Because where there's smoke, there's fire."

CHAPTER TWENTY-SIX

Callie

"Wonderful to see you, Mr. Steel," the maître d' at Aspen Grove says. "Your table is ready."

Donny and I follow him to a private table in the back of the darkened restaurant. Why do restaurants think people like to eat in the dark, anyway? I don't get it.

The tuxedoed maître d' holds a chair out for me and then unfolds and places my napkin on my lap. Cushy.

"Your server will be with you in a moment, and the sommelier will be around with the wine list."

"We won't be having wine," Donny says. "Just cocktails."

"As you wish." He bows and departs.

"I might go for a glass of wine," I say.

"Oh? Sorry. I didn't mean to be presumptuous. You said—"

"I'm kidding." I smile. "I wish I liked wine more, since it's my family's chosen business and all."

"I've told you before. Dad and Dale think I'm nuts that I don't enjoy wine and bourbon much."

Our server comes by, leaving a cocktail menu.

I glance over it. "Hmm. Pomegranate margarita. That sounds up your alley."

Donny grins. God, he's good-looking.

"It does, at that. I think I'll try one. What looks good to you?"

"It's a tough call. Either the pomegranate margarita or the pineapple martini."

"Get that one," he says. "We can taste each other's."

"Good enough." I close the menu.

The server returns and takes our drink orders, leaving dinner menus. I open mine. The prices are exorbitant. I stop myself from gasping.

"Do you like calamari?" he asks.

"Yeah."

"Good. Let's get some. Anything else?"

The calamari is twenty-five dollars. Must be squid from a royal family or something. "No. That's plenty. I don't like to fill up on bread and appetizers. It ruins dinner."

Donny laughs. "You don't know the Steels. We can eat!"

I can eat as well, but at these prices . . . Just no.

The server returns, and Donny orders the calamari.

"Are you ready to order your dinner as well, sir?"

"I'm sorry. We haven't really looked. Unless you're ready, Callie?"

"Actually I am," I say. "I'll have the Rocky Mountain Trout with drawn butter."

"Any sides?"

"Roasted asparagus, I think."

"Any soup or salad?"

And add another twenty bucks to the bill? "No, thank you."

"And you, sir?"

"Ten-ounce filet, rare, with sautéed mushrooms. Loaded mashed potatoes and roasted broccoli, please. House salad with Italian vinaigrette."

"That was easy," I remark, once the server leaves.

"Can't beat the beef here."

Steel beef is the best. We raise a little bit of beef on our ranch, but it's far from our main operation. We're mostly a winery.

Were a winery, anyway.

"Tell me," Donny says. "What were you doing at Murphy's last night?"

How does he know I was there? And why didn't he bring this up on our two-hour drive if it's bugging him? "Having a drink with Maddie. It was her idea."

"I see."

"How did you even know I was there?"

"Dale and I saw you walking with Brendan."

"Oh." My cheeks warm. "Yeah, he walked me to my car."

"Nice of him."

Donny's tone indicates something other than nice, though.

"Yeah, it was. You can't be too careful. As a woman, I mean. Walking after dark."

As a rule, I believe my words. But Snow Creek is hardly dangerous, even in the dead of night.

"True," Donny says. "I'll have to thank him."

"For what?"

"For making sure you were safe, of course."

His comment is sweet, but it grates just a little. I both want him and don't want him to worry about my safety. I've always been fiercely independent. In fact, I'd balked when Brendan offered to walk me to my car, but he insisted. And in the end, I do agree that women need to be cautious, even in a safe town such as Snow Creek.

"I already thanked him," I say.

"I'm sure you did."

His tone is . . . I'm not sure.

"What's that supposed to mean?"

"It means I'm sure you're polite and that you thanked him. There's no hidden meaning, Callie."

Right. Take words at face value. Not my strong suit. I don't want to ruin this evening just because I'm still upset about the fire and law school.

"You're right. I'm sorry."

"Are you a little on edge?" he asks. "You didn't talk much on the drive."

"I'm fine. Just . . . nothing."

"What? You can tell me."

I sigh. "I want this evening to be nice."

"Nothing will stop that. I'm really happy to be here with you, Callie."

I smile, my cheeks warming further. "I'm happy to be here with you too."

"We can go as slow as you want," he says.

Slow? We've already screwed. I'm not sure how slowly we can go at this point. I'm not sure I want to go slowly.

Which confuses me even more.

I'm hardly the screw anything with a pulse type.

And I know the man across from me is that *very* type.

Our cocktails arrive, and I take a sip of the pineapple martini, wincing slightly.

"Okay?" Donny asks.

"Yeah. It's good. Just . . . a lot of vodka." I flash back to the double screwdriver I drank last evening. Also strong. Only one, since I was driving home myself. Maddie got a ride with one of the foursome.

"You want to try mine?" He pushes the pomegranate margarita toward me.

I take a sip. It's sweet with just a tang from the tequila. "Wow. Delicious."

"You want to trade?"

I shake my head. "No. This one's yours."

"If you don't like yours, we'll get you one of these." He signals our server.

"Donny, it's okay . . ."

"Yes, Mr. Steel," the server says.

"The lady isn't crazy about her drink. Could you bring her one of these instead?" He points to his own drink.

"Of course. Right away." He takes my drink and whisks away.

Embarrassment sweeps through me. "I didn't mean you had to get me something else."

"If you don't love what you order, you shouldn't have to drink it."

"I liked it fine. It was just strong. I don't drink a lot, so I notice strength immediately."

"No problem. We can get you another—"

I gesture him to stop. "Donny, it's fine. Please."

He smiles, and my insides melt.

"I guess I'm just used to going the extra mile to get things perfect," Donny says. "My dad always says for what we're willing to pay, we should always get the best."

I nod. Not a philosophy I'm familiar with, but I'm not going to say that. He already knows.

"Sorry if I embarrassed you," Donny continues.

"It's okay. You didn't."

He smiles. "Then you're gloriously pink for some other reason. Whatever the reason, it suits you."

I look down at my napkin.

Donny Steel has a way of making me forget my troubles.

And that scares me silly.

This is a man who may wine me and dine me, take me to bed, but this isn't a man who's going to fall madly in love with me.

I have to be careful.

Really careful.

Because though I never thought I wanted to fall in love, I'm halfway there.

With a man who won't love me back.

No matter how much I want him to.

CHAPTER TWENTY-SEVEN

Donny

She looks so beautiful.

Her hair is down, all sleek and brown and gorgeous, flowing over her bare shoulders. Her dress is a basic little black dress.

Is there anything sexier than a woman in a little black dress?

Yeah.

Callie Pike in a little black dress.

It's formfitting, and the thin straps show off her milky shoulders. I love a woman with sexy shoulders.

I plan to give them a lot of attention later, back at the cabin.

I've been inside her, but I haven't had the chance to worship her body the way I crave.

That'll be remedied tonight.

A nice long night.

We'll sleep in, tangled in each other's arms, and then—

Crap.

Why did I tell Brendan I'd be over with Dale on Sunday?

After I promised myself a weekend with Callie to forget this other shit?

I'll text him later. Tell him it'll be next weekend.

Better yet, Monday evening, after my first day at work. Maybe I'll find something in the databases that will clue us in to the lien, the deed, everything.

In fact, I'll text him now while I'm thinking about it.

"Excuse me just a minute," I say to Callie as I pull out my phone. "I have to send a quick text."

"No worries," she says.

I send Brendan a quick text, and he replies right away.

Got it. But I'm tending bar Monday.
Make it Tuesday. I'm covered.

Okay.

I pocket my phone. "Sorry again." I smile. "That's the first and last interruption tonight. Now I'm focused solely on you."

She blushes. That gorgeous pink that flows over her cheeks and down her neck.

"Tell me," I say, "about everything."

"Everything?"

"Yeah. I want to know all about Callie Pike."

She chuckles nervously. "I think you know it all. We've known each other for almost two decades."

"True, but we've never really talked. I know you're beautiful. I know you're brilliant. I know you're disappointed about law school."

"One out of three isn't bad."

Self-deprecating. I find it oddly attractive.

"Three out of three. Tell me more."

"I guess I've wanted a legal career since high school, when I participated in the reenactment of *Brown vs. Board of Education* in history class. I was on the defense, and it was a real challenge to defend something I didn't believe in. I realized how powerful knowing all sides of an issue can be."

I nod. "I get it. I had the same experience doing debate back in high school."

"You were on debate?"

"Yeah, weren't you?"

She shakes her head. "I didn't have a lot of time for extracurriculars. The ranch and all."

"You guys all helped out?"

"Yup."

"We did too."

She widens her eyes.

"That surprises you?"

"No. I mean . . . I guess. A little. I mean, everyone knows the Steels have this huge work ethic, but since none of you have to . . ."

"Worry about money?"

"Well . . . yeah."

I take another sip of the pomegranate margarita. Suddenly it's a little two sweet. "We all had to learn the ropes—even Diana and me, who had no interest in staying on and working the family business."

"How's Diana doing?" she asks.

"She's good. Loves her internship."

"I'm surprised she wasn't at your party last night."

"She couldn't get away this time. Work."

She smiles. "That Steel work ethic again."

The server, Mark, brings Callie's margarita and our order of calamari.

She takes a drink.

"I'd say the Pike work ethic is every bit as strong as ours. Given that you're giving up your dream to help out in a hard time."

"I won't disagree. We do what we have to."

"Doesn't mean you have to like it," I say.

She laughs softly. "I love my family. I do. But I have zero interest in ranching and winemaking. Make that absolute zero."

"What kind of things do you do to help out?"

"I'm good at math. I help with the books. I'm also good at writing, so if we need to apply for a grant or something, that's my job."

"That skill will serve you well as an attorney," I say.

She nods. "I'm not great with people, so sales isn't my thing. Jesse and Rory help out on that end. They're both much more outgoing than I am. Very charismatic."

"Well, they're performers," I say. "Charisma is part of the equation."

She nods.

I smile. "I think you're charismatic."

She blushes. God, my dick is hard.

"I tend to say the wrong thing. Every time. I never fail." She takes a drink. "This really is delicious."

"I haven't heard you say the wrong thing yet."

"Just wait," she says. "It's guaranteed."

"So . . . Mom tells me you'll be working with us."

That adorable blush creeps into her shoulders this time. "Pretty presumptuous, wasn't it? To just go to your mom's office and ask for a job."

"I'd say it was pretty courageous."

"It was Rory's idea. That's the kind of thing she'd do. She'd get it too, with all the charisma."

"Seems you got it."

"I think your mom felt sorry for me."

"She may have," I say. "We all feel bad about the loss your family took with the fire. But even if she did, that's not why she offered you work. My mom helps out whenever she can, but she won't give out the city's resources for no reason."

She smiles. "I hope you're right. At any rate, I'm going to do the best job ever. She'll be glad she hired me."

"I'm sure she already is. I know I am."

Again with the blushing. Damn. I'm not going to be able to stand.

"I'd really like to help out as much as possible. I know it's going to be mostly errands and office work, but if I could get in on an investigation or something... Oh, never mind."

"Go ahead."

"I don't want you to think that I'm trying to get something because of..."

"Because of what?"

"Because of this, you know? You and me? If there even *is* a you and me."

I meet her gaze. "I hope there's a you and me."

"Do you? I mean..."

"What?"

"You're kind of a legend around here, Donny. You do know that, right?"

I laugh. "A legend?"

"Yeah. You, Brock, and Dave. The Three Rake-a-teers."

I nod. "I've heard that, but it's mostly Brock and Dave."

She laughs and shakes her head. "Rory actually came up with it. She and I were home for winter break during college, and we saw you, Brock, and Dave over at Murphy's, charming everyone in a skirt. You were already a Snow Creek legend, and Brock and Dave were all of eighteen, but the three of you were relentless."

A wave of embarrassment flows into me. It's new. A little disconcerting. "You seemed pretty friendly with Brock and Dave last night."

"That was all in fun," she says. "Anyway, that night, Rory said, 'there they go, the Three Rake-a-teers.' Someone in the bar overheard her, and it stuck."

"I can't defend my past, Callie."

She smiles then. "You can defend anything. You're a lawyer."

"I . . ." I pause, looking for the right words. "I don't want you thinking of me that way. Like I'm some kind of womanizing team with Brock and Dave."

She blushes. "I just mean . . . I want you to know I don't expect anything. Okay? Not a job. Or an investigation. Or a relationship. Or anything." She drops her gaze to her drink, her knuckles whitening against the margarita glass. "Crap. Told you I'd say the wrong thing."

"Callie," I say. "Look at me."

She meets my gaze, her long-lashed amber eyes burning into mine.

"I know you don't expect anything. I like you. I want to know you better. That's all this is about."

"I know."

"Good." I bite into a crisp calamari ring. "I'm glad you'll be working with Mom and me, and I'll do my best to get you some cool assignments."

She opens her mouth, but I gesture her not to speak.

"And it has nothing to do with my feelings for you or how tonight goes. Got it?"

"Got it."

"Good. Now have some calamari."

CHAPTER TWENTY-EIGHT

Callie

I'm a sucker for the dark suit, light shirt, and no tie look, and Donny Steel pulls it off better than any guy I've seen. I force my gaze from him from time to time, just to make sure he doesn't notice my intense longing.

Then I stop myself.

I don't want to play games with this man.

I'm attracted to him. Big-time. And he's clearly attracted to me.

Still, this is probably just a date to him, even if he doesn't want me to think of him as a Rake-a-teer.

So I'm determined to treat it as just a date too. I'm also determined to be myself.

I'm not charismatic like Jesse and Rory, and I'm not a big flirt like Maddie.

I'm Callie. I'm sarcastic, self-deprecating, and a little peeved about my situation.

But I'm also giving, caring, and I love my family.

I don't have the boobs my sisters have, which has always kind of pissed me off, but at least I can wear button-down shirts and little black dresses without a bra.

Not so bad after all.

I crunch on a baby squid and polish off my pomegranate

margarita just in time for Mark to slide Donny's salad in front of him.

"Can I get either of you another cocktail?" he asks.

Donny raises his eyebrows. "Callie?"

"I'll switch to Diet Coke, thanks."

Mark nods. "And you, Mr. Steel?"

"Mineral water for me, please. Sparkling with a twist of lime."

"Very good."

I can't help a smile. "Seems strange for a Steel to be having dinner without wine."

"Or a Pike," he tosses back.

"Is it weird that both our families are in the wine business and neither of us like wine much?"

"Maybe a little," he says, "but I'm my own person. Always have been."

I smile at that. "Me too." No truer words.

Dinner passes nicely. We eat without talking too much, and it seems very natural. Donny's an extrovert, but he doesn't push me to talk, which I appreciate.

My trout is delicious. Do I dare tell a Steel that I prefer fish to beef on almost every occasion? Maybe on the second date.

Mark delivers dessert menus. I ordered light, so I definitely still have room. Still, I hate to add to the bill—even though I know money is no object for Donovan Steel.

"What looks good?" Donny asks.

"All of it. What are you going to have?"

"Carrot cake, I think. Though it won't beat Aunt Marj's. She makes the best cakes this side of the Mississippi."

"That cake last night was amazing."

"Yeah. Her white cake with raspberry crème filling. That's her standard for her fancy decorated cakes."

I glance over the menu again. "Chocolate almond mousse. I admit it. I'm a chocoholic."

"Not a bad thing."

Donny motions to Mark, orders our desserts plus black coffee, and then turns back to me. "Tell me. Do you like to cook?"

I lift my eyebrows. "That came out of left field."

"Just wondering. I'm a lousy cook myself. I order takeout most evenings."

I can't afford takeout. But I don't mention this.

"Dale's a regular gourmet. Dee and Bree are both pretty good too. Even Dad can whip up a pretty good omelet. Mom and I aren't cooks though, unless you count her grilled cheese and tomato sandwiches or her chocolate cake. They're pretty legendary."

"Cooking's not really my thing. I've been living at home since college, for the most part, so my mom does the cooking."

"What's it like? Living at home as an adult."

"It's ... okay."

"I'll be moving into the guesthouse as soon as Dale and Ashley's house is ready, but that won't be for a few weeks yet. I haven't lived at home full-time since high school. It's kind of weird."

"Both of us living at home," I say.

"Yeah." He chuckles. "Not the optimal prescription for alone time."

I warm. "True."

"So we'll have to take advantage of this weekend, then."

His words arrow straight between my legs. I force

myself not to squirm.

Mark arrives with our coffees and desserts. I take a bite of mousse and let the creaminess sit on my tongue for a moment. The dark chocolate and smoky almond fill my mouth with decadence.

Donny smiles. "You have an amazing dreamy look on your face right now."

I swallow. "Do I?"

"Yeah. Must be good."

"It's wonderful. How's the cake?"

"Delicious. Not Aunt Marj's, though."

I take another bite of mousse.

"I need to get the recipe for that dessert," Donny says. "I want to bottle that look on your face."

Sparks skitter over my flesh.

"I wouldn't mind you looking at *me* like that," he continues.

"Don't I?" I try a coquettish smile, but I probably look like I have gas or something.

Don't I? God, that sounded stupid. I'm so not a flirt like Maddie.

"Not yet," he says, "but you will."

CHAPTER TWENTY-NINE

Donny

Back at the cabin, we're barely inside before I attack.

I pin her against the wall next to the door, raise her arms above her head and crush my lips to hers.

God, I want her. I've been hard all through dinner, and then that dessert. Watching her eat, that look on her face . . .

Her lips are soft and supple under mine, and she parts them, letting me take her tongue.

Man, this woman can kiss. For a moment, I wonder who taught her, but the thought erases itself and I dive in and take.

Take everything I can in a kiss.

I want to touch every part of her, kiss every part of her.

I deepen the kiss, flatten her against the wall, still holding her hands above her head. I nudge into her taut belly with my dick.

Fuck, I'm hard.

Hard as steel.

Though I don't want to, I break the kiss and inhale deeply.

Her lips are pink and swollen, her cheeks ruddy, her amber eyes heavy-lidded. I could look at her forever, but like a magnet, my lips go to her bare shoulders.

Those shoulders.

Her flesh is velvet silk, and she sighs as I trail kisses over her.

"So beautiful," I murmur, still sliding my lips over her neck and shoulders.

Everything. I want to do everything to her.

Except right now . . .

Right now . . .

I need to be inside her.

With my free hand, I lift her short dress.

Oh. My. God.

For a split second, I think she isn't wearing panties. When my fingers find lace, I realize it's a thong.

I could undress her, regard her luscious body in only a thong, but right now all I can think about is getting into that hot pussy.

Condom. Where's my condom?

To get it out of my pocket, I have to let her go.

That doesn't seem like a viable option at the moment. "Please tell me you're on the pill," I say.

"Yeah," she sighs. "Since I was— Oh! Sixteen."

"Thank God." With a free hand, I unzip my pants and pull out my cock. "I'm clean. I swear."

"Me too."

I groan, grasp the strings of her thong, and shove myself into her.

My God.

She's tight but so wet I slide right in balls deep.

She sighs against me.

I'm inside her. Inside her for the second time, and I haven't even sucked on her gorgeous breasts. Kissed her naked body.

I've never wanted a woman like this.

She deserves better.

She'll get better.

But in this moment, this pure and raw moment, I'm going to fuck her against the wall, next to the door.

It's that urgent. That necessary.

I pull out and thrust back in, and if possible, she feels even better the second time.

Better the third.

And the fourth.

Each time, she sheathes me more completely, and after two more thrusts, I'm ready to come.

Without a condom, my cock is more sensitive than ever. I shoot into her as I burst inside.

Not just my dick is involved. Every cell in my body is. I totally explode, and the contractions in my dick splatter like paint throughout my arms, legs, fingers, toes.

Fuck.

I hold myself inside her, relishing in the hazy feeling of euphoria. It's more than just condomless sex.

It's more than a fuck against a wall.

It's more.

So much more.

My rapid breathing gets under control after a few minutes, and I let myself slip out of her.

I've fucked her twice now, and I haven't yet given her an orgasm.

This isn't like me. I always make sure my partner is satisfied before I take my own pleasure. Indeed, it's part of *my* pleasure.

What the heck is wrong with me? I love women. I want women.

But this thing with Callie Pike is on a whole new level.

"Damn," I say against her neck.

She brings her legs to the ground.

"I didn't mean for that to happen," I tell her.

"I wasn't complaining."

"You should be. There's more to me than quick fucks, and I'm going to prove that to you tonight."

She moans softly.

"I just . . . You look so beautiful. Your hair." I reach toward her and sift her locks between my fingers. "It's so soft. I love the way it flows over your shoulders. And your shoulders, Callie. You have the sexiest shoulders I've ever seen."

She parts her lips, licks them.

Damn.

"I . . ."

"Yeah?"

"I need some water," she says.

"Oh. Yeah. Of course."

I pull her dress over her luscious ass and take her hand, leading her to the kitchen. I grab two glasses out of the cupboard and fill them. "Here you go."

She nearly drains the glass.

"This is a gorgeous place." She sets her glass down on the granite countertop.

"Dad bought it after Dee was born. Uncle Ry and Aunt Ruby have a place in the same complex. Uncle Joe has an actual house up here."

Her eyes widen. "Wow."

"I like our place the best. It's cozy, you know?"

"Cozy? This place is huge."

Is it? Perhaps to Callie it does seem huge. It's about two thousand square feet, with a great room and three bedrooms. Three full baths. About the same size as my loft in downtown Denver.

Tiny compared to the houses on our ranch.

Callie walks barefoot—she kicked off her strappy sandals after our quickie—into the great room. "I love the rustic decor."

"You want a fire?" I ask.

She shakes her head. "If it were the dead of winter, I'd say yes. But no, it's not necessary."

"If you want one, it's necessary."

"It's October."

"We sometimes have snow in October."

"Yeah, but there's no snow now. It's fifty-five degrees outside."

"There's nothing like making love by the fire." I smile.

"It's tempting...but no."

"Callie..."

"It's not the temperature, Donny. A fire just took a dream from me. From my family. I really don't want any flames near me."

I trail a finger over her pink cheek. "I understand."

She sits down on the leather couch across from the granite fireplace. "Wow. This might be the most comfortable piece of furniture I've ever sat on."

I plunk down beside her. "It kind of absorbs your body."

"Mmm." She closes her eyes. "I could totally fall asleep here."

Asleep? I'm nowhere near done with her. But if it's sleep she wants...

"If you're tired, we can go to bed. This couch is awesome, but the bed is better."

"Donny..."

"Hmm?"

"How many women have you brought here?"

Crap. She really wants to go there? "Why is that important?"

"It's not. I'm just curious."

I could lie to her and tell her she's the first. Or I could also lie to her and say I don't remember. Truth is, I do remember.

"Six," I say. "Including you."

Her eyes go into circles. "Six?"

"Including you," I repeat.

She says nothing.

"Does that surprise you?"

"Well . . . yeah. It surprises me that you know the actual number. And it kind of sucks that I'm the sixth. Even the fifth would be better."

"But it's better than the seventh." I smile, hoping she'll giggle.

She doesn't.

"Callie, I haven't lived as a monk."

"I know that."

"Then why'd you ask?"

She sighs. "Hell if I know."

"I respect you too much to lie to you. So I won't lie to you when I tell you that you mean something to me."

"Oh?"

"Yeah. I'm feeling something different for you. It's a . . . I'm not sure I can put it into words. All I can tell you is it's not my MO to fuck a woman without taking care of her first."

"So I bring out the selfishness in you?"

I drop my mouth open but then notice the dancing in her eyes. She's teasing me.

"I suppose you're right. I've been ridiculously selfish. And it's not because I don't want to give you pleasure. I've dreamed about sliding my lips over every inch of your body, Callie. About burying my face between those long legs and licking you until you scream. Of sucking and biting your nipples. Of . . ." I squirm, adjusting the crotch of my pants.

"Why haven't you?"

"Oh, I will. It's been my intention all along. But then I get near you. And all I can think about is being inside you. It's . . . It's like you're a drug or something, and I need a fix."

Even I don't believe the words that just tumbled out of my mouth.

That doesn't make them any less true.

"Really?" she says. "You want me *that* much?"

"Fuck yes." I trail a finger over her jawline, down her silky neck. "I want you *that* much."

"Well, then." She smiles, covering my hand with hers and bringing my finger to her lips. "Take me."

CHAPTER THIRTY

Callie

"You don't know what you're asking," he says.

"I know very well what I'm asking. Take me hard and fast, like you have before."

"Callie, I want—"

"We'll get there," I say. "Right now, I want you as you are. As you want me."

"Okay," he says, "but we're going to be naked this time."

I smile. "Then take off your clothes, sailor." I lift my dress over my head and toss it on the chair next to the couch.

My thong is somewhere over by the door in shreds, so I'm naked, my nipples jutting out like pencil erasers.

Donny's eyes go wide.

Nice.

Very nice.

"I've shown you mine," I say. "Now you show me yours."

He yanks off his jacket quickly and tosses it on top of my dress. Then his shirt. He rips it in two, and buttons go flying.

I squeal and then let out a giggle.

But not for long.

My gaze lands on his incredible chest and abs. Hairless and smooth, rippled and hard.

Oh. My. God.

"Like what you see?" he teases.

"Do you?" I taunt back.

Where is this coming from? I'm not a natural flirt, and though I know my body is nice, it's not stacked like my sisters'.

Donny Steel is bringing out the siren in me.

And you know what?

It's fun.

"I *love* what I see, Callie. You're fucking beautiful. Perfect, even."

"Ditto on that." I eye his crotch. "Keep going."

He kicks off his shoes—Donny is a Steel who actually doesn't wear cowboy boots—and unbuckles his belt. Down go his pants and boxer briefs . . .

And out springs his huge cock.

I can't help myself. I gape at it. Already I know it's big. It's been inside me twice. But actually seeing it. Ogling it . . . In the flesh . . .

It's magnificent.

Slightly darker than the rest of him, it's straight with a perfectly formed head. Two veins swirl over the top, intertwining like the marbling in a fine cut of beef.

He's a fine cut of beef all right.

Wow.

Fucking wow.

His pants and underwear join the rest of the clothes on the chair.

Then I giggle.

His eyes widen.

"The socks, Don."

His chiseled cheeks pink a bit as he looks down at his black socks. "What? This look doesn't turn you on?"

I giggle again. Because I'm so turned on. He can screw me wearing the socks, for all I care. I won't balk at it.

He peels the socks off slowly, as if he's doing a strip tease.

I giggle again.

Then I gape again. Even his feet are gorgeous. My God, he's perfect.

His thighs are hard and thick, his calves meaty and muscled. "How do you stay in such great shape? With a desk job and all."

He sits next to me on the couch and lowers his head to my ear. His hot breath makes me shiver.

"I get a lot of exercise," he whispers.

"Doing what?"

"This."

He flattens me on the couch and shoves his dick into me.

I cry out from the invasion, from the sheer pleasure.

He's doing what I told him to do. He's fucking me, and I'm enthralled.

I close my eyes—

"No," he commands. "Look at me."

I open my eyes and meet his hazel gaze. His focus is intent as he thrusts, thrusts, thrusts, sweat emerging on his hairline.

"You feel so fucking good," he says, panting.

I open my mouth to reply, but only a groan emerges—a groan that seems to come from the very pit of my soul and moves outward, flowing toward him.

"I swear I could live inside you." He thrusts. Thrusts. Thrusts. "That's how good you feel around me. So tight but so silky. Perfect fit."

Thrust.

Thrust again.

Though I'm tempted to close my eyes again and fall into a dreamland—for this must be a dream—I don't let my gaze waver from his. I lock on to him, as if our eyes are held together by an invisible beam or force.

He'll go longer this time.

After all, he just came less than a half hour ago—

"Aauugghh!" He thrusts deeply, holding himself there.

I feel him.

I feel him come.

Each spurt as he fills me.

He seems to reach my heart.

Finally, he collapses, his chest touching mine, his sweat mingling with mine. "My God."

I say nothing.

"What is it about you?"

Again, I say nothing.

"I promise," he says. "This night is far from over. You'll get what you deserve."

An ominous promise.

And one I intend to hold him to.

CHAPTER THIRTY-ONE

Donny

When I finally find the strength to lift myself from the couch, I pull Callie into my arms. She melts against me, as if perfectly molded for my body.

Everything about her is like yin to my yang. The way her pussy gloves my cock, and the way she feels against me now.

She sighs against my chest. "I could use a shower."

"Your wish is my command." I exhale. "If I can move."

She chuckles against me, her breath tickling me in a delicious way. "Not sure I can either."

We stay on the couch, cuddled, for a few more timeless moments, until—

She disentangles herself from me. "Shower. But first bathroom."

I nod. "The master suite is upstairs to your right. Bath is in back."

I gaze at her gorgeous ass as she rises and walks away, still imagining that amazing rimming I want to give her. I should get up. Go with her. Take care of her.

But my body is so relaxed. Almost numb with pleasure.

My dick lies semihard against my belly. Just watching Callie leave the room has it perking up. Twice, and I'll go again before the night is through. Already I know this. What I'm not sure I can do is take care of her first.

The situation has me seriously flabbergasted.

Callie Pike has me acting like a horny teen having his first sexual experience. Unreal.

I'm not sure how much time passes before the sound of the shower arouses me out of my haze.

She said she needed a shower.

I could use one too.

If I go up there, though, I'll end up taking her against the shower wall. In my mind's eye, I already see it happening. Wet and sleek flesh, her hair clinging to those amazing shoulders, her body melting against mine as I thrust up into her.

Yeah, there goes my dick. Hard again, just thinking about it.

Stay here. Stay here and let her shower, because if you go once more, you'll be done for the night. Three has always been my limit, and it's usually two.

The few times I've made it three times, I was quite a bit younger than my thirty-two years.

Callie deserves better.

Hell, *I* deserve better. I want more than anything to enjoy her whole body, not just her pussy.

And I want her to have an orgasm. Two, three, multiple.

As many as I can give her.

I grasp my cock in my fist, imagining her lips around it. Yeah, I want that too, and if I fuck her quickly again, I'll never know the feel of her firm lips around me—at least not tonight.

"Damn," I say aloud, rising.

I'll help her shower. That's all. I'll control myself. I've never had a control problem before. I can handle this.

Handle is my middle name. I've been handling shit with

verve since I was seven years old.

I walk out of the living room and up the staircase leading to the second floor, following the whooshing sounds of the shower.

And imagining what I'll find when I get there.

I stride into the master bath. Steam floats around me, and through the etched glass I see the blur of Callie's slick body.

She's standing under one of the two showerheads, her head tilted, her long hair plastered down her back.

I pull the door open.

God, she's better than my imagination.

The burst of cool air from the open door startles her, and she opens her eyes.

"Starting without me, I see."

She instinctively covers her breasts.

"Feeling shy?" I ask.

She moves her arms. "No."

I walk into the shower, hard as a rock but determined I won't take her here.

Determined . . . but weakening by the second.

"Beautiful." I reach forward to cup a breast. "Perfect."

Her nipple hardens at my touch, even in the hot shower.

If possible, my dick gets even harder.

"I made myself a promise," I say.

"What's that?"

"I won't fuck you in here. The next time will be slow, and you'll have an orgasm. Maybe two or three."

She smiles. "I'm not a multiple orgasm kind of girl."

"Oh?" I lift my eyebrows. "We'll see about that."

"Give it your best shot," she teases.

"I intend to." I pull her into my arms.

No. No, no, no. Not going to fuck her in the shower.

Except I *am* going to fuck her in the shower.

I may not be able to go more than three times, but that doesn't mean I can't take care of her.

I walk her backward until she's against the slick wall, the showerhead pummeling us with hot water.

She likes her showers scalding hot.

Nice. So do I.

A second later, I'm inside her, thrusting . . .

"My God, Callie. What is it about you?"

Again I dive upward into her heat. Nothing like this. Nothing. Ever. Ever again. Already my balls are scrunching, and the contractions start deep within me and pour outward from my cock into Callie's hot body.

"Coming," I grit out. "Coming again, Callie. Fuck."

I plunge into her, balls deep, and relish the pure satisfaction. The pure pleasure. The pure euphoria.

Three times. Three fucks. Four altogether.

And I'm a damned horny schoolboy.

I pant against her sleek shoulder, spent once again.

I haven't washed my hair, haven't cleaned any part of my body.

Callie stays locked against the wall, limp in my arms.

"I'm sorry," I say.

"For what?"

"I did it again. I promised I wouldn't. Fuck, Callie. I don't have an ounce of control with you."

"Who asked you to have control?"

"Damn!" I move backward so I can look into those beautiful eyes. "I did. I want to do better for you."

She smiles slightly. "I kind of like you the way you are."

"But I haven't—"

She touches her fingers to my lips. Damn. Sparks shoot through me, just from that tiny caress.

"You will. I kind of like that you don't have more control."

"Why?"

"Because it means I'm different. Different than your other . . . conquests."

I shove my wet hair off my forehead. "God, you have no idea."

"Why do you think that is?" she asks.

I open my mouth, but I don't have an answer.

I don't have an answer because I'm afraid of what the truth might be.

I might be falling for her, and that makes no sense. Donovan Steel doesn't fall for women. He enjoys women. He makes love to women. He wines and dines women. He gives women what they deserve. What they want.

But he doesn't fall for them.

Not ever.

CHAPTER THIRTY-TWO

Callie

Orgasms don't mean that much to me. I don't care that I haven't had one yet with Donny. I'm not one of those women who can come and come and come. One of my friends from college, Deb Johnson, was like that. She used to tell tales of how she could keep coming once she cracked.

Not me.

Not ever.

I'm a one-and-done girl, and I'm okay with that.

Because my one is usually pretty darned amazing.

As attracted as I am to Donny, and as experienced as he is at giving women pleasure—and I don't for a minute doubt that experience—no way will I have more than one orgasm with him.

Just isn't going to happen. I'm not wired that way.

It hasn't escaped my notice that Donny didn't answer my question.

Why does he have so little control with me?

I already know the answer on my end. Why I let him fuck me hard and fast. Because I don't have any control either. I want him inside me, capturing me, taking me.

I could say it's just chemistry. Pure physical attraction.

That's probably what it is for him.

For me, it's more. More that I don't want—more that I never wanted—at least not until I'm older and established in my career.

I love sex as much as the next person. I even like dating if the man and I have things in common and enjoy each other's company.

But a serious relationship? A long-term relationship?

I never met anyone I wanted to consider a future with.

Until now.

But I know Donny Steel. He doesn't get serious, and he's not going to change for Caroline Pike—not when he could have changed for some city beauty in Denver and didn't.

So not in the cards.

The problem? I'm there. I'm fucking there. I won't say I'm in love, but that's only because I'm stubborn.

Donny is everything. Fun. Charming. Brilliant.

And of course to-die-for sexy.

The words are on the tip of my tongue. I want to ask my question again.

Why do you think that is?

But I won't.

I will absolutely *not* ask again.

Never will I be the kind of woman who has to have her ego stroked by a man. Even though . . . right now I want that more than anything.

I grab the bottle of shampoo and hand it to him. "I'm done." I open the door, step out of the shower, and grab one of the soft forest-green bath sheets. I relish the warmth of the steamy room and the thick towel hugging my body and then grab another for my hair.

Donny squeezes shampoo into his palm while I wrap

my long hair into a turban with the towel. All my product is in my unpacked bag, but on the counter sits some leave-in conditioner. Not a brand I'm familiar with—I get all my products from Raine—but it's here. I squeeze as much water from my hair as I can and work some of the product through to the ends. A blow dryer sits on the other end of the counter in a wicker basket.

But... I need a brush or comb first. I open all the drawers, but I don't find anything.

Guess I'll go to my bag after all. I need clothes anyway. My dress, shoes, and thong are all still downstairs.

I secure the towel around my body and leave the bathroom, shutting the door so Donny will still have the warmth of the steam.

My bag sits at the foot of the bed, where Donny must have stowed it when we arrived here before dinner. I set it on the bed, open it, and pull out my lounge pants and a tank. I don't own any sexy or skimpy sleepwear. I lotion up, apply my deodorant, and throw on the clothes. Then I grab my brush and head back into the bathroom just as Donny turns off the water.

I grab a dry bath sheet and hand it to him.

"You have too many clothes on," he says.

"Did you want me to stand in here and comb my hair naked?"

"Uh... yeah. If I had it my way, you'd always be naked."

I chuckle. "Nice line."

"It's not a line."

"So you want to keep women naked. At your beck and call. Barefoot and pregnant."

"I didn't say anything about pregnant, but barefoot is good. I love your red toenails."

I look down. I don't usually paint my toenails, but Raine ran a special last week before she left town, and I took advantage of it. It was an extravagance, especially when money's so tight, but with the discount she already gives me, I went for it. Mani, pedi, facial. I had her put clear polish on my fingernails, but for some reason, the red called out to me for my toes.

Very un-Callie-like.

"Tell you what," I say. "I'll stay naked if you stay naked."

He lets out a laughing huff. "Uh . . . deal!" He pulls me into his embrace.

Then his mouth is on mine, probing my lips open, and we're kissing. Again. A firm and drugging kiss that makes me unable to think.

My hair's going to dry in a tangled mess, but what the heck? This kiss . . . Can I ever get enough of Donny? His kisses? His dick inside me?

Already I'm throbbing, my nipples erect and ready to burst out of the tank top.

Though the bath sheet is wrapped around his waist, his chest is dripping wet, and the water seeps through my tank to my skin, my nipples reacting further.

Now what will I sleep in?

But that's the last thought.

This spark with Donny Steel is everything. More than that even because I've never experienced anything like it. All thought flies out of my head until only the most pure and raw emotion remains.

Kisses.

Kisses and more kisses.

His fingers on my nipple, tugging through the damp cotton of my tank. His other hand between my legs. His erection pushing into my belly through the lush velour of the bath towel.

He breaks the kiss then.

"Wet, Callie," he whispers against my ear. "You're wet."

I sigh softly, unable to form words. Of course I'm wet. I'm wet just being in his presence.

"I'm going to suck those nipples of yours for hours," he says on a growl. "Eat that wet pussy. All of it, Callie. I'm going to do everything to you."

Words still don't come. A pink haze seems to wrap around me. Everything's foggy, and it's not the steam from the shower.

It's this. All of this. Donny's kisses. His hands. His low and raspy voice against my neck.

Then I'm in his arms, the towel drops from his waist, and he whisks me out of the steamy bathroom. My hair is still in wet knots, but I don't care.

He sets me down next to the bed and peels off the tank and lounge pants.

I'm naked again. We're naked together.

For a moment, I gaze at him. At his perfection. His corded muscles, his flawless abs, his hair—a shade darker when it's wet—still dripping from the shower.

And his cock.

Damn, it's a work of art. He walks back to the bathroom and returns with two more towels. He dries his hair with one and then dries me with the other.

Carefully. So carefully, as if I'm made of the most delicate glass.

"Get ready, Caroline Pike," he says, "for a night neither of us will ever forget."

CHAPTER THIRTY-THREE

Donny

Yeah, I'm hard again, but after three times, I can handle this.

I can give this lovely lady what she deserves.

A one-orgasm woman?

We'll see about that.

I toss the towels over a chair and set her gently on the bed. Her tits beckon me with hard pink-brown nipples. I tweak one gently. Then not so gently.

She gasps.

But she doesn't tell me to stop.

Nice.

I take one nipple between my lips, its texture like silk against my tongue. I suck gently.

Then not so gently.

A sigh tumbles out of her, like a volcanic vibration, only softer. More perfect.

"Beautiful," I whisper against her rosy flesh.

Then I suck her nipple again, finding the other with my fingers. I tug on it gently.

Then not so gently.

I love to give nipples the rough treatment, and Callie seems into it.

Which spurs me on further.

I want to spend hours on her nipples. Hours upon hours upon hours, but my cock has other ideas.

No.

A wave of determination sweeps through me.

I will *not* fuck her.

Not yet.

I will play her body like a violin, make her quiver with my bow.

I move to the other nipple, lick, suck, tug.

She squirms beneath me. "Donny," she says softly. "Feels good."

"Mmm, good, baby," I murmur, and then suck hard on the sweet nipple in my mouth.

I get a gasp out of her again. A good gasp. A turned-on gasp.

Damn, my dick.

No. No. No.

I move her so she's lying flat on the bed, supine, and I kiss down her flat abdomen to the top of her vulva. Her dark hair is neatly trimmed, not shaved like most women I bed.

And for some crazy reason, that visual turns me on even more.

I press kisses to the soft hair. And it *is* soft, not rough like most pubic hair. Damn.

Then I spread her legs slowly, even though my cock is telling me to speed things up. I'm determined to think with the head between my shoulders, not the head between my legs, as I have been.

I gaze at the pussy before me. Pink. Swollen. Glistening with cream.

I inhale.

Damn. Shouldn't have done that.

My cock is ready to explode.

But her fragrance mesmerizes me. Musky and slightly fruity. Perfect in its simplicity.

Except there's nothing simple about Callie Pike.

This perfect pussy is home to my cock, and though I want more than anything to bulldoze inside her again, I lower my head and flick my tongue over her swollen clit.

She gasps and arches her back.

Again. I lick her clit again. Again, again, again.

"Donny. God!"

I slide my tongue lower, then, over the entrance to her pussy, her folds like the satin of a flower petal. Her flavor. God, her flavor. She bursts onto my tongue with an explosion of citrusy tang—like the fragrance only multiplied a thousandfold.

"My God," I rasp against her inner thigh. "You have the sweetest pussy I've ever tasted."

"Nice line," she grits out.

It's not a line. I want to tell her that, but her pussy is right in front of me. Right at my lips and tongue, and I dive back in.

I could shove a finger in. Maybe two, and have her coming in an instant.

But then I'd have to stop licking and tasting her. Remove my tongue from inside her.

Not yet. I'm not nearly done tasting her sweet cream.

I glide over and around her folds, tug on her labia with my teeth, fuck her with my tongue. If only my tongue were longer, if I could go in deeper, taste more of her.

More. More. More.

When she grabs my head, though, I have to give her a climax.

I suck lightly on her clit while I shove a finger inside her tightness.

That's it.

All it takes.

She contracts around me, her thighs hugging my head as she comes.

"Yes! My God!"

Her voice floats around me, and she continues to contract on my finger.

I massage the anterior part of her, and she squeezes her thighs together when I find her G-spot. I add another finger, determined to show her she's capable of more than one orgasm.

Except this first one hasn't stopped yet.

She's still going as I lick her clit. It throbs beneath my tongue.

Her cream erupts on my lips and chin, and I . . .

I . . .

"Fuck," I growl, as I climb over her and thrust inside.

She's still climaxing, and she milks my cock with her sweet contractions.

I thrust.

I thrust.

I thrust and thrust and thrust.

Four more times.

Five.

Six.

And then—

"Damn, Callie," I grit out as I burst. "You're fucking amazing."

I lie there a moment, resting my weight on my arms so I don't crush her. I stay embedded in her body, my cock so sensitive I can't bear to move it.

Her eyes are closed.

"Look at me," I say.

They flutter open. Her expression is dreamy.

"You're amazing." I kiss her lips lightly.

"Mmm. You too."

"I wanted to do more. Give you more."

"Mmm. Told you. One and I'm done. It was wonderful."

I smile. "I can give you more than one. The problem is I have to keep from fucking you to do that. Clearly, I'm not capable of restraint when it comes to you."

"I haven't been complaining."

I kiss her again and then roll onto my side, pulling her into my arms. "In the morning. In the morning, you'll have more than one. I promise."

She sighs into my shoulder and closes her eyes again. "I'm just happy to be here."

"Me too, baby."

Then I add to myself, *God, you have no idea.*

★ ★ ★

Freaking phone.

I open my eyes to the morning sunlight streaming in through the skylight in the ceiling.

Right. I'm in Aspen. At the cabin.

Callie . . .

Where's Callie?

The door to the bathroom is closed. She's in there. And

my phone is ringing. Where the hell is my phone?

Screw it. I'll ignore it. It's Sunday morning. Nothing can be that important.

Finally it stops.

And then starts again.

Damn. Where is it?

I sigh as I sit up in bed. Is it in my pants? And my pants are ... downstairs. But I wouldn't hear the phone so clearly if it were downstairs.

Or maybe I would. I have the ringer on the loudest setting.

I walk out of the master suite to the staircase. From the loft above, I see my pants on the floor. The phone stops again.

Then starts again.

For God's sake! Who the hell is bent on bothering me on a Sunday morning? I walk down the stairs, and the ringing gets fainter.

Okay, not in the pants.

Back into the room. Callie's back in bed, holding my phone. "It was in the bathroom," she says. "Looks like it's your brother."

"No. The brother I know and love would never interrupt me when he knows I'm on a special weekend with you. He knows I'll make mincemeat of his face if he does that."

"See for yourself." She tosses me the phone.

Yup. It's Dale. I decline the call, and then I see that he's also texted me about a hundred times.

Okay, three times.

Call me. Urgent.

Shit. Dale wouldn't say urgent if it wasn't urgent. "Sorry,"

I tell Callie as I walk out to the hallway to return Dale's call.

"Where the hell have you been?" Dale says.

"Good morning to you too. Is everything all right?"

"I'm sorry. My head's not on straight right now. I know you're with Callie, and I'm sorry, but... Fuck, I don't want to lay this on you."

"What is it, Dale? You're scaring me."

"It's Dad," he says. "He's been shot."

I drop the phone, and it clatters onto the hardwood floor.

Callie sprints out into the hallway. "Donny?"

I can't speak to her. Can't even acknowledge her presence as she picks up my phone and hands it to me.

"Donny, what's wrong?"

I shake my head as I tighten my fingers around the phone and place it to my ear.

"Don! Are you there?"

Dale's voice. Dale. My brother.

My father.

"He's in surgery," Dale says. "I'm in the city with Ashley. We're at the hospital. Bree and Mom are with us."

"Is he ..." I can't do it. Can't even say the words.

"His prognosis is good. The bullet went through, but it grazed his liver."

"But what? Who? How?"

"We don't know. He was in the north quadrant early this morning, probably on a morning run. It's Sunday, so only a skeleton staff was on duty. Dad was alone."

My mouth drops open. No words. No words at all.

"Whoever it was got away. He was on our property and got away. I swear to God, Don ... I'll fucking kill him."

My father. My good, strong father. Who would want to

hurt him? On his own property?

"We've talked to the cops," Dale continues. "They're on a manhunt, but Dad hasn't been able to talk to them. We don't know anything else."

"How... How did you find him?"

"It was just chance. One of the hands was out on a jog as well and found him."

"Donny?" Callie says hesitantly.

"Don," Dale says into my ear. "Things look pretty good here, but this is serious. Someone was on our property and tried to kill our father."

"Mom?" I say.

"She's holding it together. She's better now that she knows the prognosis is good."

"Bree?"

"A mess. We're all a mess, Don. You need to get here as soon as you can."

I gulp. "Yeah. We're on our way." Then the phone falls from my hand again.

Callie bends down and retrieves it for me once more. "What's wrong?" Her pretty face has turned white.

"My dad," I say, my tone robotic. "My dad's in the hospital."

Her hand flies to her mouth. "What happened? Is he okay?"

I shake my head. "He's not okay. He's been shot. Someone put a bullet in my father."

CHAPTER THIRTY-FOUR

Callie

Donny's lips are a grim line as we drive home. He's speeding as much as he can, and I don't blame him.

All this time, I've been caught up in my own head, thinking the Steels are golden. That nothing bad ever happens to them.

I want to reach out to Donny, grab his hand. Anything to let him know I'm here for him. That I wish I could help. But I don't know what to do, really. My father is big and strong like Talon Steel. What would I do if someone shot him? If he were lying helpless on an operating table?

One thing is certain.

It's time for me to stop thinking others have it better than I do. I love my life. So I can't go to law school yet. So what? I'm only twenty-six. The law can wait.

I'll still show up tomorrow to do my job, even though Donny and Jade probably won't be at the office. They'll be in Grand Junction with Talon.

Where they should be.

Donny pulls into the long driveway leading onto Pike property. He stops at my parents' ranch house and moves to open the door.

"Don't," I say. "Just get back on the road."

"I'll walk you up."

I place my hand on his corded forearm. It's ice cold. "It's okay. Please. Let me do this for you. Get to your father."

He smiles and gives me a quick peck on my cheek. "Thank you, Callie. I . . . I'll make this up to you."

"Don't concern yourself with any of that right now. Will you call me, though? Let me know what's going on?"

He nods, and I leave the car. In a flash, he's peeling out of the drive and roaring onto the road.

I choke back a few tears. We already know that Talon's prognosis is good. He'll most likely be fine, but until I hear for sure, I'll worry. I heave a sigh as I head toward the door and then open it and walk in.

"Hey, you." Rory walks out of the kitchen. "Did you have a nice time in Aspen?"

She doesn't know. "Where are Mom and Dad? Jess? Maddie?"

"Maddie headed back to school with Angie and Sage. Jess is over at Dragon's, working on music. Mom and—" She gasps. "What's wrong, Cal? You look like you've seen a ghost."

"It's Donny's father. He's been shot."

Rory's pretty brown eyes go wide. "Oh my God. What happened?"

"Shot early this morning while he was out running. A hand found him. He's in surgery." I gulp. "Things look good."

"Thank God. Who would do such a thing?"

"I don't know. I really don't know. Donny's beside himself."

"Of course he is. I'm so sorry, Callie. Here. Let's get you some tea or something."

I follow Rory into the kitchen, and she puts the kettle on the stove. Tea. Mom always used to give us a cup of hot tea with milk and sugar when we were upset.

It won't work this time, but Rory's intentions are good.

"I'm not going to be any good for anything until I hear from Donny." I sit down at the kitchen table. "I told him I'd go with him, but he brought me here instead."

"Don't take that personally," Rory says. "It's family time."

"I know. I just wish I could do something."

"You can let him deal with this in his own way," she says. "You hungry?"

We raced out of the cabin without breakfast, but my stomach is a pit of despair. "I couldn't eat," I tell her.

"Just the tea, then."

I pull my phone out of my purse and set it on the table, eyeing it as if it's about to explode. Another half hour, and Donny will arrive at the hospital in Grand Junction. He'll call me.

Except he may not. He'll be busy with his family.

With his mom, who he's very close to.

With his brother, who he's equally close to in a completely different way.

With his sister.

Then there's Diana in Denver. Is she driving out? Probably. I didn't ask. It's not my business, really. None of it is.

Donny and I have had one date. One. Sure, we fucked in his library at home, and we fucked a ton in Aspen, but it still only equals one date.

No commitment. No nothing.

One date.

Mom walks in then, her eyes heavy-lidded. "I just heard about Talon. Your father got a text from the sheriff."

I nod. "Donny's going to call me when he knows more.

He's on his way to the hospital now."

Mom sits down at the table just as the teakettle whistles.

"Tea for three, coming up." Rory turns toward the stove.

"You think you're safe on your own property." Mom shakes her head. "Now I'll worry every time one of you is out there working."

"Who would have anything against Talon Steel?" Rory asks. "The Steels do so much for the town."

"It could just be random," Mom says.

"On private property?" Rory shakes her head. "I don't buy it. Someone targeted Talon, but why?"

I have no answer to my sister's question.

I have no answer to any question at the moment.

"I'll head over to the Steel place," Mom says. "See if there's anything I can do."

"They're all at the hospital, Mom," I say.

"Right. Of course. Maybe Darla needs some help."

My mom means well, but we all know there's nothing we can do for the Steels that they can't do for themselves. They have unlimited resources.

"There's nothing we can do," I say softly.

I'm right. If there were, I'd be doing it.

Doing it for the man I love.

Yeah, I love him. I'm not ready for this, and I doubt he'll ever return my feelings, but I love him.

How do you fall in love after one date?

Beats me, but it happened.

I love Donovan Steel.

And there's nothing I can do for him.

CHAPTER THIRTY-FIVE

Donny

"Donny! Thank God!" My mother launches herself at me.

I return her embrace for a few seconds until she finally pulls back.

"The doctor was just here. He's in recovery now. They won't let me see him until he's awake. Out of the anesthesia."

"Hey, Don," Dale says.

I hug both him and Ashley, and then Brianna.

"Diana?" I ask.

"She's on her way." Bree's face is swollen and tearstained.

"She shouldn't be making the drive alone," I say.

"I agree," Mom says, "but what alternative is there? A flight would take longer at this point. At least you're here now. For good."

I nod. I'm here because Mom asked me to come. To be her assistant city attorney and take over when she retires. It wasn't in my plans, but I'll do anything for family, especially Mom and Dad. If I could go back in time and throw myself between Dad and that bullet, I'd do it without hesitation.

"Do we know anything else?" I ask.

Mom shakes her head. "Whoever did this is long gone. The hand who found him is Jed Michaels. He's only been with us since July. He was laid off after the fire, but he stayed on property and was out on an early jog. Thank God. What if no one had happened by? What if—"

"Stop it, Mom. Don't put yourself through that."

She nods, swallowing. Her pretty face is red from crying, and her blue eyes are swollen and bloodshot.

"I got you a suite at the Carlton," Dale says to Mom. "It's open-ended. Darla's packing a bag for you, and Willow will drive it over."

"Don't bother Willow," Mom says. "She's been through enough."

"My mom's glad to help," Ashley says. "She knows what you're going through."

"At least my husband's alive." Mom attempts a smile. "Please thank her for me. But I only need the bag, not the suite, Dale. I'm not leaving your father's side."

"You need a decent bed, Mom," I say.

"The only thing I need is my husband. To be here for him. What if something happens in the middle of the night? What if—"

"Stop," I say gently. "Please."

She sniffles and nods. "You're right, Donny. You always are."

"Jade, let's go get a cup of coffee or something," Ashley says. "You need to get out of here."

Mom shakes her head. "I can't."

"Ashley's right, Mom," Bree agrees. "Come on."

The two of them manage to get Mom out of the waiting area. I'm not sure how they did it. Then Dale turns to me.

"We need to talk, Don."

I sigh. "I know."

"Shit's going down, and it's not funny anymore."

"I don't think it was ever funny, Dale."

"You know what I mean. Shit's getting uncovered, and all of a sudden our father gets shot?" He shakes his head, frowning. "I don't like it. Not one bit."

"Of course you don't like it. None of us do. Our dad was *shot*."

"You know what I mean."

"You think this is all related?"

"Don't you? You're an attorney, for God's sake."

Uncle Ryan and Uncle Joe burst in then, putting a halt to our conversation.

"Hey," Uncle Joe says. "Why didn't anyone call us sooner?"

"We tried," Dale says. "No one was answering. He's out of surgery, in recovery. Things look good so far."

"Thank God," Uncle Ryan says. "Mel and Ruby are parking the car. We all came together."

"We can't see him yet. Not until he's conscious," I say.

Ryan nods. "Where's your mother?"

"Bree and Ashley took her to get coffee. She's... Well, she's doing as well as can be expected."

"She's strong," Joe says. "Marj and Bryce are on the way. Damn. How can something like this happen?"

Dale shakes his head. "Fuck if I know. But if I ever find the son of a bitch, I'll rip his head off with my bare hands."

"Get in line." Uncle Joe's eyes darken.

That look. Uncle Joe's dark side. Everyone knows about it, but no one talks about it. We all just stay away from him when he goes red.

A nurse pushes through the double doors and heads straight for Dale. "Mr. Steel, your father is awake." She looks around. "Where's your mother?"

"She went to get coffee with my wife and sister," Dale says. "I'll text her. Can my brother and I go in now?"

"Sure, but only for a few minutes. Then your mother only."

Dale and I follow the nurse back to the recovery room.

"He's in and out," she says, "but his vitals look good. He's got a long recovery ahead, but he's strong and in excellent health."

My father—my strong and robust father—lies on a hospital bed, and two IVs, one in his hand, the other in his arm, entwine around him. A pulse ox machine beeps. It shows ninety-one percent.

I nod to the nurse. "That's low."

"It's normal for coming out of anesthesia," she says. "Trust me. He's doing well, all things considered."

I nod again, though her words give me no comfort as I watch her leave the room.

"Hey, Dad," Dale says.

Dad's eyes flutter open. "Your mother?"

"She'll be here soon," I say.

"How are you doing?" Dale asks.

"My heart's beating," Dad says. "I'll take it."

I regard my brother. He and Dad are so close. This has to be killing him. But he's got a look of pure steel on his face.

He's angry.

Angry that someone did this to Dad.

I am as well, but Dale . . . No one does anger quite like my big brother. Not even Uncle Joe.

"We're going to find whoever did this," Dale says. "I swear to you, Dad."

"You let the police do their job, son," Dad says. "Don't go

all vigilante on me."

"I won't," he says.

A month ago, I wouldn't have believed Dale, but I believe his words now. Ashley has calmed my brother. Sure, he'll want to take this on himself, but he won't. He has someone else to think about.

The nurse returns. "Your mother is back and wants to come in. I'll need to ask you two gentlemen to leave."

I nod. "I understand. Come on, Dale."

"Take care, Dad." Dale squeezes Dad's unencumbered hand. "We love you."

"Yeah," I say. "You got this."

And I hope I'm right.

I've never seen my father look as weak as he does in that bed.

Dale and I leave as Mom rushes in.

"Let's get a coffee," I say to Dale. "We need to talk, and I don't want to do it in front of the rest of the family."

He nods. "Got it."

CHAPTER THIRTY-SIX

Callie

Mom, Rory, and I head over to the Steel house anyway, Mom carrying a loaf of her homemade sourdough.

"The gift of bread signifies you'll never go hungry," Mom says.

Words she's always said to us when she bakes bread for people. Words she heard from her own mother, and words I'll probably say to my own children someday out of habit. If I ever learn to bake homemade bread.

The Steels were never even close to hungry, but I get it. Mom feels she has to do something.

"Mrs. Pike," Darla says, opening the door for us once we arrive, "how nice to see you. Rory, Callie."

"Please, Darla, it's Maureen. How are you holding up?"

"As good as I can. Please come in."

Mom hands the loaf of bread—still warm—to the Steels' cook and housekeeper.

"I'll just put this in the kitchen," Darla says. "Please excuse me."

She returns a few minutes later, a weak smile on her pretty face.

"What can we do?" Mom asks.

"Pray," Darla says. "I honestly don't know what else to do."

My phone beeps with a text. I pull it out of my purse. From Donny.

Dad's in recovery. Doing well so far.

I heave out a relieved sigh. "Thank God. Donny just texted me. Talon's in recovery and doing well."

Darla crosses herself and then shakes her head. "I'm not even Catholic."

"Please let Jade know we're here for her," Mom says to Darla. "Anything she needs."

I stifle a scoff. I don't mean to be sarcastic at such a horrid time, but what on earth could Jade need that we could give?

"I'm sure she knows," Darla says. "Thank you for the bread."

"Is there anything we can do for you, Darla?" Rory asks. "Callie and I are great with a vacuum."

Darla smiles. "No. That's my job."

I like Rory's idea. "Not today," I say. "Take the day off. If Raine weren't out of town, we could send you into town for a beauty treatment, but since she is, take a warm bath. Read a book. The library is stocked full of great fiction."

I warm. Probably shouldn't have said that. Why would I know what the Steel library holds? Oh, because Donny Steel fucked me up against one of the shelves . . .

"That's a wonderful idea," Mom says, not seeming to notice my library comment, thank God. "Let my girls help you today. I'll pitch in as well. Donny will be hungry when he gets home tonight. I'll cook, and Rory and Callie can get the house in shape."

"I couldn't—"

Mom gestures for Darla to stop. "It's the least we can do. You work so hard around here, and I know you're just as worried as the family. You *are* family, Darla. Let us take care of you."

"What about Mr. Pike?"

"I already have dinner in the Crock-Pot at home," Mom says. "Frank will be fine. Besides, we'll be done here by dinnertime. Right, girls?"

"Right," Rory says. "Just point us in the direction of the cleaning supplies and vacuum."

"I don't know how to repay you for this." Darla sighs and melts into a living room chair. "I wasn't sure how I was going to get anything done today. Sunday is normally my day off, but with everything going on . . ." She shakes her head. "Thank you all. Thank you so much."

Rory hands off the vacuum cleaner to me. For some reason, my weird sister actually enjoys scrubbing toilets. I'm glad to take care of the hardwood and rugs. First, though, I head into the kitchen with Mom. I'm wondering . . .

"Mom?"

"Yeah?"

"Maybe . . . Maybe I could cook dinner for Donny."

She smiles. "Oh? Miss I Hate Cooking?"

"I do a few things well."

"You do, but I'm not sure the Steels have Trader Joe's Moo Goo Gai Pan in the freezer."

"Cheap shot, Mom." Though she's right on target. "Did you not notice the shelf of cookbooks behind you?"

"I suppose you think all there is to cooking is reading a recipe."

"Isn't there?"

She laughs softly. "Go for it, Caroline. Choose your recipe. But first you'd better check the freezer and pantry and see what's available. The kitchen is yours, my queen. Good luck."

I sigh. Donny deserves a well-cooked meal when he comes home after such a trying day. I could try. I might even be successful. But I'm just as likely to produce something inedible.

"You win, Mom. You cook. I'll vacuum."

She smiles.

"Just make something good for Donny, okay?"

"Do you know what he likes?" she asks.

Not really. I've eaten one meal with him. He had calamari and a steak.

I smile and meet Mom's gaze.

"Beef," we say in unison.

I leave Mom to her domain and lug the vacuum down the hallway to the master bedroom. Jade will probably stay in Grand Junction tonight, but I'll vacuum anyway, on the off chance she comes home with Donny.

After the master and two guest rooms, I come to a room filled with unpacked suitcases.

This must be where Donny's staying until Dale and Ashley move out of the guesthouse.

I inhale.

I can smell him—that intoxicating mixture of woods, cloves, and law books. Okay, so I don't actually know what law books smell like, but I imagine that the leather musk on the fringe of Donny's scent comes from those voluminous tomes. Everything's mostly online now, but I love the look of a bookshelf lined with casebooks. The kind you see on those old TV legal dramas.

I always imagined my office would look like that someday. My office.

Wow. I have a new job to begin tomorrow.

And already I know the investigation that will be the top priority.

Who shot Talon Steel?

CHAPTER THIRTY-SEVEN

Donny

Brown swill. That's what this hospital coffee tastes like. Fucking brown swill. But it's hot and burns my throat, which is oddly comforting at the moment.

"Did Dad ever take you to that dive bar on the other side of the city?" Dale asks.

"Oh, yeah." I take another sip of the brown swill. This must be what dirt tastes like. Actually, it's not. I tried dirt once when I was five because Dale told me it was crushed-up Oreos.

Fucking big brothers.

"Did he tell you why?"

I nod. "It was my twenty-first birthday. Something about his guardian angel named Mark."

"It was Mike."

"Right. Mike."

"I went back there recently. I'm not sure what I was looking for. My own guardian angel, maybe. I didn't find one."

"Sure you did."

He lifts his eyebrows.

"Ashley. Her name is Ashley. She's your guardian angel."

Dale huffs softly and shakes his head. "I won't put that kind of pressure on my wife."

"What *is* a guardian angel, anyway?" I ask. "Just someone

who watches over you. Sees that you're happy. Sounds like Ashley to me."

"I don't believe in guardian angels," he says bluntly.

I scoff. "Neither do I."

"Then what was that nonsense about?"

"Oh, that nonsense was real," I say. "You found someone to make your heart complete. Maybe not a guardian angel. Maybe not even a soul mate. But a heart mate for sure."

"Can we get back on topic, please?" Dale says with a hint of irritation.

Okay, more than a hint of irritation.

"Sure. What was it?"

"Dad's dive bar."

"Right. What about it?"

"I went back there recently. I was a mess, totally searching for answers about our birth father, why he could possibly do what he did to us. Answers about Ashley. The fire. Everything. I felt like my world was ending."

"But it wasn't."

"No. But now, with Dad getting shot . . ."

I nod. "I get it."

"Anyway," he continues, "I got the feeling from Dad, all those years ago, that he found something there. I was desperately trying to find the same thing."

"And you didn't."

"Right."

"Dale, what's this about?"

"The bar," he says. "It got me thinking. The answers we're seeking aren't there, Don. Not at that particular bar. But they *are* in a bar."

I nod, taking another sip of dirt water. "Right. Murphy's."

"Yeah. They start with that lien."

"I'm on it first thing tomorrow morning."

He nods. "That's what I was hoping you'd say, and dare I say it? Dad's shooting may work in our favor."

I set my ceramic cup of swamp root onto the Formica table more harshly than I mean to. "The fuck?"

"Mom will be here in the city with him until he comes home, which won't be for a few days, at least. You'll have the office to yourself."

"Not exactly. The investigator, the secretary. And Callie."

"Callie?"

"Yeah. Apparently Mom hired her to be some gopher or something."

"Fuck." Dale rakes his fingers through his hair, making it look like a lion's mane.

"She's cool, Dale."

"I know that, and I know you've got the hots for her. It's just… This has to stay between us."

I nod. "Got it. And I agree."

"Which means you need to access records without anyone else in the office knowing it."

"If Mom's not there, I'll be the boss. Shouldn't be too difficult."

"Any way you could give everyone else a few days off?"

"Yeah." My voice drips with sarcasm. "That won't look suspicious or anything."

He sighs. "I know. You'll make do."

"I can be discreet," I tell him. "Nothing to worry about."

"And we're supposed to pull up Brendan's floor Tuesday," Dale says.

"Yeah."

"We need to get him to leave town. Whatever else might be under his floor, I sure as hell don't want him to know about it."

"Good point. Exactly how do we get him to leave town? And then I suppose you're suggesting we just break into his place and remove his entire floor, all while the bar is teeming with patrons one floor below?" I shake my head. "Not happening, Dale."

"What if we could make it happen?"

"How would we do that?"

"You go into the database tomorrow. Find a problem with… I don't know. His liquor license. Get it suspended for a few days."

"That would shut the bar down, but it wouldn't get Brendan out of the building."

"A potential gas leak, then. Or a code violation in the building. Brendan has to stay at the hotel and close down the bar for a few days."

"And if there's no gas leak? No code violation?"

"Then you manufacture one."

My jaw drops. "Who are you and what have you done with my brother?"

"I've been known to breach ethics now and then."

"Exactly when?"

He sighs. "A few times."

"Meaning you ran a red light once? Or you didn't stop for a jaywalker?"

"For fuck's sake, Don. Are you with me or not? There's something going on. Our father's been shot."

"I'm an officer of the court," I remind him. "I can't intentionally break the law."

"Right." Dale sips his coffee, takes a bite of his donut. "It was worth a shot."

"Of course," I say, "I might be able to bend it a little."

CHAPTER THIRTY-EIGHT

Callie

I could learn a lot about the man I've inadvertently fallen in love with. All I have to do is look inside his suitcases.

Trespass.

A big-assed trespass.

So easy. I'm in here vacuuming. No one would know or even suspect, especially if I keep the vacuum running. Mom's busy in the kitchen. Darla is relaxing in her room in the other wing of the house. Rory's scrubbing mildew somewhere.

So tempting.

But already I know I won't do it. That's not my style. I don't violate others' trust.

Especially not the trust of someone I love.

I force the vacuum over the navy area rug, and then I change to a lower setting for the hardwood. Donny's room is large, but still, it doesn't take long to get it vacuumed. Just a bit of dog hair here and there. Plus some sunflower seed shells.

Funny. I just learned something about Donny. He likes sunflower seeds.

Big damned deal.

I could learn so much more by snooping through his luggage.

"Stop it," I say out loud. "Don't even go there."

Rory peeks into the room. "Did you say something, Cal?"

My heart skips a beat. "Just talking to myself. I guess I'm done in here."

"I'll do the bathroom, then." She strides in, holding a bucket full of rags and cleaning solutions.

A lightbulb shines over my head. "I'll do this one."

"You sure?"

"Yeah. Take a break."

"This is the last one." She shoves the bucket into my hands. "I'll go help Mom finish up in the kitchen."

Once my sister is gone, I take the bucket and head into the bathroom Donny's using. Not that I think blond hairs in the shower are going to give me some amazing clue about the man I love, but for some ridiculous and unknown reason, I don't want my sister—or anyone else—cleaning his bathroom.

Go figure.

If possible, the bathroom smells more like Donny than the bedroom. On the marble counter sits a bottle of cologne. Aspen Grove. That explains Donny's woodsy scent. Doesn't explain the law book fragrance, though. I chuckle out loud. Must be in my head.

I begin in the shower, which is bigger than my whole bathroom at home. Next to the shower is a jacuzzi bathtub. A sex bathtub. That's what I call those kind of tubs. Big enough for a threesome for sure.

Damn. Why did I have to have that thought? Donny's a known womanizer. He's probably had a threesome. Maybe even a foursome.

Geez.

The tub is sparkling, however. As I suspected, Donny's a shower guy. I can't imagine him lounging in a bubble bath by himself.

Though I wouldn't mind him lounging in a bubble bath with me.

I open the thick glass door to the shower. It's in good shape, given Donny's only been home a few days and he spent last night in Aspen with me. Only a few stray blond hairs. Still, I disinfect the floor and walls, scrub the glass door until it shines. He uses American Crew three-in-one shampoo, conditioner, and body wash.

Very Donny Steel.

Next, I tackle the counter and double sinks. Donny clearly uses the sink closer to the shower, as that's where his cologne and toothpaste sit. My reflection stares back at me in the mirrored cabinet on the wall above the sink.

Without thinking, I open the cabinet.

I'm just cleaning, right?

Inside is some ibuprofen and a glasses case. Does Donny wear contacts? I don't know. These could just be readers, but why are they in the medicine cabinet?

No, Donny doesn't wear contacts. If he did, I'd see contact lens supplies somewhere in the bathroom, and there aren't any.

I absently pick up the glasses case and open it.

I widen my eyes. Inside is not a pair of glasses but a key.

It looks like a key to a safe-deposit box somewhere.

Again, nothing odd. Lots of people have safe-deposit boxes.

Lots of people don't hide the keys in a glasses case, though. Or do they? I don't have a clue.

"Not your business, Callie," I say aloud again.

I close the case and replace it on the shelf, close the door to the mirrored cabinet, and then spray Windex and wipe it until it's free of all streaks.

Already the guilt is eating at me.

I give the floor of the bathroom a quick once-over and gather the cleaning supplies. I need to get out of here before my curiosity compels me to snoop further.

So he has a safe-deposit box. So he keeps the key in a glasses case.

So what?

I gather everything and leave Donny's bedroom quickly. Rory and Mom are still in the kitchen. I hold up the bucket.

"Where does this go?" I ask.

"Not sure," Rory says. "Darla gave me everything before she retired to her room."

"I hate to bother her, but I don't want to just leave it out for her to put away later."

"Your call," Mom says. "She probably won't consider it a bother. Her room is down the other hallway at the very end. It goes off on another wing. Sort of."

I nod. I'm familiar with that hallway. The library is there. But I didn't realize there was another wing. This house goes on forever.

"Jade told me they added the servants' wing after Diana was born," Mom continues. "They needed a live-in nanny for the kids."

Of course. A live-in nanny. Makes sense, when you're billionaires.

I carry the bucket and begin my walk down the hallway, inching closer to the closed door of the library with each step. Funny how the doors all loom in the distance, as if my perspective is being challenged.

Then in a flash I'm past the library. Things return to

normal, and at the end of the hallway, I veer slightly right.

Here it is. The servants' quarters. I feel like I'm in a Victorian novel or something. Who has servants' quarters these days?

Quick answer—the Steels.

Darla's is slightly ajar. I knock quietly. "Darla?"

"Yeah?" comes her voice. "Come in."

"Sorry to bother you. Rory wasn't sure where these supplies go."

"Just set them down. I'll take care of it."

"Please. I don't want you to bother. Just tell me where."

"You're very sweet. There's a supply closet on the other side of the hallway. It's the only unlocked door."

"Got it. Thanks, Darla. Again, sorry to bother you."

"You're no bother, Miss Callie. Have you heard anything else about Mr. Talon?"

"Nothing new. I don't want to text Donny and bother him."

"I'm sure he'll tell us if anything changes. Thank you again for all your help."

"We're happy to do it. Let us know if you need anything else, okay?"

"For sure."

I close the door and leave Darla in peace. Her eyes were red and puffy. I wonder if we did the wrong thing, taking over for her. Now she has nothing to do but worry and feel sad.

I let out a heavy sigh.

Funny. You do what you feel is right.

When it could very well be wrong.

CHAPTER THIRTY-NINE

Donny

My phone buzzes at six a.m., and I jolt out of bed.

"Hello?" I nearly scream into the phone until I realize it's the alarm, not the ringer.

Dad's okay. Just to be sure, I turn off the alarm and call the hospital for an update. Once I'm assured he's still doing well and resting comfortably, and that Mom is in the room with him, sleeping in the recliner, my heart beats a little more normally. I resist the urge to text Mom. She needs to sleep while she can.

I need to go to the office. For now, I'm the acting city attorney.

An acting city attorney who's going to finagle a gas leak or code violation at Murphy's Bar . . .

Fuck me. How did I get to this point?

What is my family involved in?

And why?

Think of something nice, Don. Let your mind go to a better place, for God's sake.

Callie, of course.

She, her sister, and her mother left me a delicious meal of beef stroganoff, homemade egg noodles, and sugar snap peas last night. Apparently they showed up and took over for Darla so she could have her day off.

Amazing neighbors, especially after all they've been through.

The meal was wonderful and rivaled Darla's cooking. I tasted love in every mouthful.

God, that sounds hokey. But it's no less true.

I'm not in love with Callie Pike. Not really. Of course, how would I know if I were? I've never been in love.

All I know is that she's crept into me like no other woman ever has.

And the fact that she came over here and took care of me...

Yeah, yeah, her mother and sister were here too. It wasn't just Callie. I need to remember that before I go all head over heels for her.

That's not my style, anyway.

The hot shower helps. Eases away some of my tension, thank God. Once I'm suited up and ready for work, I head to the kitchen.

"Morning, Mr. Donny."

"Hi, Darla. Coffee?"

"Coming up. You want eggs and bacon this morning?"

"I'm not really hungry."

"I understand, but you have to eat."

"You're right. Just some scrambled eggs. Maybe a piece of Maureen's sourdough toasted."

She nods and bustles around, getting to work on my breakfast. "Any news?" she asks.

"I just talked to the hospital when I woke up. He's resting comfortably. Mom, of course, stayed with him instead of going to the suite Dale booked for her."

"I'd expect nothing less," Darla says.

"Me neither."

Dale doesn't get our mother like I do. No way will she leave Dad's side, even if it's best for her.

I eat the breakfast Darla prepares. Maureen's sourdough is nearly as good as Ava's. I can still taste, even though I'm not particularly hungry.

Last night's dinner was also delicious. I wouldn't mind trying it when I'm not worried sick. And I'm not just talking about Dad, though he's the major part of my worry. I'm worried about what secrets my family is hiding.

And what the consequences might be.

My father is a good person. The best. So are his brothers. So are Aunt Marj and all the spouses.

So I wonder... How much of what I uncover will be a surprise to them as well?

But...

People wear masks all the time. As an attorney, I've seen my share of good people go bad.

But not my family. Not the Steels.

Not possible.

"I'm heading into the office," I tell Darla.

"What time would you like your dinner?" she asks.

"The usual time is fine. No reason to change your schedule to suit me. If something comes up and I won't be home, I'll give you a call."

She nods. "Have a good day." She smiles weakly.

I smile in return. Weakly as well. "I will. I'll try, anyway."

★ ★ ★

It's seven thirty, and I'm not the first to arrive. The building opens at seven for early court appointments, and when I walk upstairs to the city attorney's office, I find Callie sitting in the waiting area, dressed in black pants and pumps, a white blouse, and a pink cardigan.

I smile. "You're early."

"I wanted to make a good impression on my first day. How's your dad?"

"He's good. I called the hospital this morning. Mom won't be in for a few days."

"I figured."

"So I guess I'm your boss." Normally my voice would have a teasing tone at those words. Not today. I'm too worried and tense. "Did Mom show you where you'd be working?"

"Not really."

"Okay. We'll set something up." I pull out the key to the office that Mary vacated. "Come with me."

She walks with me to the office. I unlock the door and walk in. It's a corner office, not quite as big as Mom's. I flip the light switch. "Have a seat."

"When do the others come in?" she asks.

I can't help a chuckle. "I don't have a clue. It's my first day too."

"Right." She smiles. "I just thought your mom might have..."

I sigh. "I'm sure she would have if she'd foreseen the current circumstances."

Callie blushes. "I'm sorry."

"Hey, it's okay. We've all had our share of unforeseen circumstances lately."

"I'm so glad your dad's doing well."

"Baby, so am I."

She bites her lip at my endearment.

"Sorry," I say. "I suppose we should keep things professional here."

"Yeah." She nods.

"So." I take a seat in the leather chair behind the oak desk. "I have no idea what's going on today. I hope my mom doesn't have to be in court this morning, because if she does, I need to go in her place, and I don't know what any of the cases are about."

"The secretary will know."

"Right. She'll probably be in soon. In the meantime... what did Mom say you'd be doing?"

"Filing, errands. Whatever needs to be done while the rest of you are busy, I guess." She bites her lip.

"Something wrong?"

"No. It's just... Like I've said before, I think your mom might have hired me because she feels sorry for me. For our whole family."

"My mom wouldn't do that. I mean, she'd want to, but she wouldn't."

"Oh?"

"Yeah. Trust me. I know my mom better than anyone. Sometimes I think I know her better than my dad does, even. You have to remember that my mom grew up very modestly, like Dale and I did before the Steels adopted us. She knows how it would feel to have someone do something out of pity, and she wouldn't do that to anyone else. If my mom hired you, it's because we need you."

She smiles. Sort of. I'm not sure she believes me, but I know the truth. My mom would totally *want* to do everything, but she wouldn't out of respect.

"So," I continue, "that means there's something for you to do around here. I guess we'll figure out what."

The secretary, Alyssa, bustles in then. "Hey, Don," she says. "Is Jade coming in?"

Shit. She hasn't heard. "Not today. Probably not all week. My father was... He was shot yesterday."

Her hands fly to her mouth.

"He's okay," I say. "He's going to make it, but Mom's at the hospital in Grand Junction with him."

"Thank God. But Jade's due in court in a half hour."

I sigh. "I guess that's on me, then. I'll go down and explain the situation, get the cases continued until I have a chance to get up to speed. By the way, this is Callie Pike. She's going to be our new..."

Callie smiles. "Jack-of-all-trades?"

I return her smile. Life sucks at the moment, but Callie Pike gives me a reason to smile. "That's as good a description as any. Callie has a degree in criminal justice and is going to law school next year."

"But I'll do anything to help," Callie pipes in. "Filing, whatever. Alyssa and I went to school together, by the way."

"Good. Then you already know each other."

Alyssa nods. "It's great to have you here, Callie. I can find you some stuff. You want to come with me?"

Callie rises. "Sure. Are we done here?" she asks me.

"Yeah, go ahead."

She follows Alyssa out of the office.

"You want your door closed, Don?" Alyssa asks.

Yeah, I want my door closed. I'm about to commit a little fraud. But, "No, that's okay. Get me today's court schedule, please. I don't want to look completely ignorant when I go in front of the judge in half an hour."

"Right away. I'll set you up in the system so you can access everything."

"When you say everything, you mean all the databases, right?"

She nods. "We have access to all state and local information just in case we need it."

"Thank you."

Perfect.

Just perfect.

CHAPTER FORTY

Callie

Alyssa sets me up in the cubicle next to hers. The investigator, Troy, has the other cubicle. The two offices, of course, belong to Donny and Jade. It's a small building. Snow Creek is a small town. The other side of the second floor houses the administration for the town. Parks and recreation—a department of one—and the mayor and city administrator—department of two.

Oddly, the city attorney's office has more employees than the other two offices put together. The police department is next door and consists of a sheriff and two officers. Yeah, they're called officers instead of deputies. Go figure.

Are there that many legal issues in such a small town?

Apparently.

I'm about to learn all about them, which is cool. Anything to dip my hand in the pot of my career choice.

"You can start with some filing." Alyssa hands me a stack of documents. "Everything is by case number. It's all online, but Jade likes to keep hard copies of everything too."

"Got it." I get to work.

A half hour later, Donny whisks by. "Everything going okay?"

"Yeah. Fine."

"Good. I'm going down to court. Back in an hour or so."

I nod and can't help watching his posterior as he heads toward the staircase.

Nice. Very nice.

Alyssa peeks her head into my cubicle. "Do you mind going for coffee?" she asks.

I stand. "Not at all. Don't you have a machine here?"

"We do, but it's in Jade's office. She's the only one who makes coffee. She's weird about her coffee, so none of us use it. Plus, her office is locked."

"No problem. You want me to hit up Rita's?"

"Yeah. Vanilla latte for me, black coffee for Troy, and— Crap. I don't know what Donny likes."

"Black coffee," I say absently.

"Great. And whatever you want, of course."

"Sure, no problem."

Alyssa throws some bills down on my desk. "I'm taking it out of petty cash."

Is that kosher? I don't ask. I just take the money and head out of my cubicle, down the stairs, and through the glass doors, nodding to reception.

"Oh, you got the job!" the receptionist says.

"I guess I did. Coffee girl."

I don't mean to sound self-deprecating. It's just kind of how I am. I'm truly thrilled to have the position, even if it means I'm using my criminal justice degree to get coffee.

Hey, if I'm the coffee girl, I'll be the best damned coffee girl out there.

Rita's Café and Coffee Shop is right across from Ava Steel's bakery. The rich fragrance of fresh bread wafts toward me. I got up early and skipped breakfast. One of Ava's almond croissants sounds heavenly. I take a quick detour and walk into the bakery.

Ava herself is at the counter. "Hi, Callie. What are you doing all dressed up today?"

"I'm working for your aunt and cousin at the city attorney's office. Out on coffee duty."

"Sorry. I don't serve coffee. Only bottled natural spring water." She smiles.

"I know. I actually couldn't resist the smell of the fresh baked goods. I'd like four almond croissants, please."

"Coming up." Ava pulls four of the delicacies out, wraps them in tissues, bags them, and hands them to me. "Enjoy."

"Uh . . . aren't you forgetting something?"

"I'm sorry. Did you want something else?"

"No, but how much do I owe you?"

"Oh." She blushes until her cheeks are nearly the color of her pink hair. "Gratis."

I shake my head. "I insist on paying."

"I wouldn't dream of it—not after all your family's been through."

My jaw drops. I don't know whether to yell at her or hug her. I'm equally insulted and uplifted. I open my mouth to insist upon paying, when Brendan Murphy opens the door and walks in.

"Well, good morning," he says jovially. "How are the two loveliest ladies in Snow Creek?"

Without thinking, I look around the bakery. No one else is here.

"I mean you, Callie. You and Ava." Brendan chuckles. "What are you dressed up for?"

"I work here. I mean, not here at the bakery. At the city attorney's office."

"Oh, hey, that reminds me." Brendan turns to Ava. "Talon still doing okay?"

Ava nods. "Last I heard. My dad's still in Grand Junction with him. Mom came home last night."

"Donny heard this morning," I add. "All's good."

"Thank goodness." Brendan shakes his head. "It'll never feel like we don't have to look over our shoulders in this town. I'm not sure I like the idea of you working alone here," he says to Ava.

"I'm not alone. Luke's in the back. Maya will be in later."

"Still…"

"Ava, I need to get back." I plop my credit card on the counter.

"Please, Callie. My treat."

I can argue this until sundown, but not in front of Brendan and not when Alyssa is expecting me back with coffee. "Okay, thank you so much. But next time, I pay. Okay?"

Ava smiles. "Okay."

"See you, Brendan."

He nods as I walk out the door and across the street to Rita's.

Rita's is hardly bustling, though the sheriff and one of his officers sit at a table in front, sipping coffee.

"Hi, Sheriff," I say.

"Hello, Callie. You look nice."

"Do you have anything on the Talon Steel case?" I ask.

"We're looking into it."

I nod. "Thanks. I can't believe it happened."

"Neither can any of us."

I wave goodbye, head to the counter, and place the coffee order.

And I wonder, for the first time since we moved here twenty years ago.

Is Snow Creek safe?

CHAPTER FORTY-ONE

Donny

The judge granted my requests for continuances into next week, when Mom returns. Or if she doesn't, I need to be up to speed by then. Since they're all misdemeanors, no problem. Hell, I've tried multimillion-dollar corporate cases. A few traffic mishaps won't be any issue. I probably could have shot from the hip today, but I wanted to get back to the office.

To dive into the databases.

To find the best way to get Brendan out of his place for a few days and get the bar closed.

Yeah, I'm really going to do this. I, Donovan T. Steel, attorney at law, am going to manufacture a crisis for Murphy's Bar.

I like the Murphys. Always have. So yeah, I feel some guilt here. But my first allegiance is and always will be to my family.

The Steels, who took my brother and me in and gave us a life we never imagined. No, it didn't erase what happened to us those few months prior, but it gave us a lot we wouldn't otherwise have.

A knock on the door jars me out of my thoughts. "Yeah? Come in."

The door cracks open, and Callie peeks in. "Coffee. And an almond croissant."

I'm not hungry, but she's sweet to bring it. "Thanks."

She sets the coffee and roll on my desk. "Black, right?"

"The only way to drink coffee." I take the plastic lid off and inhale. "Rita makes a good cup. Doesn't beat my mom's, though."

"Yeah. Alyssa said no one else is allowed to make coffee here."

I can't help a chuckle. "That sounds like Mom. She swears no one can make it like she does. So, Callie to the rescue, huh?"

"Rather Rita to the rescue. And Ava. The croissants are from her place."

"Ava nearly put Rita out of business when she opened up two years ago. Rita had to expand to a café, and her saving grace is that Ava doesn't sell coffee."

"Yeah, why is that, anyway?"

"Hell if I know. If I know Ava, it's because she didn't *want* to put Rita out of business. Ava is a champion of the underdog, including herself. She opened her place all on her own. Wouldn't take any money from her parents."

"Champion of the underdog, huh?"

"Yup." I take a sip of the coffee. Delicious, but not the Jade Steel masterpiece. Hell of a lot better than the brown swill I drank at the hospital yesterday, though.

"I can believe that. She wouldn't take money for the croissants." Callie sighs.

"Ah... And you don't want her feeling sorry for you because of what your family lost in the fire."

"Bingo."

"I get it. I do. But this is a small town. A friendly town. We take care of each other. And Ava's been known to nurse baby birds back to health. She's the caringest of all the Steels."

"I don't think *caringest* is a word. Did you see it on the bar exam or something?"

I smile. Damn, Callie Pike is adorable. "Legal licensing. We're allowed to make up words. It's in the handbook. About a quarter of the terms in *Black's Law Dictionary* were made up by lawyers, and they caught on."

"Right." She shakes her head, smiling subtly.

"God, you're cute. You know, there are actually women who would fall for that."

She scoffs. "Not on my watch."

"Nope, not on your watch. As for Ava, just take her gesture for what it is."

"Charity?" Callie asks.

"No, Callie. Kindness. That's Ava to a T."

She sighs. "I know. Enjoy your coffee. I guess I'll get back to work."

"What are your plans for lunch?" I ask.

"Sitting in the park with my turkey sandwich. Unless it's too chilly. Then sitting at my desk with my turkey sandwich."

"Sounds like a plan. Call Ava and order a turkey sandwich for me. She knows what I like. I'll join you."

She laughs, shaking her head. "Turkey? Not Steel beef?"

"Hey, I'm a well-rounded eater. Plus...I like all meat. I really don't have a preference among protein. Remember when I told you never to tell Dale and my dad that I'm not all that crazy about wine and bourbon?"

She nods.

"Don't tell them I like turkey as much as beef, either. It'd kill them."

"You're something."

"I'll take that as a compliment."

"That's how it was meant." She walks through the door. "Open or closed?"

"I have some calls to make, so closed." Not calls so much as databases to explore and doctor.

God, what am I getting into?

Callie closes the door.

And I freeze.

Literally. Okay, not literally. As an attorney, I understand the power of a word's actual meaning. But I seriously go numb. I want my fingers to get on the keyboard, to start tapping and searching.

But the magnitude of what I'm about to do freaks me out more than a little.

Dale. I need to call Dale. He's probably at the winery with his Syrah. It's nearly done fermenting, and he's getting ready to age it, first in a barrel and then in bottles. I don't know the actual process. The winery is usually full of noise. Will he even hear his phone?

I make the call on my cell.

"Yeah, Don?"

The sounds of the winery buzz in the background. "Sorry to bother you while you're at work."

"Not a bother. What's up?"

"I'm here. In my new office, and Alyssa just set me up to access everything."

"Yeah?"

"So it's time. I have to figure out how to get Brendan out of the building and close down the bar for a few days."

"And you're having second thoughts."

I scoff. "Of course I am! I'm an officer of the court, and I'm about to commit fraud. Plus . . ."

"What?"

"If we force Brendan to shut down the bar, he and his family lose several days of income."

Silence for a moment. "Yeah," Dale finally says. "I guess we didn't consider that."

"I know. I feel like shit about it. I just thought about it because Callie's here. Ava gave her free croissants, and she took it the wrong way, of course. But it got me thinking. The Pikes have lost a lot of income this year. Do we want to do that to the Murphys?"

"Of course not. But we can't really compare the Pikes to the Murphys. The Pikes have lost a whole season of income, plus more because they'll have to purchase grapes for future seasons until their vines are producing again. The Murphy's'll lose three days of income. Tops."

"Yeah, but three days might be a lot for them. How much can you make from a bar in a small town?"

"Look it up."

"Huh?"

"You have the world at your fingertips, Don. Look it up. Access their tax payments to the state. That'll show their income."

"Fuck," I say slowly.

"Yeah, it's a huge invasion of privacy," Dale says. "I get it. But think of the bigger picture here."

My brother is right. Neither he nor I like this plan, but unless we can come up with something better, we must do what's necessary to protect our family.

I sigh. "Got it. I'll do what has to be done. What if I find out they'll suffer if they're closed for a couple days?"

"Then we'll make sure they don't suffer."

"Yeah. I suppose it won't be the first time the Steels take care of the town."

"No, it won't be. I've got nothing against the Murphys, but we have to find out what's out there. If we don't, it could bite our family in the ass in the future. Do you want to leave that for our kids to deal with?"

"Kids?" I drop my mouth open. "Is there something you're not telling me?"

He chuckles. "No. We're not pregnant. Ashley wants to finish her doctorate first. But we will have kids, and so will you, Don. So will Diana and Brianna. Do you want to leave this mess to them?"

"No," I say. "It's bad enough that it's been left to us. Why would Mom and Dad do this?"

"For our protection," Dale says, "but Mom and Dad aren't the ones who should take the blame for all this."

"I know. Grandpa. Brad Steel."

"Right. I'm not convinced Mom and Dad and the rest of them even know the extent of what we might find. Otherwise, I know for damned sure they wouldn't have left it for us to find."

"Yeah. Okay, Dale. I'll start some research. I'll let you know what I find. What I'm able to accomplish."

"Thanks. I've got my phone's ringer set to the loudest setting, so if you call, I'll hear it."

"Got it. Talk later."

No longer frozen, I fire up the computer and set up my accounts with the information Alyssa gave me.

First things first. I need to know what damage I'll potentially be doing. Time to research the information on Murphy's Bar.

I sift through databases and documents and find

Murphy's does a darned good business. Of course, it is the only bar in Snow Creek, though some of the restaurants also serve liquor. However, the income from the bar has to support Brendan and his parents, who've retired, and his aunt and her daughter. If all their business and residential mortgages are paid, the earnings from the bar will suffice. Still, I need to know more. What salary does Brendan take? What does he pay the other employees?

Shit.

The deeper I dive, the deeper I must go.

I hate this. I truly hate this.

But I'm all in now.

CHAPTER FORTY-TWO

Callie

"Second time in a day!" Ava gushes when I walk into the bakery.

It's noon, and the place is packed with lunch diners. Ava waves me over to her to bypass the line. I feel a little awkward.

"Here's Donny's sandwich." She hands me a white paper bag.

"What do I owe you?"

"Jade's office has an account for her lunches. I put it on that."

I nod. "Great. Thanks."

"Anything for you?"

I wave my brown paper bag at her. "Brought my own today."

She laughs. "All right. Enjoy!"

I leave the bakery and head to the park. Donny is supposed to meet me here for lunch. I find a bench and sit. It's a lovely October day, sixty-two degrees and sunny. We get over three hundred days of sunshine a year in Colorado. That alone puts a smile on my face today.

Alyssa kept me fairly busy my first morning, but it didn't escape my notice that Donny stayed behind his closed door for two hours. I knocked a few minutes ago, told him I'd pick up his sandwich and that I'd be in the park. He nodded and smiled.

Now, though, as I sit here alone... Is he coming?

I can't help myself. I pull his sandwich out of the bakery bag. It's twice the size of mine and smells heavenly. If he doesn't get here soon, I may have to take a bite.

For now, I munch on the sandwich I prepared myself before work this morning. Deli turkey breast and avocado on rye. One of my favorite combos, but all I can think of is the delicacy Ava prepared for Donny.

I finish my sandwich, take a sip of my Diet Coke, and then stare at the white bag again.

Irritation niggles at me. Is Donny standing me up? If so, why should this sandwich go to waste? I pull it out of the bag, unwrap it, and take a bite.

Gah! It's delicious. Smoked turkey breast, bacon, tomato, green leaf lettuce, and yeah, avocado. All bound together with something that resembles mayonnaise but tastes so much better, like it's infused with chipotle or cumin or something.

I can't help myself. I take another bite but stop chewing as I look up and see Donny walking briskly toward me.

I swallow quickly and take a big gulp of Diet Coke to get it down.

"You're late," I finally say.

He chuckles. "Is that my sandwich?"

I thrust it toward him. "Yeah. Sorry. I wasn't sure if you were coming... and it smelled so good..."

"It's okay. I apologize for being late. I was looking through documents, and I lost track of time. It's kind of a lawyer thing. Did you leave me any?"

"I only took two bites."

"I thought you had a sandwich."

"I did. It was about a third the size of yours, though."

"Ava's creations are the best." He takes a bite. "Mmm. The Donny."

"That's your sandwich?" Ava has sandwiches named for each of her family members. "So your family does know how much you love turkey, then."

"They know. They just don't know I love it as much as beef. Ava can't just serve roast beef sandwiches, you know."

I smile and slide a bottle of water toward him. "I got you a water, too."

He swallows. "Thanks. So how's your first day going?" He takes another bite.

"Good. About what I expected. Nothing too mentally challenging, but that's okay. I'm glad to be working."

He nods, swallowing. "I might be able to help you with a mental challenge."

I perk up instantly. "Yeah? I'm your woman."

He smiles. "I certainly hope so."

Warmth rushes to my cheeks. God, I'm probably turning about a billion shades of scarlet. "I didn't mean . . ."

"I know exactly what you meant, Callie. I'm teasing."

I'm both relieved and disappointed.

He goes on, "I need a friend in the office."

Friend? I'm just a friend? More disappointment. "I'm your friend, Donny."

"I know. What I mean is . . . I need someone I can trust."

"I'm sure you can trust your mom."

"Sure," he says, though he doesn't sound quite sure. "But she'll be out for a week at least with Dad, and I hardly know Troy and Alyssa."

"You don't?"

He shakes his head. "I've been in Denver for over ten years."

"Right." I nod.

"Anyway, I'm..." He looks over his shoulder and then back at me. "I'm doing some research, and I'm going to need some help."

"Research? Of course. That'd be great."

He pauses a moment, staring into my eyes. "You look beautiful."

I warm again. "Thank you."

"You know, it's hard to concentrate when you're so lovely."

Again with the warmth. I'm certainly the color of a beet by now.

"Research?" I say again.

"Right." He blinks and then gets serious. "Callie, I need to be able to trust you."

"Of course you can trust me."

"You know, of course, that as an attorney I'm bound by ethical guidelines. Confidentiality. All that kind of stuff."

"Yes, of course."

"And as an employee in the office, you're bound as well."

I nod. "Of course. I'm a sealed book, Donny. Seriously."

He smiles. "I believe you are."

"So what do you need? I'll do anything."

"Really? Anything?" He waggles his eyebrows.

"Well...within the bounds of the office." I warm again. "Though I'm not averse to other stuff either."

He smiles. "Glad to hear that. This weekend we'll put that to the test. Right now I'm talking about some research that has to be kept completely secret. Just between you and me."

I drop my mouth open. "Oh?"

"Well, Dale will know. He and I are working on some stuff together."

"Okay. What kind of a case is it?"

"It's not a case."

"But you're the city attorney . . ."

"Acting city attorney, and yes, I'll stay on top of all that. But Callie, I need someone to do some . . . personal research."

"I wouldn't feel right taking a paycheck to do anything personal."

"Not a paycheck from the city, of course. You'll be taking a paycheck from me."

"Oh. I guess that's okay. As long as it's not during working hours."

He sighs. "It might be. And it might require using city resources."

I bite my lip. "I don't know, Donny . . ."

He grabs my hand, rubs his thumb into my palm. "Forget it. I shouldn't ask."

I should be relieved. Indeed, I am. But I also want to help him. I love this man, and if there's something he needs, I want to provide it.

After a few minutes that seem like hours, I finally say, "Donny, what's all this about?"

CHAPTER FORTY-THREE

Donny

Donny, what's all this about?

A loaded question if there ever was one, and my earlier conversation with my brother haunts me as well.

"She's cool, Dale."

"I know that, and I know you've got the hots for her. It's just... This has to stay between us."

I nod. "Got it. And I agree."

Except I no longer agree. I meant it when I told Callie I needed a friend in the office. I need help to do this, because Mom is otherwise occupied, and I have to make sure the office runs smoothly without her, which means I won't have as much time as I need to deal with...other things. Dale was right that Mom's absence gives me opportunity, but after my first morning, I've also realized it gives me responsibilities that I wouldn't otherwise have.

I gaze into Callie's lovely amber eyes. Concern reflects back at me. Friendship.

Questions.

Questions she has the right to demand answers to, especially if I'm going to drag her into this.

"I need to find out who shot my father," I say.

She widens her eyes. "Of course. Anything I can do to

help. Count me in."

"It wasn't an accident, Callie."

"Are you sure?"

I nod. "Pretty darned sure. He was on our property. He was over on the northern quadrant of the beef ranch, not a place where he usually goes, which means someone was watching him."

"Do you have any fencing around the perimeter of your property?"

"Yes and no. We let our cattle graze pretty much everywhere because our property is so vast. That said, we do have perimeter fencing, but it's only four feet in height."

"Any barbed wire or anything?"

I shake my head. "No. That might harm the cattle."

"It wouldn't harm the cattle if it were higher."

"True. I guess we've just never felt the need before, you know? Besides, our property is all accessible via county roads." I sigh. "Maybe it's time to protect ourselves better, but that's not even the issue at this point. The deed has been done."

"Any news on your dad?"

"Yeah. I just talked to Mom before I came here. She called, and that's when I realized I was late for our lunch. Sorry again about that. He's doing well. He'll be in the hospital for another day or two, and then he'll have home care for a week or so after that."

"Your mom will probably want to stay with him."

"Yeah. She already said as much, which means I'm the acting city attorney for at least a week, probably more."

"Not a bad thing."

She doesn't know how right—and wrong—she is. "I have a chance to do some research. Find some answers. I need to take advantage of that, Callie, but I also need to do all my mother's work at the same time, which is where you come in."

She nods. "I understand."

I hope I haven't made a huge mistake. The last thing I want is to put Callie in an untoward position, but I need help with this. Dale is busy with his wines, and I don't want to involve anyone else yet. Callie is here. In my office. With a background in criminal justice and an eagerness to learn the ropes.

She's perfect to assist me on this stuff.

I don't approach this lightly. In fact, I've been considering it all morning, going back and forth in my head.

I believe she's trustworthy.

I believe it because . . . I love her.

I fucking love her.

All morning long, as I tried like hell to find some valid reason to shut down Murphy's for a few days, my mind kept returning to Callie and the thought of asking her to help me.

That's when I knew.

I love her.

I'm in love with her.

I wouldn't have considered asking for her help if I didn't love and trust her. I believe she trusts me. Does she love me? I don't know yet. I'll find out soon.

I need her love. More than I ever thought I could need anything. At the moment, though, what I need is her trust.

Plus, I'll pay her, and I know she can use the money.

"How does sixty bucks an hour sound?" I ask.

Her eyes nearly pop out of her head. "Sixty bucks an hour?"

"Yeah. It's standard in the industry for research and assisting an attorney."

"It sounds amazing, Donny, but what about my *actual* job?"

"What's my mom paying you?"

"Not sixty bucks an hour."

"You'll still do your work. Trust me. Alyssa will run out of things for you to do. When she does, you come to me."

She swallows. "Okay. I feel kind of funny about this."

I sigh. "Believe me, Callie. So do I."

"Then why...?"

"Because my father was shot. My father could have been killed. And there are things going on that I need to be aware of if I'm going to protect my family."

She nods then. "Okay. I get it. I'd do anything to protect my family too. It's why... Well, it's why I won't be going to law school. My family needs the money."

"Which is exactly why I know I can trust you, Callie." I cup her cheek. "Thank you."

"I haven't done anything yet."

I smile and press my lips to hers lightly. "You've done more than you know."

★ ★ ★

Back at the office, I continue to research the Murphy property. Unfortunately, the Murphys have done yearly upkeep to keep everything to code, they're up to date on all their taxes, and they've passed every health inspection with flying colors.

Damn.

They're not giving me a lot of room to find fault here.

I laugh out loud. A deep and sarcastic laugh. Here I am, an attorney, wishing that a family in my town—a good and honest family—somehow screwed up along the way.

I'm totally in the Twilight Zone.

I sigh. A gas leak, then. A manufactured gas leak. That will get Brendan off the property and out of business until it's fixed.

Man, I was really hoping I could find a legitimate reason to shut them down.

Fortunately—or unfortunately, depending on how you look at it—I do have some contacts at the energy board from a case I worked on a couple of years ago. Even if I have to grease a few palms, I'll be able to get this done.

I plug the number into my cell phone.

"John Lambert, please," I say when a receptionist answers. "Donovan Steel calling."

A few seconds pass.

"Donny!" John's big voice booms into my ear.

"Hey, John. How are things?"

"Good, good. I hear you packed up and moved back to the slope."

"I did. A favor to my mom."

"I can't believe you gave up your track at Bishop Helms," he says. "Then again, since when do the Steels need to worry about money?"

Classic John Lambert. He's a good guy, but definitely willing to bend the rules for the right price. His money comment cements it.

"I need a favor," I say.

"Sure. Of course. Anything for the man who got me out of that defamation lawsuit. What can I do for you?"

"I need you to create a fake gas leak on a property in Snow Creek."

Silence for a few, until—

"I'm listening."

"I won't go into detail unless you want me to. Probably the less you know about the reasoning the better."

"Don, this is pretty substantial."

"I know. I wouldn't ask if it weren't necessary."

"Everything okay out there?" he asks.

"For now. I want to keep it that way."

Silence again as he pauses.

Finally, "You got it, Donny. Give me the relevant information, and I'll let you know when it's done."

"How will it go?"

"I'll get someone from the office in Grand Junction to pay the property owner a visit."

I inhale. Exhale. Inhale again. "John, I was hoping you could take care of it yourself. I don't want to include any more people than necessary. I'll make it worth your while. Put you up at the Carlton in Grand Junction, wherever you want. But I want *you* to be the one to visit the owners and serve the papers."

Another pause.

"All right. All right. I can get a few days off. What's the point of working for the government if I can't slack off on the job, right?"

I force out a laugh even though this is far from funny. "When can you serve the papers?"

"Tomorrow good enough?"

"Yeah. Tomorrow's perfect."

"Got it. I'll put it all together and get on a flight to Grand Junction tonight. I assume the Carlton suite will be waiting?"

"Absolutely. Plus a car and airfare. And whatever else you need."

"Can't think of a thing. Except now you owe *me* a favor, Don."

"Yeah. I know."

I hate owing favors to people outside family.

It never ends well.

CHAPTER FORTY-FOUR

Callie

As Donny predicted, Alyssa and Troy run out of things for me to do by three, so I knock on his still-closed door.

"Yeah? Come in."

I open the door and walk in. Donny's hair is mussed, as if he's been ruffling his fingers through it nonstop. He smiles when he sees me.

"Hey," he says.

I bite my lower lip and close the door behind me. "I'm free."

"I sure hope so." He smiles lasciviously.

There go my cheeks again. Sparks galore. "I mean, Alyssa doesn't have anything else for me today. And since there are still a few working hours left..."

He inhales. "Right. Yeah. I have plenty, Callie."

"What can I help you with, then?"

"I'm going to give you access to the databases, but it's imperative that Alyssa and Troy not know what you're working on. Do you know if there's a VPN set up on your computer?"

"I have no idea, but it's easy enough check."

"Good. Make sure there is one. If not, we'll get one installed quickly. Then I need you to do a search of all the property in and surrounding Snow Creek."

"Okay. What am I looking for?"

"Liens." He clears his throat. "I want to know if the Steel family holds any liens on any property. I already know you'll find one."

"Oh?"

"Yes. Apparently the Steels hold a lien on Murphy's Bar."

I widen my eyes. A lien on Murphy's? Why?

Donny's gaze turns serious. "Not that I think you need reiteration, but I'll say again that this all remains between you and me."

"Of course." I frown.

"Good."

"Can I ask something?"

"Anything."

"Why does your family have a lien on Murphy's?"

He shakes his head. "Callie, I don't have a fucking clue."

"Ah." I sit down in a chair across from him. "I'm beginning to understand what's going on here."

"I'm not sure you do," he says, "because I don't understand it myself."

"Probably because the rumors never get to you."

"Rumors? About the Steels owning the town? Of course they get to me. It's a small town. It's just not true." He sighs. "At least I never thought it was. My parents always said they were nothing but silly rumors because we were a rich family."

I hesitate a few seconds, wondering if I should bring up what's on the tip of my tongue. Then I begin. "Remember that football rivalry between you and Jesse?"

"Yeah. It was stupid. We played on the same team, for God's sake."

"Just high school drama," I say, "but there's one thing

Jesse never quite got over."

"Don't tell me. I got MVP."

"Yeah. He thought, as quarterback, it should have gone to him."

"Wide receivers score the points, Callie."

"True enough. But Jesse threw every one of those passes to you. He even got college offers but wanted to pursue his music instead."

"I got college offers too, Cal."

"I know. But Jesse actually got an offer from Wyoming. A D-1 school."

He raises his eyebrows. "I know. He was good. Damned good."

"So he thinks you got MVP over him because the Steels funded the team that year."

"MVP is chosen by the coaching staff. My family had nothing to do with it."

"Maybe not. But maybe the coaching staff wanted to make sure the Steels kept funding the team. You do still fund it, don't you?"

"I don't have a clue. I'd have to ask Uncle Bryce. He's the CFO and is in charge of what we fund. Or Brad or Henry. They run the foundation."

"It doesn't matter whether you're still funding the team or the school or whatever. My point is that the rumors about your family owning the town had to start somewhere. If you have a lien on Murphy's . . ."

"Yeah. I know. Why do you think I'm asking you to look into this? There's shit I don't know that is popping up from seemingly nowhere."

"And you think your father's shooting has something to

do with all of this?"

"I'd be a fool if I didn't consider that possibility."

My skin goes cold, and despite my long sleeve cardigan, I rub my upper arms to ease the chill.

Someone got shot. Someone could have died.

What am I walking into?

Still, I love this man. I want to help. I don't want to see him lose his father. I don't want to see him lose anyone or anything.

"All right, Donny. I'll get started." I rise.

"Just a minute," he says.

I sit back down. "What?"

"I don't want to sound like a broken record here, but it's really important that this all remain between you and me."

Slight irritation spears into me. Donny means well, but how many times do I have to say it?

"I understand."

He opens his mouth to speak, but I gesture him to stop.

"You know how close I am to Rory. To my mother. I promise I won't say a word to either of them."

"I'm not concerned about Rory or Maureen."

I lift my eyebrows. "Who else would I tell?"

He pauses a moment. Then, "I'm talking about *my* mother."

"Jade?"

"She's the city attorney. She's the person who hired you."

He makes a good point. How can I keep this from Jade? "If she doesn't ask me straight out, I won't say anything."

He sighs. "I don't want to lie to my mother any more than you do, but she can't know about this."

"I'm sure she's just as anxious to find out why your father was attacked."

"Of course she is, but that's not the point. My parents have kept some stuff from me. From all my siblings and cousins. For our own protection, I'm certain, but things are coming out."

"Donny," I say, my tone as serious as it gets. "If I'm going to be in this with you, maybe you'd better start at the beginning."

He rubs his forehead. "You're right." He rises, walks to the door, and flicks the lock.

My stomach tightens. A locked door? Who would walk in? No one but Troy or Alyssa. Why would it matter? We'd just stop talking, right?

He sits down behind his desk and then stares out his window for a few seconds that drag on like hours.

"Donny?" I finally say.

He faces me then. Meets my gaze. His hazel eyes are troubled. "Let's get out of here."

"It's only three thirty."

"I'm the boss, Callie. I say we're done for the day. Besides, if I'm going to give you the lowdown, I don't want to do it here."

"Why not?"

"I don't know."

"You don't think the office is . . ."

He shakes his head. "No, of course not. I doubt we're bugged. Why would we be? The only people in this town who can afford to sneak in and bug a city office are the Steels, and if that were the case—" He stops abruptly.

"What?" I ask.

He rises quickly. "Let's go." He walks briskly to the door and unlocks it.

I follow him out. What else can I do?

"We're calling it a day," he says to Troy and Alyssa. "Take

the rest of the afternoon for yourselves."

Troy lifts his eyebrows. "Everything okay? With Talon?"

"Yeah. I checked in with Mom an hour ago. He's still doing well."

"Thank God," Alyssa says. "Why are we shutting down early, then?"

"Because it's my first day, and I need to get to Grand Junction to see my dad."

"We can still stay—"

Donny stops Alyssa. "I love you guys. Really. Most city employees would be gunning to get the rest of the day off. Please. Go. Enjoy yourselves."

"All right." Alyssa shuts down her computer and grabs her purse. "Thanks, Donny."

"Don't mention it."

Donny and I wait until Troy and Alyssa are gone, and then we leave as well.

"To the park," Donny says.

"What for?"

"So I can tell you what you want to know."

CHAPTER FORTY-FIVE

Donny

"Nervous?" I ask Callie.

She inhales. "I'm fine."

"Then why are you shivering?"

"Am I?" She rubs her arms and then squeezes her hands together. "Maybe just a little chilly."

"It's sixty-three degrees."

"Okay, okay. I'm a tad nervous. I want to help you, Donny. But frankly... Frankly you're scaring me a little."

I draw in a breath. "That's exactly what I don't want to do." Though I'm a little scared myself, as well, which is more than freaky. After my childhood horror, there's not much that scares me. Almost losing my father is at the top of that very short list.

"I know. I mean, I know you wouldn't scare me on purpose."

"Damn." I rub my forehead against a headache that's threatening to erupt. "You want to get out of here? Go..." I chuckle. "Where the hell would we go? We both live at home."

She smiles shyly.

"The hotel. I'll get us a room."

"Donny, I..."

"I know. I'll tell you. I just... I don't want anyone to see us."

"Ashamed to be seen with me?" she says, trying to tease, but her voice cracks a little.

Yeah, she's really nervous.

"Everyone already knows how I feel about you. This is a small town, Callie. Donny Steel and Callie Pike are already an item." And I'm in love with her, but that has to wait.

"Are we?"

"I hope so."

She blushes again. Damn, that pink that spreads over her cheeks is like a fucking love glove on my cock. She's so damned hot.

"Look," I say. "I'm not going to pretend I don't want to fuck you into next week right now. I do. I'm hard as a rock already. But that's not what this is about. I want to be somewhere where we won't be interrupted. Where no one will overhear us."

She nods tentatively. "So if we go to the hotel, we won't fuck. Got it."

I grin. "I didn't say that."

She returns my grin, her cheeks still pink, her countenance still slightly rigid. "Then you're going to have to buy me dinner first."

★ ★ ★

We grab takeout from Lorenzo's and then go to the Snow Creek Inn. Callie deliberately looks away as I check us in and get the key card for our room. Funny thing... We're actually here to talk, not to fuck.

I mean, sure, we'll probably fuck too, but that's not the main reason for shacking up at the hotel. If I'm going to tell Callie the reasons for the research she's going to do, I need to be assured of privacy.

Once inside our room, Callie takes the bag of takeout from me and spreads it on the small table next to the window. "Crap. We forgot to get drinks."

"No problem. There's a machine downstairs. Let me guess. Diet Coke?"

She smiles. "If they don't have it, water's fine too."

"Got it." I leave the room and make my way downstairs again.

"Nice," Patrick Lamone, the clerk, says when I walk by reception. "Callie Pike. I'd do her."

The hair on the back of my neck springs into action as jealousy spears into my gut. Who does this guy think he is? I vaguely remember the Lamone family, but Pat was just a kid when I left Snow Creek. "I'm going to forget you said that, Pat."

"I'm just saying—"

"Maybe I didn't speak loudly enough. Say anything like that about Callie again, and I'll knock you unconscious."

"You mean you're not tapping that?"

"You're skating on really thin ice, Lamone. I'm not kidding."

"Easy, Steel. I don't want any trouble."

"Then you should have kept your mouth shut about Callie."

"Come on, man. Everyone knows the Pike girls are easy."

Rage unfurls in my gut. "Everyone like who?"

He's pulling something, but I'm not sure what. Rory Pike is in a committed relationship, last I heard. Callie has never been known as anything other than an intelligent woman with a goal, and Maddie is the honorary fifth member of the awesome foursome of Bree and three of my cousins, and while they like to have their fun, they're certainly not easy. They'd better not be, anyway.

"Everyone, man. Surely you've heard."

"Heard what, exactly?" I say through clenched teeth.

"The story of the Pike girls. Rory and Callie."

"Let's say I haven't."

"I've tapped Rory Pike, and she fucking enjoyed every minute of it. And Callie was waiting her turn, but we didn't get there."

This is unreal. I'm ready to yank Patrick Lamone right over the counter and beat his face into a pulp, but it occurs to me that he's not smart enough to make this shit up.

"You're saying you've been with Rory Pike."

"Yeah. Back in high school, and she loved it. Women can't fake that shit."

I'm too angry to laugh in his face, but man, does he have a lot to learn about women. But dumbasses never learn.

"Maybe you're telling the truth," I say, "and maybe you're not. Doesn't really matter. One goof-up in your bed doesn't make the Pike girls easy."

"You haven't heard about Callie, then."

Pat Lamone's an idiot, no doubt, but as much as I want to walk away, I can't. "What about Callie?"

He looks around. Why, I'm not sure. The hotel's vacant except for us. Then he lowers his voice. "She and Rory fucked their way around high school. Ask anyone."

"I'm asking *you*," I grit out.

"Why do you think she couldn't look me in the eye when you guys checked in? She knows I know."

"My family had students at that school almost every year. If there were any rumors about the Pike sisters, they would have gotten back to me." I curl my hand into a fist. *One more word, Lamone. Just one more…*

"Dude," Pat says. "Everyone knows about the Pikes."

"Everyone knows *what* about the Pikes?"

"They're gold diggers. All of them. Willing to sleep their way to the top."

I try to hide the surprise on my face. What the hell is he talking about? He's so wrong. We couldn't get them to accept our help, other than through the foundation, after the fire. And Callie's already afraid my mother hired her out of pity.

"You're barking up the wrong tree, Lamone."

"Don't say I didn't warn you."

I walk closer, my stomach hitting the counter. "If I hear one more word come out of your mouth, or anyone else's, about Callie, Rory, or any other Pike, I will personally run you out of this town."

"Easy, Steel. I don't want any trouble."

"Then you shouldn't be spreading lies."

"Lies. Yeah. Think what you want."

"Do I have your word you'll never mention the Pikes again? Because if I don't, I'm going to pull you over that counter and take all the anger inside me out on you."

"Anger? What are you so fucking angry about?"

"Other than the shit coming out of your mouth? My father was shot yesterday, asshole."

His eyebrows nearly fly off his forehead. "Talon Steel was shot?"

"Yeah, someone tried to off my father. And I'm so fucking angry I can't see straight. And right now, you're a worthy target for all that rage."

"Look," he says. "I like you guys. I've always liked the Steels. And the Pikes. I got nothing against any of you."

"Interesting way of showing it. Spreading rumors."

"They're not—"

I grab him by the collar before he can finish. "You don't want to take me on, Lamone. I'm bigger and stronger, not to mention meaner, than you could ever hope to be."

"Easy," he chokes out. "Let go of me."

I let him go harshly, and he nearly falls to the ground. He would have if he didn't grab the edge of the counter.

I leave him there and go back to the room.

"Where are the drinks?" Callie asks.

Fuck. The drinks. Now I have to go back down there. "Machine isn't working." Man, I hate lying, especially to Callie, but if I go back down there, Pat Lamone may not live to see another day.

"No problem," Callie says. "Tap water's fine."

"Tap water it is," I say. "Maybe one day the Snow Creek Inn will begin stocking minibars."

Callie laughs sweetly. "That'll be the day."

I fill two glasses with tap water when a thought spears into my mind.

Do the Steels own this place? Other places in town?

And why haven't I thought of any of this before?

We're billionaires. Fucking billionaires. Sure, we have many other investments, but the money to fund them had to come from somewhere.

Who the hell makes billions raising beef?

CHAPTER FORTY-SIX

Callie

I'm going to tell him.

I'm going to tell Donny Steel that I love him. I'll make sure he knows I don't expect his love in return...though I hope I get it.

No. I'm going to tell him so he knows without a doubt that he can trust me with what he's about to tell me.

My word is good, of course.

But words can lie. I'm not lying to him when I tell him he can trust me, but he doesn't know that. I want him to know for sure he doesn't have to hold back with me.

So I'm going to confess my love.

And hope like hell he doesn't run away screaming.

He hands me a glass of water, and I take a long sip. It's cold. Sort of.

"I ran it until it got as cold as it gets," he says. "Maybe when this place adds minibars it can add an ice machine as well. We're living in the nineteen forties here."

I swallow. Yes, I'm going to tell him. Now. Right now.

"Small towns are like that," I say instead.

Right. Like I'd know. I've never lived in any other small town, and I was in grade school when we moved here. I have no substantial memories of our time in Denver. *Quit stalling,*

Callie. Tell him.

"You made a comment earlier," he says, "about the Steels funding the high school football team."

I nod. "It's true, right?"

"Probably. Honestly, I'm not part of the family business, so I don't know what we fund and what we don't. I'll ask Dale."

"He's part of the business?"

"Yeah, of course. He runs the winery with Uncle Ryan. After this season, it'll be his baby."

I nod. "He runs the winery, but does he do anything on the business end?"

"Meaning?"

"Does he know where the money goes?"

Donny takes a drink, swallows. "Good question." He pauses a moment. "You know, none of us ever questioned the money thing growing up."

"Why would you?"

"That's the point, I guess. We wouldn't." He pauses again, takes another sip. "I really shouldn't talk about this stuff."

"I love you," I blurt out.

Then my jaw drops. Damn. Damn, damn, damn.

A smile spreads over his face.

"I shouldn't have said that." God, my cheeks. They're going to burst into flames.

"I don't mind."

I open my mouth, but... No words. I can't think of one damned thing to say. I can't take it back because it's true. I could apologize, but how does that look? I'm not sorry I love him. Am I sorry I said it? Kind of, but kind of not.

I really, really wish for him to say it back, but I won't push. I'll never push. I don't need his love badly enough to beg for it.

Never in a million years will I beg a man to love me.

We sit in silence, drain our glasses of water. The baked ziti sits congealing in its foil containers, its robust aroma filling the small room. It's starting to nauseate me.

Just when I think we'll die in here, never having said another word to each other—

"I love you too, Callie."

I blink, as if for some reason my eyes are connected to my ears and if I move them enough times I'll hear the words again.

"What?"

He reaches toward me, more tentative than usual, and trails his index finger down my hot cheek. "I love you too."

"You do?"

"Why wouldn't I?"

"I ... Uh ... I don't want you to say it just because I said it." *God, shut up, Callie.*

"I don't say anything unless I mean it. Especially something of that magnitude."

"I just ... I just wanted you to know you can trust me."

"I do know. I knew before you said you love me. But now I really know."

"That's what I wanted."

"And I love you too, Callie. I mean it. I realized it today when I was thinking about asking you to help me with this stuff. You're different from every other woman I've been with. I've never wanted anyone quite like I want you. I can't get enough of you. I'm hard just being in your presence. But that's the physical stuff, which is great, but I also love your mind. Your self-deprecating sense of humor. Your ..." He sighs. "Just you, Callie. Caroline Pike. I love you."

He kisses me then.

It's passionate but soft, not like our other kisses that have been so primal and urgent. This one is different. It's just as powerful, but it's full of emotion as well.

Raw emotion.

And as I part my lips and take his tongue with mine, I forget why we're here.

I forget about what he's about to tell me. About secrets. About rumors. About…

Just this kiss.

Life is just about this kiss.

We're already sitting on the bed, so it's not long until we're lying side by side, working each other's clothes off and writhing together naked.

I love you. I love you. I love you.

The words float inside my mind, inside our kiss, above us in fluorescent pink lettering, around us in a cloud of lust and love.

I'm in love.

For the first time in my life, I'm in love.

And he loves me back.

Our lips slide together, our tongues tangle and swirl. His fingers find my nipple, pluck at it, sending sparks straight between my legs.

Sparks. Oh, the sparks!

Donny Steel and I could light a bonfire with all our sparks.

His cock is hard against me, and I reach down, grasp it firmly.

He groans into my mouth.

I take the lead, then. Something I like to do but don't do often in sex, because… Well, I don't know exactly why. Don't care at the moment.

I maneuver him so he's flat on his back, and then I rise and straddle him, teasing his dick with the wet folds of my pussy.

"Damn, Callie," he grits out. "Just fuck me. Damn."

I slide down onto him. God, sweet completion. Though my instinct is to ride him hard, ride him fast, I stay still for a silent moment, letting him fill me, reveling in the fullness.

The sweet and perfect fullness.

Then he grips my hips and lifts me until his cock head peeks out against my folds and thrusts me back down.

"God," he groans. "Fuck."

I do ride him then. Fast and furious, as if my life depends on it. He grabs my boobs, squeezes them, plays with my nipples.

"You're so beautiful." He reaches behind me and yanks the band out of my low ponytail.

My hair falls like a soft curtain over my back, like a warm waterfall cascading through me and around me.

I ride and ride, taking him inside me so deeply I swear he's touching my heart.

And he is.

Emotionally he is, and—

I'm on my back now. He flips me so quickly my perception is skewed.

He looks down at me, plunging inside me, and meets my gaze. His hazel eyes are burning.

"Fuck, I love you," he says. "I love you, Callie."

"I love you too, Donny."

And oh, I do. He takes charge, fucking me hard. Fucking me fast. Sweat emerging on his brow, sliding down his forehead.

He thrusts, thrusts, thrusts, and—

The friction on my clit catapults me into a climax. A long and perfect climax.

"That's it, baby. Come all around me. Come for me. Only me."

He thrusts again. Again. Once more.

"Fuck!" He clenches his jaw. "God, so good."

He stays embedded in me then as we climax together. Together.

"I love you," I say on a sigh.

"I love you too. Always."

★ ★ ★

I'm not sure how long we stay joined. I think we sleep. Maybe. Perhaps it's just a haze of love and lust.

Finally, I hear Donny's voice in the edge of my consciousness.

"We should probably eat if we're going to have the energy to do this again."

A chuckle leaves my throat. "I suppose so. Don't want to get up, though." I snuggle closer into his shoulder.

"I hear you. I could stay like this for maybe . . . forever."

I smile against his warm skin. "Me too."

More moments pass, until I finally move. "Nature calls." I head to the bathroom. When I'm done, I grab one of the robes on the hook on the door and wrap it around myself.

"You look comfy," Donny says when I return to the bed. "Though I prefer you naked."

I grab the bag from the table and pull out the foil containers. "I suppose it's too much to expect the Snow Creek Inn to provide plates and flatware, huh?"

He laughs. "Definitely too much."

I hand him a container and a plastic fork. "This is it, then.

Cheers."

He laughs again. "I've never heard anyone say cheers for food. Only drinks."

"I've kind of always marched to the beat of my own drummer."

"One of the many reasons why I love you, Caroline."

"You should know, then, that I detest the name Caroline."

He laughs once more. "It's a gorgeous name for a gorgeous woman, but I hear you. I detest the name Donovan. That's why I'm a thirty-two-year-old man who still goes by Donny."

I return his laughter. "I guess we have a lot in common."

"Baby, I know we do." Donny pulls the top off his container. "Ah, congealed mozzarella. Can't beat it."

"We should have eaten first," I say.

"Nah. Sex always takes priority. But I'm going to need some carbs now, so cold ziti will have to do."

We eat in silence, both knowing what's coming next. More sex.

And then . . .

The talk. What we came here for.

Maybe it will get my mind off seeing Pat Lamone working the reception desk.

That brought back memories.

Memories I thought were buried.

Between what Donny asked me to do and the return of Patrick Lamone . . .

Even the love of Donny Steel doesn't take away my fear.

Or my anger.

CHAPTER FORTY-SEVEN

Donny

I never expected to come home to Snow Creek and fall in love.

Not that I intended to make Callie Pike a one-nighter. I wouldn't do that to a friend and neighbor. She deserves better.

I figured we'd have some fun, stay friends. All that.

If I had any doubts earlier, hearing her say the words flushed them away. My thoughts weren't just thoughts. They are reality.

I love this woman.

I love Callie Pike.

Caroline Pike and Donovan Steel. What a fucking mouthful.

We'll always be Callie and Donny until we're old and gray.

Old and gray. Damn, I really am in love.

I polish off my ziti and drink another glass of water. Callie leaves a little in her container.

"Want the rest?" She holds it out to me.

"I'm stuffed. Maybe later."

"So . . ." she teases. "More sex?"

"Always."

She parts her robe but then stops. "Or maybe . . ."

"Yeah?"

"We should talk." She gasps. "Not about the future or

anything. I didn't mean—"

"I know, Callie. I know what you mean. The future can wait. We came to talk about my father. My family. The things I need you to look into."

She nods. "Right."

"Not that we shouldn't consider the future," I add.

She smiles. "I don't expect anything from you. Only your love."

"I know that. We'll see how things go before we start talking about the future. About you and me."

"Right. But Donny"—she bites her lower lip, and damn, I want to bite it for her—"I'm worried. About you. About your father. About . . . lots of stuff."

"So am I, baby. So am I. Which is why I have to do this research. If my dad is keeping things from me, I have to find out if I'm going to help."

"Why not just ask him? I mean, he's not up to it right now, but couldn't you ask your uncles?"

"Dale and I have talked about that. We're not sure they even know some of the stuff."

"How could they not know?"

"I don't know much about my grandfather, Bradford Steel, but there's something there. Call it lawyer's instinct. I feel it in the marrow of my bones."

She listens raptly as I tell her what I know. How Uncle Ryan has a different mother. How Brad Steel apparently quitclaimed all his assets to Ryan only, but the deed was never dated or recorded. How he had a brother that apparently only Uncle Joe knows about.

Her eyes go wider with each word.

"You okay?" I ask.

"Just wondering what I've gotten into."

"I'll protect you, Callie."

"Wait, wait, wait... You think I need *protection*?" Her mouth drops open.

I cup her cheek. "I think we're about to unearth some serious stuff. That's all. I don't know what we'll find, but I'm not expecting it to be all wine and roses. Know what I mean?"

She nods, her jaw quivering just a bit. "Okay." She inhales.

She's frightened, and I wonder, for a moment, if something other than my situation has her on edge.

"You can bow out," I say. "I won't hold it against you. I swear."

"I know that, but I'm in now. And..."

"And what?"

"I love you, Donny. And you love me. That means we're in this together. No matter what."

I smile and press my lips to hers, easing them open. After the short kiss, I pull back. "Thank you."

"For what?"

"For your confidentiality. For your kindness." I pause a moment. "For your love."

"You don't need to thank me for any of that. Of course I'll keep anything confidential. And I like to think I'm kind to everyone. As for the love, it's in my heart and requires no thanks. It just happened, and I'm glad it did."

"I am too." I kiss her again. "I honestly never thought I'd feel this way about anyone. Not for a while yet, anyway."

"Me neither. I had this idea I had to focus and get through law school before I could have a real relationship."

"Callie..." My mind whirls back to Pat Lamone's allegations about the Pike sisters.

"Hmm?"

"How well do you know Pat Lamone?"

She pauses a moment, some of the color draining from her cheeks. "I don't. I mean, I recognized him at the reception desk, but it's not like we're even on a 'hello' basis."

"And Rory?"

"What about her?"

"How well does she know him?"

"I don't know." She clears her throat. "I think he was a year ahead of her in school. No, he was between us. A year behind her and a year ahead of me. Why do you ask?"

"He said something that made me want to pummel him."

"Oh? What?" She looks down at her lap.

"He said he had sex with Rory in high school." I leave out the part where he said Callie was waiting in line.

Her eyes nearly pop out of her head. "What? He's a liar."

"I know. Why do you think I was ready to bash his skull in?"

"Rory wasn't exactly a nun during high school. She experimented a lot before she came out as bisexual. But Pat Lamone?"

"I'll go right back down there and finish the bashing," I say. "No questions asked."

She shakes her head. "Don't bother. Snow Creek has always been a rumor mill. I guess none of us hear the rumors about us, though."

I nod. "Maybe that's where we should start, then, and it'll help me with this research we have to do. Tell me all the rumors you've heard about the Steels over the years."

"And you tell me the ones about the Pikes."

"Honestly, I haven't heard any about you... until this evening. From Pat."

"What did he say? Other than the lie that he slept with Rory?"

I inhale. I don't want to tell her, but I must. I inhale once more. "That the Pike sisters are easy."

She drops her jaw. "I had sex with one guy in high school. One!"

"Rumors aren't necessarily true," I say. "I hope you remember that when you tell me what you've heard."

"What else?"

"That you're gold diggers."

"You know that's not true!"

"Yes, I do. I honestly don't know where anyone got that idea."

Callie stays silent a moment.

I stroke her soft cheek. "What is it?"

She sighs. "I don't like to think about high school."

"Why not?"

"It was tough for me. I wasn't the big man on campus like you were. Rory was popular and talented, and I was a nerd."

I chuckle. "You were never a nerd."

"Donny, you were long gone from high school when I was there. I was a mess. It was a nightmare. Plus, there was—"

She stops abruptly.

"What?" I ask.

"Nothing."

"It's not nothing, Callie. What?"

"I don't like to talk about it. I don't even like to think about it."

"Think about what?"

"It's so easy for you. Has anything ever been hard for you, Donny?"

I go numb. She doesn't mean her words to ignite anger. I try to remember that, but I ultimately fail as I curl my fingers into fists.

I draw in a breath and hold it. One. Two. Three. Four. Fi—

Then I burst. I fucking burst.

"Easy?" I shout. "Really? You don't have a fucking clue what I've gone through in my life. Don't even start with that."

Callie's face goes white. That lovely blush that I adore is wiped out. Clean as a slate.

"I hope you've never endured what I've endured," I continue, my voice full of rage. "How dare you, Callie? How fucking dare you?"

Her lips quiver. "You're a Steel. A Steel. Nothing bad happens to Steels."

"For fuck's sake. My father is in the hospital. Someone shot him!"

Her mouth drops. "God, Donny, I'm so sorry. I don't know why I said that."

"You said it because you are angry. I get it. I'm angry too."

Her eyes gloss over with unshed tears. "I'm so sorry. I didn't mean—"

"Yeah, you did. You meant it all."

She gulps. "I didn't. Please believe me."

Rage engulfs me, though. I'm ready to explode right here in this stupid-ass hotel room with no minibar.

"Donny…" She reaches toward me.

I back away. "I love you, Callie, but I can't do this right now."

"If you'd let me explain—"

"Explain what? That you think all us Steels shit gold bricks? Remember one thing. I wasn't always a Steel, Callie.

I came from somewhere else, and you have no idea what I went through."

She shudders visibly and wraps the robe around herself more tightly. "Donny, I love you too."

All these years, I've prided myself on being able to put my past behind me. I've watched Dale struggle with what he thought came easy to me.

Truth? It was never easy. It took a hell of a lot of work on my end, but I was determined not to live in the past. The Steels gave Dale and me a future, and I wanted it. I wanted it, and I made sure I got it.

"I can't," I say. "I can't do this tonight. We'll talk in the morning."

She nods. "I'll get dressed and go home."

"You don't have to," I say. "You can have the room for the night. I'll go."

"Or we can both go."

"Perfect," I say, gathering my clothes. "Meet me for breakfast at Ava's tomorrow at seven a.m. We'll talk once we've both cooled off."

She nods. "I love you."

"I love you too."

The words are true. Undeniably true. But there are things Callie doesn't know about me. Things I'll have to tell her if this is going to work.

And...

I have the distinct feeling there are things I don't know about her as well.

CHAPTER FORTY-EIGHT

Callie

I knock softly on Rory's door when I get home. "Ror? You awake?"

The door opens, and a yawning Rory looks back at me. "Cal? What are you doing up this late?"

"I just got in. Sorry to wake you."

Another yawn splits my sister's pretty face. "S'okay. What's up?"

I walk into her room and close the door behind me. "Some shit's going down."

"Like what?"

"I ran into Pat Lamone tonight."

Rory wipes the last of the sleep from her eyes and widens them. "Shit. How?"

"He's back in town, apparently, working the evening shift at the Snow Creek Inn."

"How can he be back in town?"

"Hell if I know. I had to act all innocent with Donny, like I hardly remembered him."

"Did he buy it?"

"I think so. He was more angry about other stuff."

"Like what?"

"I think…" My heart hurts. It hurts so badly for the man

279

I love. "I think he and Dale must have gone through some serious stuff before they came here. Like really bad."

"I guess we always suspected."

"Maybe you did. I didn't give it a thought, which makes me feel about an inch tall right now."

"Damn, Callie. You're in love with him, aren't you?"

I nod, sniffling back tears.

She pulls me into a hug. "It'll be okay. We'll work it all out."

"How can we? Why is that jerk back in town?"

"I don't know, hon. But I'll find out." She sighs. "I have some news myself. It's not good."

I pull back. "What? What happened? Is it Talon Steel?"

"No, no. He's still fine, as far as I know. It's Raine."

"Oh my God. What happened?"

"She's fine, as well, but she's decided to stay in Denver. A former colleague offered her a partnership in his new day spa. She'll be in charge of the salon. It's too good an opportunity for her to pass up."

"Ror, what are you going to do?"

Rory pauses a moment. "I don't know. Except that I think I do."

"I wouldn't blame you if you wanted to get far away from this place."

"But the family. The fire. They need me. And you, Cal. If Pat Lamone is back in town, you and I need to stick together."

I gulp audibly. Rory's right, but I can't be selfish. "Raine needs you too."

"I don't think she does, Cal. I don't think we're in that place."

"But you live together."

"We do. Or did. But lately . . ."

"What?"

"Things have been a little tense, like I told you. She can't seem to get over the fact that I'm bisexual and she isn't. Plus, apparently Willow White has offered to buy Raine's business here, so other than me, there's no reason for her to stay."

"You're a pretty big reason."

"I shed a tear or two earlier tonight, but I feel okay now. I think our time has passed. We weren't each other's forever."

I say nothing. I'm not sure what to say.

"Have you found your forever?" she asks.

I simply nod. I have. Whether Donny feels the same way after tonight is up in the air, but at least he loves me. He said it, and I believe him.

One silly fight doesn't change that.

But it does bring the current issue back to light.

"I'm sorry about Raine," I say, "and Donny and I will work through our issues. But Pat Lamone . . ."

"Right." Rory nods. "I guess we gather the group together."

"Some of them don't even live here anymore."

She nods. "Carmen Murphy is still here. And Jordan."

Carmen Murphy. Brendan's cousin, born to his unwed aunt, Ciara Murphy. And Jordan Ramsey, Rory's and my cousin, who was in Pat Lamone's class at school.

Pat Lamone.

There were others, but he was the worst.

He tried to destroy us.

He failed.

But now he's back.

CHAPTER FORTY-NINE

Donny

It's after midnight when I drive up to the home belonging to Jonah and Melanie Steel, my aunt and uncle.

I came here on a whim.

Uncle Joe.

He's the oldest of Bradford Steel's children, and Brendan mentioned him by name when he told us about another Steel heir, a brother to Brad.

If anyone has answers, he does.

I sit in the driveway and make the call.

After four rings, I get a groggy, "Hey, Donny. You okay?"

"Uncle Joe. Sorry to bother you so late."

"No bother. Is it Talon? Is anything wrong?"

"No, Dad's fine. I just checked in with Mom a little over an hour ago."

"Thank God. What's up, then?"

"I'm here. Outside your place. I want to talk to you."

"What for? Can it wait until morning?"

I clear my throat. "No. I'm sorry. It can't."

"Okay. Give me a few minutes. I'll let you in."

I turn off the motor and walk to the door. A few minutes later, Uncle Joe appears in a robe, unlocks the door, and lets me in. His dogs bound around my ankles. I give them some love before he lets them out.

He leads me down the hallway to his office and sits down at his desk. I sit across from him.

"What's this all about?" he asks.

"It's about a lot of stuff," I say. "But first and foremost, it's about Bradford Steel's brother."

Uncle Joe raises an eyebrow. "What about him?"

I cock my head. His reaction surprises me. "You're not going to deny he exists?"

"Why would I do that?"

"Well . . . because none of us knew he existed until a few days ago."

"How did you find out about him?"

"I'll be happy to tell you how, right after you tell me why no one ever talks about him. We all assumed Brad Steel was an only child."

"He was a half brother. My grandmother was in an accident after she had Brad and she couldn't have any more children."

"So his father had an affair? Or what?"

"Apparently."

"Apparently? That's all you have to say?"

"Donny, my father was . . ." He pauses, clears his throat. "I was about to say he wasn't a good man. But that's not the whole truth. In many ways he *was* a good man. He just did some really bad things."

"Okay. What's this got to do with his brother?"

"Half brother."

"Half brother. Whatever." Uncle Joe's use of the term *half brother* like it means something perplexes me more than a little. After all, Uncle Ryan is only *his* half brother. Why does that make a difference at all?

"Where is this coming from?" he asks. "And why in the middle of the night?"

"Because Dad got shot. That couldn't have been an accident, and I'm finding there's a lot of family stuff that we don't know."

"I'm sure your father has his rea—"

"It's not just Dad, and you know it. Dad has started to tell Dale and me a few things. Things he says you guys all decided to keep from your kids."

Uncle Joe flattens his lips into a straight line. "We had our reasons."

"That's a cop-out."

"It's not a cop-out, Don. Those decisions were made out of love. For you and your brother. For Henry, Brad, and Diana, who were so young, and for the rest of them that were still unborn at the time."

"Well," I say, "those decisions are coming back to bite us all in the ass."

"What do you mean?"

"I mean...I found out about Brad Steel's half brother, which you say was never a secret, but I call bullshit. So it's only a matter of time before I find out more."

"Donny," Uncle Joe says, "sometimes the past is better left buried."

"According to whom?"

"According to people who have lived through it and don't want it dredged up."

"I see. And those people would be...?"

"I'm sure I don't have to spell it out for you."

"I get it. You're protecting us. That's a noble cause, for

sure, but my father's been shot. On his own property. He was on the northern quadrant of the beef ranch, Uncle Joe, a place he hardly ever goes. On a Sunday, when the workers are reduced to a skeleton staff. This wasn't an accident."

Uncle Joe sighs. "I've already talked to Ryan and Bryce at length about this. We've come to a conclusion. A theory, rather."

"And...?"

My phone buzzes.

"Damn!" It's John at the energy board. At this hour? But I have to take it. "Sorry," I say to Uncle Joe, and then, into the phone, "Yeah?"

"Sorry, Donny. I know it's late."

"It's tomorrow, John. The day you're supposed to— Do that thing we discussed."

"Sorry. The flight got canceled, so I had to drive. I just got in and got settled in the suite."

"Glad you're comfortable." I resist an eye roll for Uncle Joe's benefit.

"I was hoping to get to use the suite for more than a couple hours, but whatever."

"Stay an extra day on me."

"Thanks, man. I appreciate it. I've got the paperwork in hand, and I'll drive into Snow Creek first thing in the morning to serve the papers and get the bar evacuated and shut down for a few days."

"Good enough. Make it between ten and noon. Brendan Murphy usually closes the bar, so he won't be up yet. Then I need you to go over to the Snow Creek Inn and arrange for a room for Murphy while his place is shut down."

"I don't have author—"

"Don't worry about it. It's all on me. Got it?"

"Got it."

"You'll be well taken care of."

"Thanks, man."

"Now go get some shut-eye."

"Will do. Thanks, Donny."

"Don't mention it. I owe you."

"Not a bad position to be in," he says.

No shit. I end the call and turn to face Uncle Joe. "You were saying? About a theory?"

"Never mind."

"Are you kidding? You can't dangle that kind of bait in front of me. This is my father's life we're talking about."

He sighs. "All right. But don't tell your father I told you. This is only between Ryan, Bryce, and me so far. Your father is out of the loop. We don't want him to worry. His only job is to heal."

"Agreed," I say. "So what's the theory?"

He meets my gaze, pauses, and then clears his throat. "You want some coffee or something?"

"Are you fucking kidding? It's the middle of the night. No, I don't want coffee. I'm hoping I might get two hours of sleep before I have to get up again."

I can't help a soft scoff at the thought. Right. Like I'm sleeping tonight at all. No way in hell. I won't be able to stop my mind from churning.

"Good enough." Uncle Joe plunges his hands into the pockets of his robe. "I really shouldn't say anything without talking to the others."

"Please. Don't even go there. This is Dad. My dad."

He nods. "Right. You're right."

"What is it, then? What's your theory?"

He pauses again, and I'm ready to grab him by the throat, when finally—

"It's our feeling that your father wasn't meant to be shot. At least not yet. The target"—he rubs his temples—"was me."

★ ★ ★

No way will I sleep tonight, so I head to Dale's. Yeah, he's still a newlywed, and yeah, it's the middle of the fucking night, but damn it, this can't wait. He's still keeping something from me, and tonight I need to be armed with every fact at my disposal.

I don't bother texting. I just pound on the fucking door. His rescue dog, Penny, barks until she recognizes me. Then she pants and wags her tail through the window.

One minute passes. Two. I pound again. Three. Four—

The door jerks open. My brother stands there looking like a madman with his long hair in disarray.

"What the fuck, Don?"

I walk in without an invitation. "Let's chat."

"In the middle of the damned night?"

"Yeah, in the middle of the damned night." I make my way to his office and walk in, taking a seat.

"You've got some nerve."

"Dale, I've got a Mack truck rolling over my brain inside my head, I just arranged for someone from the energy board to illegally close down a bar, and Callie and I had a humdinger of a fight, not to mention what Uncle Joe just laid on me, so don't even start with me."

"Uncle Joe?"

"Yeah. Apparently, he, Ryan, and Bryce think Joe was the

target of our mystery assassin, and I have to admit, it makes sense. Dad was in the north quadrant, which is Joe's domain."

"Fuck." Dale runs his fingers through his already messed-up hair.

"Now get in here, sit your ass down, and spill whatever's left that you haven't told me."

"It's nothing, Don."

I grit my teeth. "I'm in no mood for lies, Dale. No fucking mood."

His facial features soften, then—a mixture of love and determination.

I've seen the look before.

All those years ago, when he safeguarded me. When he was taking what was meant for me. All those years, he protected me, and at what cost? Himself. He took the beatings, the rapes, the torture so I wouldn't have to.

He's protecting me still, and it needs to stop. Without all the information, I can't do what has to be done.

"Please." I soften my tone. "I need this. I won't be able to sleep until I know all that you know."

"I've told you all I know," he says. "Dad didn't elaborate."

"Then what are you hiding? Because I know you, Dale. I *know* you."

He clears his throat. "I've thought about whether to tell you my last secret. It's not something you need to know, but it's something I feel you should know. Even if you end up hating me."

I widen my eyes. "Hate you? I could never."

"You haven't heard what I'm about to say yet."

"Fine." I'm too tired to argue. "Shoot."

He inhales. "It's not that easy."

"You can tell me anything. We've seen each other at our worst, Dale. At our very worst. We don't need to have secrets."

"This is a big one, Don."

"It's not too big to share with me. I promise."

"God, if you only knew..."

Dale's forehead wrinkles, and he rubs at his stubbled jawline. He's troubled. Both happy and content—due to Ashley and his newfound love, no doubt—and troubled. It's an odd look.

We're a hugging family, but Dale and I aren't touchy-feely brothers. Despite this, I reach forward and grasp his forearm. It's cold as ice.

He yanks it away. "No. Not until I get this off my chest."

"Okay."

"I know you're trying to comfort me. Tell me it's all okay, and I believe it will be. In time, anyway."

I go rigid. Something's up. Something big. "Dale, whatever it is, it *will* be okay."

"I'm not sure you'll be able to forgive me."

"Forgive you? For what? You've taken care of me your whole life. Even when I've gotten sick of it."

"I can't take this to the grave. I've tried. I held it inside me for so long that it got buried. But then... Ashley..."

"What about Ashley?"

"She opened up something in me. Let it all loose. It's been wonderful, but parts of it were also terrible. Horrific, even."

"Dale"—I force a chuckle, trying to ease the situation—"you're not making marriage sound all that great."

He shakes his head vehemently. "That's not what I mean at all. My feelings for Ashley kind of exploded inside me. Brought out the bad with the good, if that makes sense."

"Sure, it makes sense." Sort of.

"I've debated whether to tell you this thing this thing I buried inside myself for so long. Aunt Mel and Ashley say it's my decision. Dad says—"

"Wait a minute," I interrupt him. "Whatever this thing is that concerns me, three other people know about it?"

He swallows. "Yeah. They do. But I only told them recently."

I'm not sure whether to be angry. My brother is so strong. Way stronger than I am. But whatever this is, it's bringing him to his knees.

So I won't give him shit about telling others before me. Aunt Mel is probably acting as his therapist, Ashley's his wife, and Dad... Well, he and Dad are close the way Mom and I are close.

I get it.

I could make it easy for him. I could tell him that whatever it is, I forgive him. I no doubt will. I can't imagine anything Dale could do that I wouldn't forgive. But I can't. I have to know everything. Going into what we're about to with any blind spots could be very detrimental.

"This isn't easy, Don."

"Few things in life are easy," I say. "But if this is eating you up inside, just tell me. We'll work it out."

He nods then.

And he begins to speak.

As he enunciates each word, I go back in my head. Back to a place I never let myself think about. Never let myself remember.

"It was that last time," he says. "Right before we were rescued. They took me." He clears his throat. "And then they took you."

I nod. Trying not to think about it even as he continues speaking.

Because that last time...

It was horrific. More horrific than all the others combined. But probably not more horrific than what Dale went through. He saved me so many times. Begged them to take him instead of me. Fought for me. Struggled, bit, kicked to keep them from touching me.

"The last time," he says, "when they tried to take you, but I made them take me instead."

I nod. Then I gulp. "Dale, I don't want details. Please."

"I won't give them to you. I'll say only this, Donny." He swallows, pauses, swallows again. "They broke me. That time. They finally broke me."

"They broke me long before, Dale. That's nothing to be ashamed of."

"I'm not ashamed of it," he says. "Not of being weak."

"You shouldn't be. You were a little boy. We both were."

"I know that. And I've forgiven myself. I just hope you can forgive me."

"For what? I don't understand, Dale."

He clears his throat. "That last time. They broke me. You don't want details. I won't give them to you. Suffice it to say, everything they'd done to me previously was like nothing. It was...pure torture, and the only way they would stop was if..."

"It's okay. Go ahead."

"Was if I told them to do it to you instead."

My stomach drops. I remember that last time. It was hell because it was prolonged, but it wasn't anything they hadn't done to me before. It was...

No. Can't go there.

I don't think about this. There's a reason I don't think about this.

"I forsook you, Don, and I'm sorry."

Forsook. An interesting choice of words. My brother didn't choose this word by accident.

He felt he had abandoned me. Offered me up to the wolves to save his own hide.

I swallow. Though I expect to feel angry—especially after everything else this evening—I don't. I feel . . .

Helpless.

Just as helpless as I felt when we were stolen from our home that day, thrown into that cold concrete room.

But I wasn't helpless.

I had Dale.

And Dale had . . .

Dale had no one.

Seconds pass. Then minutes.

"For God's sake, Don, say something. Anything."

I open my mouth, hoping I'll find words. Nothing comes.

"I don't expect your forgiveness," he says.

Those words slice straight into my heart. "It was so long ago, Dale. Of course I forgive you. You protected me. Always."

"Except that time."

I swallow. "Except that time. But if it helps . . . God, I hate thinking about this."

"I know. I'm sorry."

I clear my throat. "If it helps, they didn't do anything different to me that time. They . . . God, I can't say it."

"I know. I remember Aunt Ruby gave you a bath because you told her you hurt down there. And you tried to—" He closes his eyes, shakes his head harshly "So I know what they did to you, Don."

"But they had done it before."

"Are you saying they didn't . . ." He clears his throat. "Do it with something . . . sharp?"

I gasp, my jaw dropping. "No! My God, did they—"

He gestures for me to stop. "Please, don't even say it. It's okay. *I'm* okay. Now. Better, even, knowing you didn't endure that."

"All these years, you thought . . ." I shake my head.

"Yes. But now I know. Now I've admitted what I did, and you forgave me."

"Is it forgiveness you're after, Dale? Or is it redemption?"

"It's forgiveness. I have nothing to redeem myself for. I was a child. We both were."

I nod. "I'm glad you see it that way. We're okay, Dale. We're okay, and we always will be."

"You've always been okay. But I am too. My last secret is out. Thank you for your forgiveness."

"There's nothing to forgive. We were children. And Dale, you were as strong as any ten-year-old child could have been in those circumstances."

He nods. "I know that now. Thanks to Ashley, Dad, Aunt Mel. And now you."

"No," I say. "Thank no one but yourself. You're the strongest man I know, Dale."

My brother smiles. A full smile—one I've seen so seldom over the years but that I've seen a lot more since Ashley came into his life.

He's happy.

And he deserves that.

★ ★ ★

I'm chilled yet numb as I stand in front of my mirror to brush my teeth.

So much to process for one evening.

God, my head. I'd swear Paul Bunyan is inside swinging his ax through my skull and into my brain.

Ibuprofen will ease it. Maybe.

I pull open the mirrored door to the hidden medicine cabinet—

What is that? I pull out a glasses case. I don't wear glasses. Never have. I do wear sunglasses, but I've never left the case inside this cabinet. Besides, I don't even recognize this brown leather case.

I unsnap it and open it.

Nestled inside the black lining is a key.

A key to what?

The key chain has a number and address etched on it. A bank in Denver.

This is a key to a safe-deposit box.

And I don't have a safe-deposit box.

CONTINUE THE STEEL BROTHERS SAGA WITH BOOK TWENTY

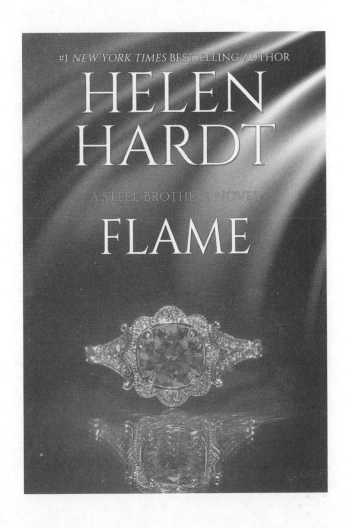

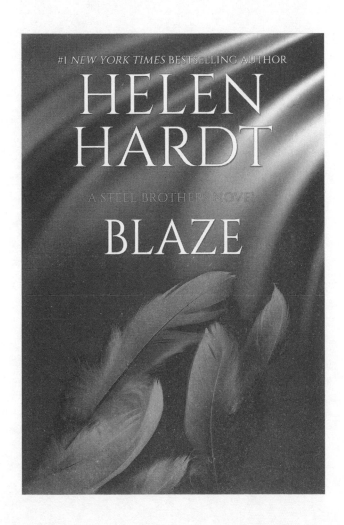

MESSAGE FROM HELEN HARDT

Dear Reader,

Thank you for reading *Spark*. If you want to find out about my current backlist and future releases, please like my Facebook page and join my mailing list. I often do giveaways. If you're a fan and would like to join my street team to help spread the word about my books, please see the web addresses below. I regularly do awesome giveaways for my street team members.

If you enjoyed the story, please take the time to leave a review on a site like Amazon or Goodreads. I welcome all feedback. I wish you all the best!

Helen

Facebook
Facebook.com/HelenHardt

Newsletter
HelenHardt.com/SignUp

Street Team
Facebook.com/Groups/HardtAndSoul

ALSO BY HELEN HARDT

The Steel Brothers Saga:
Craving
Obsession
Possession
Melt
Burn
Surrender
Shattered
Twisted
Unraveled
Breathless
Ravenous
Insatiable
Fate
Legacy
Descent
Awakened
Cherished
Freed
Spark
Flame
Blaze

Blood Bond Saga:
Unchained
Unhinged
Undaunted
Unmasked
Undefeated

Misadventures Series:
Misadventures with a Rock Star
Misadventures of a Good Wife (with Meredith Wild)

The Temptation Saga:
Tempting Dusty
Teasing Annie
Taking Catie
Taming Angelina
Treasuring Amber
Trusting Sydney
Tantalizing Maria

The Sex and the Season Series:
Lily and the Duke
Rose in Bloom
Lady Alexandra's Lover
Sophie's Voice

Daughters of the Prairie:
The Outlaw's Angel
Lessons of the Heart
Song of the Raven

Cougar Chronicles:
The Cowboy and the Cougar
Calendar Boy

Anthologies Collection:
Destination Desire
Her Two Lovers

ACKNOWLEDGMENTS

I don't know about you, but I'm loving the Pike sisters! Callie and Rory are writing themselves. I can't wait to see what happens with Callie and Donny next. We're about to delve into the history of the Steel family, and it's not all going to be pretty, as you can imagine, but Callie and Donny do provide a bit of comic relief. I love it when a couple I create has that kind of chemistry.

Huge thanks to the always brilliant team at Waterhouse Press: Jennifer Becker, Audrey Bobak, Haley Boudreaux, Keli Jo Chen, Yvonne Ellis, Jesse Kench, Robyn Lee, Jon Mac, Amber Maxwell, Dave McInerney, Michele Hamner Moore, Chrissie Saunders, Scott Saunders, Kurt Vachon, and Meredith Wild.

Thanks also to the women and men of Hardt and Soul. Your endless and unwavering support keeps me going.

To my family and friends, thank you for your encouragement. Special shout out to Dean—aka Mr. Hardt—and our amazing sons, Eric and Grant.

Thank you most of all to my readers. Without you, none of this would be possible.

Flame is up next!

ABOUT THE AUTHOR

#1 *New York Times*, #1 *USA Today*, and #1 *Wall Street Journal* bestselling author Helen Hardt's passion for the written word began with the books her mother read to her at bedtime. She wrote her first story at age six and hasn't stopped since. In addition to being an award-winning author of romantic fiction, she's a mother, an attorney, a black belt in Taekwondo, a grammar geek, an appreciator of fine red wine, and a lover of Ben and Jerry's ice cream. She writes from her home in Colorado, where she lives with her family. Helen loves to hear from readers.

Visit her at HelenHardt.com